Lip Lock

Lip Lock

Susanna Carr

BRAVA

KENSINGTON PUBLISHING CORP.
http://www.kensingtonbooks.com

BRAVA BOOKS are published by

Kensington Publishing Corp.
850 Third Avenue
New York, NY 10022

All Kensington titles, imprints, and distributed lines are available at special quantity discounts for bulk purchases for sales promotion, premiums, fund-raising, educational or institutional use.

Special book excerpts or customized printings can also be created to fit specific needs. For details, write or phone the office of the Kensington Special Sales Manager: Kensington Publishing Corp., 850 Third Avenue, New York, NY 10022. Attn: Special Sales Department. Phone: 1-800-221-2647.

Brava and the B logo Reg. U.S. Pat. & TM Off.

ISBN 0-7582-1081-7

First Kensington Trade Paperback Printing: December 2005
10 9 8 7 6 5 4 3 2 1

Printed in the United States of America

To Hilary Sares,
with thanks for her guidance,
her patience, and most of all
for her wicked sense of humor

Lip Lock

Chapter 1

If she didn't get something to eat, her coworkers would have to take cover!

Molly Connors oh so casually strolled toward the executive kitchen. She darted her gaze side to side, making sure the coast was clear. Seeing no one around, she walked into the kitchen as if she owned the place.

She glanced around the rich cherry cabinetry and the dark granite counters. The place was empty. Whew!

She wasn't up to creating a credible excuse. The food staff could probably care less, but it was the executives on the floor that took offense. They acted as if one had to be a club member to enter.

She opened the door to the stainless steel refrigerator, scanned the labels on the fancy jars, and slammed it closed. Weren't there any leftovers? She hadn't eaten all day—unless you counted the day-old Halloween candy, which she didn't—and was in desperate need of something other than a Tootsie Roll. Her stomach was growling so loud it could be heard over phone conversations.

She peered inside a small ceramic serving dish and found a fortune cookie still in its wrapper. Good enough. Molly grabbed the treat, the cellophane crackling loudly in the silence. She cracked open the cookie and stuffed a jagged piece in her mouth.

Molly closed her eyes and sighed as she tasted the almond flavor. It was good, but it wasn't going to blur the sharp edge of hunger. She needed something more. Something substantial.

She broke off another section of cookie and vaguely wondered about her fortune. Molly frowned when she saw there was no slip of paper.

"That's not even funny." She glared at the cookie and stuffed it in her mouth.

She might be down on her luck right now, Molly silently admitted as she munched, but that didn't mean she was stuck there. She knew it was only temporary, although getting a second opinion would have been nice.

It didn't even have to be about her upcoming work review. She knew that was in the bag. When she started working at Ashton ImageWorks, they promised to increase her pay raise after three months' probation. She followed the rules. She was here every day and on time.

Now if she could make it to Friday without starving to death . . .

Molly opened the pantry door and scanned the contents. There was nothing. Not unless she could cook it undetected and get back to the reception desk in five minutes.

She started opening and closing the cabinet doors. She opened the one under the sink. Sheesh! Her *kitchen* was smaller than this.

The cupboards were almost as bare as the ones in her apartment. What was that about? Hers were bare because she'd been waiting for payday. These shelves were empty because the kitchen was too big.

She opened the cabinet over the sink and nearly jumped for joy when she saw a jar of marinated olives. It wasn't sweet, it wasn't from a vending machine, and it was a fruit. Or was it a vegetable? Who cared? Right now it was her lunch.

She struggled to open t..
jumped back before it drip..
for a towel. She pulled open..
the huge preparation island. Bi..
paper towels way back just as s..
the kitchen.

"Sure thing, Kyle."

Shoot! Molly wanted to stomp h..
the chief financial officer. He was an o..
ignore his need to establish a caste syste..
she couldn't, since he made it clear she wa..
the system.

"I'm going to grab something to eat."

Molly looked around frantically. She had t..
found her in here again today, he was going to..
and she was going to come up empty-handed. Aga..

"I'll see you at the meeting."

Molly dove in after the paper towels. Ow! May..
kitchen *was* bigger. She winced as her knee hit the w..
There went her new pair of pantyhose.

She slammed closed the cabinet door with her free han..
and caught her knuckle. Molly muffled her cry and stuffed
her pinched finger in her mouth just as she heard Glenn's
foot hit the kitchen's tile floor.

Okay, Glenn, she thought as her fingertip throbbed at
the same beat as her skinned knee. *Just get in, get out, and
don't go looking for paper towels.*

She heard him walking around. He wasn't opening anything as far as she could tell. Just . . . pacing.

Go. Pain bloomed from her lower back and shot up her
spine. *Just go away. Shoo.*

The door swung open.

Finally. Molly wanted to sigh with relief but she couldn't
move her shoulders. She didn't think she could stay this
squooshed up much longer.

have you been?" Glenn whispered fiercely.

Molly's head shot up and caught the hard wooden
winced and pressed her lips shut.

ldn't get away."

was this? Another person? *Come on, people. Don't
e important work to do?*

who was the woman? It wasn't Annette, the only fe-
xec, and therefore acceptable in Glenn's eyes to walk
he executive kitchen. It must be someone high in ad-
stration.

he suddenly heard the squeak of shoes on linoleum.

"Kiss me," Glenn ordered.

Excuse me?

She heard the smack of lips on lips.

Whoa! Not good. Whoever the woman was, she was really
stupid. Molly had made some hideous career moves in the
past, but even she knew this was professional suicide.

"I want you," the woman said.

Duh.

"I want you right here and now."

No, you don't. You really, really don't.

"Someone might walk in," Glenn said.

"I know. That's the idea."

"Julia—"

Julia! Molly's eyes widened. No way. And here she thought
the engineering coordinator was a class act who had it all
together. A little bit snooty, but Molly assumed that meant
the woman had standards.

"You want me?" Julia asked in a purr. "Take me now."

No. No. No. Molly frowned as she heard the rustle of
clothing and the muffled breathing. She nearly jumped out
from her hiding place when she heard the thud above her.
Felt it. The island shook.

Molly flattened her hands against the walls. Were they

doing it on top of her? On the island? Where people prepared the food?

Okay, new rule. She was not eating anything from this kitchen unless it came with a tamper-proof seal.

"You naughty girl. You're not wearing any panties."

I really didn't need to know that. She wanted to cover her ears, but couldn't reach them.

"You're dripping wet."

Didn't need to know that, either.

And then she heard the sounds. The slap of skin, a few slurps, and something like gnawing. The cabinetry creaked and groaned under their weight. At least she was already in the standard earthquake position.

Why does this feel just like home? Every night she could hear the bed springs go wild in the apartment upstairs. She probably would have never noticed it if her neighbor wasn't a prostitute who did most of her business at night.

"Oh, God," Julia whimpered. "That feels good."

I don't care.

"I'm going to come."

Thanks for the warning, Jules. Like I couldn't predict that.

She heard the muffled sobs and felt the frenetic pounding above her. Her neck hurt and the back of her head was probably going to be permanently dented.

And then . . . silence. Blessed, peaceful silence, if you didn't count the hum of the refrigerator. Or the hard, labored breathing, but she was trying to block that out.

"God, that was great."

Says who?

"Oh, Glenn . . ."

Enough pillow talk. Leave before I get a charley horse.

"You're still so hard. So big."

That image was going to scar her fragile psyche. Wasn't

it enough that every time she saw the engineering coordinator she was going to look for nonexistent panty lines? Or that every time she heard a mule bray, she'd think of Julia?

"I want that monster in me. Right now."

Oh, for crying out loud, get a room!

"Take me in your mouth."

Molly leaned a little more to the left and carefully opened the jar of olives. This might take a while.

She plucked a fat green olive from the jar and wondered if there ever was going to be a day when she had it all together. When she'd be sneaking into the kitchen for sex instead of a garnish. Desperate for a condom instead of a condiment.

It was doubtful. She nibbled the olive, thinking a dry white wine would have gone well with her lunch, as Julia reduced Glenn into mumbling baby talk.

"Oh, yeah," Glenn crooned. "Just like that."

The only way she'd have a rendezvous in the executive kitchen was if she planned to meet Kyle Ashton. She smiled as the image of his tall, lean, and muscular body popped into her head. The light green eyes. And that mouth! Full and wide, that was made for kissing.

Yep, Molly decided as she shifted, flattening the rolls of paper towels with her hip as she tried to find a more comfortable position. She'd do Kyle anytime, anywhere. No questions asked.

Now if he just knew she was alive, she'd be all set.

Kyle dropped the file on his assistant's desk and walked out of her office when he caught a furtive movement from the corner of his eye. He turned sharply and looked down the long hallway just in time to see Julia slink out of the kitchen.

The woman looked flushed. Rumpled. Like her hard, brittle edges had gone soft. She tugged at her sophisticated black suit jacket and smoothed her sleek blonde hair. If he didn't know better, he'd think Julia just had sex. But he had to be wrong, which wouldn't be a surprise. It'd been a while since he made a woman look that way.

Exactly three months, now that he thought about it. Ever since Molly Connors walked into his office.

From the moment she flashed him a wide smile and her left cheek dimpled, he knew the receptionist was going to be trouble. He had no idea how much. Or what kind.

He automatically glanced at the reception desk. He felt the familiar mix of relief and disappointment when she wasn't there. The security glass doors that separated her work station from the rest of the offices never diluted the energy that crackled from her. Sometimes he wondered if it only served to magnify her allure. Make it seem brighter. Less attainable.

Kyle rubbed his hand over his eyes and almost missed seeing his friend Glenn walk out of the kitchen. Disheveled, red in the face, and sweating profusely. Glenn was looking down as he zipped up his trousers.

What the hell? Anger roared through him as he watched Glenn retreat to his office.

That goddamn liar. Kyle gritted his back teeth before he said it out loud.

The chief financial officer could not keep his pants on. Never had, never would. Kyle used to think it was a phase, but now he knew it was part of his character.

Glenn's trysts and encounters were annoying. Even inconvenient. But lately, it'd been nothing but drama, and was creating major problems at work. One of these days, it was going to put them in a legal mess.

If he had been any other employee, the guy would have been dismissed. But Glenn was one of the founders, not to mention Kyle's oldest friend.

Supposedly more than a friend. When Kyle confronted him with the problem a week ago, Glenn swore he wouldn't do anything to hurt the company. Even went so far as to say, "Kyle, you are like a brother to me. I wouldn't do anything to disappoint you."

And he fell for it. Not only was the guy screwing around, but right under his nose. Kyle shook his head in self-disgust and strode down the hall, determined to confront Glenn.

So he could be lied to again? Listen to promises his friend had no intentions of keeping? Kyle slowed his pace and looked at the kitchen's swinging door.

He hesitated, but if he went into the kitchen, what did he expect to see? Pots and pans thrown all over the floor? Food smeared on the refrigerator in the shape of a body print?

He didn't want to see any evidence of raw passion. He wanted some proof that he was wrong. That he was jumping to conclusions. That Glenn had meant what he had said.

Kyle pushed open the door and halted when he saw Molly Connors crawling out of the cabinet door.

"Oh!" She yelped as she tumbled to her knees. "Uh . . ."

He stared at her, his throat squeezing closed at the unexpected sight of her. She flipped her wavy brown hair from her eyes, the golden red streaks catching the overhead lights. Her hair fell to her shoulders, free from pins or product. It beckoned for him to touch.

"Hi?" she said as she rose to her feet.

He couldn't stop staring. The lavender silk blouse looked soft and fragile as it caressed her shoulders and curves. The darker lavender tweed skirt should have concealed the gentle slope of her hips, but instead it emphasized her small waist.

"I was hunting for"—she looked at the jar of olives in her hand—"paper towels."

He didn't say a word. His eyes traveled down her long legs, noting the laddered nylon at her knee. He paused when he saw the black heels. They seemed out of place with the outfit, but he didn't know why.

She rolled her eyes as her complexion turned pink. "Not that these are paper towels."

There were two possibilities of why she was in the cabinets.

"I mean"—she gestured wildly with her hands—"I know what paper towels look like."

Either she was not too bright . . .

"They're paper. On a roll." Her cheeks were streaked bright red. "With . . . with holes on both sides."

Or she was a voyeur. He wasn't sure which answer he preferred, but he was leaning to the first one.

A third possibility hit him. Threesome. He was surprised that didn't occur to him first.

"Okay, I'll shut up now." She pressed her lips into a tight, straight line.

"I'm looking for Glenn," he finally said.

She quickly looked at the kitchen island. "Mmm." Nodded her head but kept her lips firmly sealed.

"Have you seen him?" he prompted her.

She opened and closed her mouth. "*Seen* him? No."

The lie irritated him. "You sure?" he asked as Molly became more flustered. He took a step closer to her. "He was going to be here."

"Haven't seen hide nor hair of him." She winced and turned crimson. "Just got here myself."

He felt his eyebrow arch. "You did?"

She slowly blinked. "Yep."

"When?" Kyle stood in front of Molly. He caught a whiff of her scent. He couldn't place it, but it made him think of something sweet and delicious.

He reached out and Molly went still. He felt the tension soaring, arcing between them. Heat flared and boomeranged.

Kyle's fingers brushed her hair. It was softer than he anticipated. He wanted to curl his hand into the waves and get tangled.

Molly's sharp intake echoed in his ears and he reluctantly let his hand drop. "This was in your hair," he said gruffly, showing her the sliver of wood.

"Oh." She grabbed the long splinter and held it in her clenched hand. "Uh, it must have happened when . . ." She drifted into silence.

"Paper towels," he explained for her.

"Right." Her voice was a whisper.

"Molly"—his voice was soft but carried a bite—"how could you have missed seeing Glenn when he was right here in the kitchen with you?"

Her eyes widened and she blinked rapidly. "I, uh. Well. Okay, I was in the cabinet." She motioned defiantly at the island. "I didn't see anybody else in there."

"*What?*" Kyle heard what she said. He just couldn't believe it.

She set the jar down. "I need to get back to my desk. If I see Glenn, I'll let him know you're looking for him."

Kyle stared after her, unable to tear his gaze away until the door swung shut. What was it about Molly Connors that made his head spin?

And why did people find the need to lie to him?

Why had he been concerned about lying? It was no big deal, Kyle decided a half an hour later. So what if he questioned his oldest friend's word, or if the receptionist didn't tell him the truth? What was the saying about the devil you know? Yeah, he'd take that over the nameless, faceless people out to destroy him.

He leaned back in his chair and faced his three top advisors across the conference table. Glenn, Timothy, and Annette had been through it with him from the start. Together they had achieved the impossible and amassed power, respect, and a fortune.

But today, he felt vulnerable. Like he was the under-dog—the one thing he swore he would never be again.

"Our security procedures are expensive as it is," Glenn said. "We don't need to add on anything else."

"Glenn, you're not getting it," Timothy, the head of security, said from across the conference table. "Last night we caught a low-level computer programmer walking out of the building with the blueprint in his backpack. Obviously, we need to go on lockdown."

Kyle's stomach tightened and pinched as the rage billowed inside him. Someone almost got away with the intellectual property for their upcoming product. It was his most innovative work. He had spent years coming up with the artificial intelligence for a program to analyze the content of a picture. Any picture.

And he almost lost it.

Sure, he was going through the process of getting it legally protected. But his idea was at its most vulnerable from the time they created the blueprint to the time they get it patented.

It would be hell if they lost all they had researched and developed. If they missed out on the partnership with plaza+tag, the revolutionary community on the Internet, they would stagger from the bad hit.

But if their competitor stole the idea and patented it as their own . . . The possibility ate at Kyle's gut like acid. He refused to let that happen. Ashton ImageWorks would never pay the competition millions of dollars for the use of one of his ideas!

"I thought the blueprint was online," Glenn said. "And you had to use a password to get to them."

"Parts of it are," Kyle explained. Glenn never understood computers, which was how their friendship developed. They met in college when Kyle had to tutor him. "And some of the specs of the blueprint are not available online. Like the highly sensitive ones that we don't want leaked."

Glenn rolled his eyes. "A lot of good that did."

Kyle felt the reluctant smile tug at his mouth. "You know the green book I'm always carrying around? That's the blueprint this programmer tried to take out."

"Why didn't he copy it?"

"Because," Annette interrupted, "it's on a specially treated green paper that makes it very difficult to copy."

"Oh." Glenn paused as he mulled over the information. "How many of these blueprints do we have to keep track of?"

"There's only one." It was a thick book with hundreds of thousand lines of code.

"One?" Glenn looked back and forth at the others, obviously wondering if he heard correctly. "For the whole company? Just one book?"

"Yes," Annette said, "we all have to share."

"In this book is a log of every programmer who has looked at the blueprint and why they looked at it. They have to be approved each time by a manager."

Glenn's mouth dropped open. "This is your idea of a secured system?"

"It has sensors embedded in the pages," Timothy said. "It's like trying to take a book out of the library before you checked it out."

Glenn practically sputtered with outrage. "And not once did anyone think of going high-tech security?"

"No one has swiped the blueprint before this."

"Uh-huh." Glenn rubbed his eyes with the heels of his hands. "And you really wonder how a nobody got the book?"

"The programmer is the fall guy," Annette decided with

her usual intensity. Right now the blonde radiated with deep anger. "No way was he working alone."

"Don't be too sure," Timothy said.

"He didn't have the security clearance," she pointed out. "He didn't work for anyone who did. He would have raised red flags earlier."

"So you think he had an accomplice?" Glenn asked.

"I think he *was* the accomplice," Kyle said. "We have to look higher. All of those who have access are under suspicion. We'll find the connection that way."

"You do know what this means?" Annette said.

Glenn hunched his shoulders as if he were bracing himself for the impact. "No."

"This programmer wouldn't have made a ballsy move unless he already had made contact with a buyer."

Silence wavered in the conference room until Glenn slapped his hands on the table. "Shit."

"Our competition now knows what we want to do with our product," Annette continued. "And we don't know how much info they have of ours to make their own blueprint. It's going to be a race against the clock."

Timothy rubbed the back of his neck and exhaled. "Which company do you think it is?"

She shrugged. "The image processing software industry is very small, very competitive, and—"

"Very hot," Kyle finished. "We need to use that to our advantage."

Annette stiffened and then groaned. "I don't like the sound of this."

Kyle drummed his fingers on the polished table as a plan began to form. "It's time for our potential partners to pay us a visit."

"Are you insane?" Glenn asked, wide-eyed.

Possibly, Kyle decided. The idea bordered on deranged,

but he couldn't play it safe. Going on the defensive would be a bad move. "It's only a matter of time before word gets out that we had a security breach."

Timothy tossed his hands in the air. "Which is why we need to lock down."

"No." Kyle was adamant on this point. "That makes us look panicky."

"That's because we are," Glenn muttered.

Kyle pinned his friend with a cool stare. "Which is why we have to look confident, but not careless. We're going to invite the owners of plaza+tag, show them around, and get the deal."

"Show them around?" Timothy was horrified. "Have them tour our company so they can, what? Take pictures with their cell phones?"

"We have to gain their confidence," Kyle said. "And make sure they won't want to do business with anyone else."

"They'll screw us," Annette predicted.

Kyle rose from his chair. "They'll have to take their turn. This is our plan and we're running with it."

Molly was just about to turn off her computer when her boss pushed open the glass door. She pulled her hand away from the shut-off button and tried to look busy as Sara hurriedly approached her.

"Did you confirm the meeting?" the executive assistant asked in a breathless rush.

Oh . . . shoot! Molly felt her insides twist but kept her expression blank. "With the outside advertising agency?" she asked carefully.

"Yes, that one." Lines formed on Sara's forehead. The woman always appeared frazzled and anxious, from her curly red hair to her chewed fingernails.

Molly smiled brightly. "Of course."

"Good! What a relief." The phone buzzed and Sara

leaned over the reception desk. Molly slowly rested her elbow on a stack of papers.

"That's my line. I'll get it here." Sara reached over and grabbed the phone. "Sara speaking. Oh!" She checked her watch. "I didn't realize . . . I'll be right down. Okay . . . okay. 'Bye." The phone went down with a clatter.

"I forgot to tell you that I have to leave early," Sara said with a grimace. She hurried to the glass door, slid her ID badge across the security pad, and yanked open the door. "I have another doctor's appointment. I bet I used up all my sick leave for the year."

"No problem," Molly called out, frozen in place. "I have everything under control."

She didn't move even after her boss reappeared. "Do you have any questions before I go?" Sara asked as she crossed the spacious, modern reception area, carrying an overflowing tote bag.

"I got it covered."

"Thanks," Sara said as she headed for the stairwell. She pushed the heavy door with all her might. "I'll see you tomorrow."

" 'Bye!" Molly kept her smile intact until the door closed with a metallic click.

Dang it! Molly lifted her arm and grabbed the to-do list. She glared at the unchecked item: confirm ad agency meeting.

She slapped the notepad onto her desk and covered her face with her hands. She could do this. Cover her tracks. She was practically a pro at it.

Molly looked at the clock. It was almost five. How much did she want to bet everyone at the ad agency was gone for the day?

She punched in the numbers, gnawing her bottom lip as she devised her story. Her mood brightened when a live person answered on the other end.

"Hi, this is Molly Connors from Ashton ImageWorks. I'm following up on a message I left earlier today. I haven't received a reply." She closed her eyes, silently apologizing for whoever was going to get blamed for the "breakdown" of communication.

But by the time she hung up the phone, the meeting was confirmed. Molly scratched the task off of her list with a swipe of her pencil, hoping she didn't get anyone in trouble. She had a feeling that kind of karma was going to turn around and smack her good one of these days.

"Where's Sara?"

Molly's heart lurched into her throat at the sound of Kyle's low voice. Her arms and legs suddenly felt floppy as she felt an electric rush scream through her veins.

"She's . . ." Didn't Sara say she used up her sick leave? Molly didn't want to get the executive assistant in trouble. "She's in a meeting."

Molly risked a look at him. He was really too handsome. All hard lines and angles from his slanted cheekbones to his uncompromising chin.

It was too distracting. Made her mind go to mush. She could vaguely remember what she was talking about. "It's going to last a few hours and she said she'll go home afterward."

Kyle frowned. "What meeting?"

Oh, why did you have to go and ask that? Molly was about to concoct a meeting. It was on the tip of her tongue when she decided not to take the chance. She always blathered like an idiot around Kyle Ashton.

"I don't know," she said as she systematically turned off her computer. "Would you like me to find out?" *Say no, say no, say no . . .*

She felt his piercing gaze. Molly didn't need to see if he was watching her. Her skin stung with awareness.

"No," he said slowly. "You can go home."

Hey, that ESP thing can work. Molly smiled big at Kyle. "Good night."

"Good night, Molly."

Oooh. Her shoulder blades twitched as her spine tingled. There was something about the way he said that. Low and husky and full of promise. She was still buzzing from it on her bus ride home.

What was it about that guy? Molly rolled her eyes at the rhetorical question. Well, yes, his body was to die for, but it was the way he moved. She sensed power—real power—lurking under iron restraint.

That command of his senses probably made him amazing in bed. She wanted to experience it, but most of all she wanted to shatter his self-control. She wanted to face the fierce wildness he kept hidden.

Like that was ever going to happen. She'd seen his choice of women. Debutantes, heiresses, celebrities. Receptionists weren't on that list.

And that was fine. Sure, it was. She didn't need the drama. She already had enough in her life. Like which bill she should pay this month. The water bill or the power bill? Eenie-meenie-minie-mo.

The Kyle Ashtons of the world didn't bother with that sort of thing. Molly laid her head against the cold bus window and stared out into the darkness. Heck, he probably *owned* water and electric companies.

Nor did the Kyles of the world date women like her. She might spend her days on the luxurious executive floor, but she spent her off hours in a cockroach infested "studio" apartment. She took extreme measures hiding that fact. It took her a while during her long job hunt, but she eventually got smarter about her appearance.

Her manicure was as homemade as her haircut, but no one looked closely enough to see the mistakes. The knock-off designer shoes had black marker scribbles to conceal the torn leather. She might never repeat an outfit, but that was only because she'd figured out the complicated system of abusing every exchange policy at the trendy boutiques. Even her perfume was an imposter fragrance.

Most days she felt like she was walking on a tightrope, but it wouldn't be like that for much longer. Friday, to be exact. Then she'd get closer to paying off that horrendous debt her good-for-nothing ex-boyfriend left her with. Maybe even make a dent in her medical bill.

Let's not go crazy here, she thought wryly as she got off at her bus stop.

She usually tried not to think about it and push it to the back of her mind. Not so much out of denial, Molly decided as she hurried down the block, but out of survival. If she thought about it, she'd crack. Break. Lose the strength to fight back.

And then where would she be? Because there was no one backing her up. Fighting at her side or fighting for her.

"Molly!"

Molly stopped and looked up at the apartment building kitty-corner from hers. She saw her friend waving at her from an open window. "Hi, Bonita."

"Can you look after my kids tonight while I go to the Laundromat?" she called across the street.

"Yeah, sure." Not like she had anything exciting going on. Plus, Bonita had cable television. Unlike herself, ever since her good-for-nothing ex-boyfriend racked up a thousand dollars on her cable bill. All from watching porn, and all within a month before he left. She didn't even *want* to know how he managed that.

Molly trudged over to her mailbox and unlocked it. It was crammed with letters, and not the good kind. She scanned through the items. Bill. Bill. Overdue notice. Bill. Junk mail. Wait, what was this?

She tore the envelope and quickly read the letter. The library was coming after her with a collection agency over a late book? She slapped the paper against her leg and sighed. What was this world coming to? She'd returned it.

Molly slowly walked down the steps to her dark and dank basement apartment. That letter was just one more thing pulling her down. On top of another and another. And then Molly saw the sheet of white paper taped onto her door.

Oh, great. Three guesses on who it was from. Her psychotic neighbor telling her to keep the noise down? Her landlord springing another surprise inspection? A letter from Ed McMahon saying he dropped by because she won the sweepstakes?

She got closer to her door and stopped. Molly read the first bold line as every ounce of air squeezed out of her lungs.

Eviction notice.

Chapter 2

She heard the elevator bell ding. Of course. The day she wanted to make some personal calls before she clocked in, people showed up to work early. This was how her luck worked.

Molly placed the phone down and sat up straight. It was showtime. Keep the personal drama hidden.

The elevator doors slid open, revealing her boss and the engineering coordinator. "Good morning, Sara. Julia." Molly kept her eyes off of the engineer coordinator's bottom as the woman walked past her desk. Panty lines, or the lack thereof, were none of her business.

Julia barely glanced at her. *Fine*, Molly thought. *No skin off my nose. And, by the way, you sound like a barnyard animal when you come.*

"Morning, Molly," Sara said. "How are you doing?"

"Fantastic!" Hmm. Those behavior specialists in the media were wrong. You didn't start feeling fantastic after saying it. "And you?"

Her boss sighed heavily and leaned against the high edge of the reception desk. "Busy, busy, busy."

Molly tried to look sympathetic, but Sara always talked about how busy she was. As if no one else had as much on their plate as she did. Molly knew that was why she'd been hired, but it could get annoying. She bet that Sara was disorganized rather than indispensable.

And she would love to see if Sara could handle her personal to-do list. Like throwing herself at the mercy of her landlord without anyone overhearing. Calling in favors from her friends who had little money to spare. If Sara had a list like that, she'd really start complaining.

"Kyle invited plaza+tag to visit, and I need you to make arrangements," Sara informed her. "He plans to show them around, dazzle them. You know, give them the works."

"When are they arriving?" Molly asked, jotting down notes on her scratch pad.

"Thanksgiving week."

Molly paused. The worst week to make any travel arrangements. Did bosses sit around and brainstorm impossible challenges for their staff?

"Okay," Molly said with a serene smile, "tell me what you need and I'll get started." *In between calling pawn shops . . .*

"Thanks, Molly. You're a big help."

"That's what I'm here for," she answered brightly. And the only reason she came to work today. Well, that and the unlimited long distance phone service.

An unwelcome thought occurred to her. "Oh, hold on!" Molly said. "Work is going to be closed on Thanksgiving and that Friday, right?"

"Officially," Sara said as she adjusted the tote bag strap on her shoulder. "Some of the executives will probably work through it like always, but the administrative staff isn't expected to."

"And are the guests visiting during that weekend? Don't they want to celebrate Thanksgiving?"

"I guess not," Sara said with a shrug, and headed toward the glass door. "But you have nothing to worry about. Do you have big plans for the holiday?"

Molly shook her head. "No."

"What are you going to do?"

"Soup kitchen." *If her luck didn't change real soon.*

"Wow," Sara said, coming to a halt. "Really?"

Molly winced and her stomach did a free fall. She didn't mean to say that out loud! What all did she say?

"Now I feel selfish for booking a ski trip to Whistler. Eh, what should I expect from a girl like you."

"Like me?" She dropped her pen and heard it clatter onto her desk. What was that supposed to mean? Her ribs squeezed her lungs; her nerves zeroed in for a crash landing.

Sara winced and splayed her hands out in apology. "Oh, don't take it the wrong way. It's just that, well, I know you don't say anything . . ."

Splat! Her nerves felt like they were spewed everywhere. Molly wrapped her arms protectively around her midriff before she doubled over. "You *know*?"

"I started picking up clues here and there," Sara said, clearly uncomfortable about saying anything, "and then it became obvious."

"It did?" Clues? What clues? She had been so careful. What tipped her off? Had she said something? Was someone trying to garnish her wages? Did she smell?

"It's nothing to be ashamed of," her boss said as she backed up to the glass door.

Was she kidding? Molly felt her skin burning. She was furious with herself for getting into such a deep hole of debt. Sure, most of it was medical bills because she had no insurance when she got pneumonia, but her finances were in dire straits before that. Getting sick just took her over the edge.

It would take years for her to crawl out of debt. She would've liked to blame it on her good-for-nothing ex-boyfriend, her series of dead-end jobs, and her bad luck.

But the fact was, she'd messed up and she was paying for

her own stupidity. As far as Molly was concerned, that wasn't something to toot her own horn about. Only until she could pay back every dime would she be able to hold her head up high.

"Don't worry, I won't tell anybody."

"Thank you." She struggled getting the words out of her constricted throat.

"I don't know why you're hiding it," Sara said as she swiped her ID on the black security box next to the door.

"I want to keep my job." Was so afraid to say it out loud, to show how much she wanted it, that she nearly choked on the words. To her horror, Molly felt her eyes sting. She bet her nose was turning red.

Sara scrunched up her face. "No one is going to fire you because you're a trust fund baby."

Molly froze in mid-flinch. *Trust fund baby*? Was she joking? She stared at the other woman through squinty eyes.

"I promise," she said as she yanked open the door.

She was afraid to move, to do anything that would straighten out this turn of events. But her boss seemed sincere. "O . . . kay."

"It'll be a secret just between us girls," Sara decided as she walked into the executive floor's inner sanctum.

Relief flooded her so fast it hurt. "Thank you!" she called after her boss.

Oh, good grief! People thought she was a trust fund baby? Molly pressed her hand against her mouth to keep from laughing like a lunatic.

Well, if that was how people wanted to see her, who was she to disappoint? She'd do her best.

Trust fund baby.

If only.

Sara pushed the door open and dashed through the reception area, making a run for the elevator. "I forgot! I'm late for a meeting. Kyle is going to kill me."

What else is new?

"Can you start looking for hotels?" she asked, hitting the up button. "Nicest penthouse suites you can find."

"Sure thing." Molly grabbed her pen, noticing her hand still shook from the heartfelt relief. "Days?"

"Monday to Monday," she said. "You'll have to look up the dates.

She wrote it down with a flourish. "Got it."

"Love that scarf of yours, by the way," Sara said as she stepped into the elevator. "Where did you get it?"

"One of my travels." *To the consignment shop.*

"Yeah, where's it from?"

Molly remembered the care label. "Bangladesh."

"Wow." Sara looked impressed. Molly was impressed she pronounced the country's name correctly. "Oh, I should be back in an hour."

"Okay." Molly watched the elevator door close and sank into her chair. She was so going to burn in hell for each and every one of her lies.

Why'd she do that? It just came spilling out of her mouth and she apparently had no shut-off valve. *Stop trying to push the image down her throat!*

Trust fund baby. Molly clucked her tongue and grabbed for the phone. Yeah. Just watch this trust fund baby work the cash advance stores.

"Anything else, Kyle?" Sara asked, her fingers flying over her keyboard.

He scanned the faces along the conference table. He had just updated his top executives on what they needed to know about the attempted theft, and they watched him, everyone on their best behavior.

And Kyle wondered how much could they be trusted.

His mind wandered to the first time someone stole one of his ideas. He had been in high school when he and his friends came up with a groundbreaking idea. It had been a fun and wild time until the big software companies started sniffing around.

Those friends were long gone. The moment they could, those guys took the idea, the credit, the money, and ran.

Kyle never mourned the energy and sacrifices he made for that idea. And he now made more money every day than the lump sum his friends had received. But he missed the innocence he once had, and the freedom that went with it.

He didn't know what happened to those friends, and wasn't interested in looking them up. They did teach him a valuable lesson, though. He had to watch his back.

"Kyle?" Sara prompted.

"No, we're done." He stood up, reminding himself that he wasn't that high school kid anymore. He was now in a position of power.

He craved power more than seeing his ideas come together. It was what pushed him to become a leader in computer software. He achieved his goal, but not the invincibility he thought would go with it.

As he headed for the back steps, he heard Timothy calling for him. Kyle hesitated. He didn't want to talk to the guy, even though he was probably one of his closest friends.

But that was the problem, Kyle thought as he turned to face Timothy. Rumor had it that the head of security was the unofficial source for a tell-all book about Kyle's rise to power.

Kyle considered it a betrayal, and the possibility was strong enough that he was investigating to see if the rumors were true.

To him, Timothy's revelations were more than releasing proprietary information. Kyle's business dealings, his successes and failures, were private. He would've liked to keep it that way.

It had nothing to do with image, or if he had to hide any shady dealings. He hadn't done anything illegal. At the time, he thought wryly. Some of those actions were against the law now.

The head of security wove through the other executives to catch up with him. "Are you going to the game tonight?"

"No, I have work to do."

Timothy's mouth dropped open. "This is the playoffs!"

"You'll have to tell me how it was," Kyle told his friend as he took the back stairs to the executive floor.

"You're taking this workaholic thing too far!"

Kyle ignored the words echoing in the stairwell. He knew some people thought he was driven—too driven—and they were right. He'd do whatever it took to be king of the hill.

He would never be at a disadvantage again. He needed to be in control of his surroundings. In control of his creation. And he'd sacrifice everything to get that.

He stepped onto the executive floor and walked by the reception desk. He automatically glanced over, prepared for the fierce attraction to hit him, when he saw Molly talking to Curtis Puckett, one of their elite programming architects.

She glanced at him and stilled. A hectic blush crawled up her skin before she darted her attention away.

His own body reacted. Kyle felt tight and alert. Ready to pounce. What was wrong with him? Why did he feel like a primal animal ready to mate around this woman? There was nothing overtly sexual about her.

But there was something about her eyes. The brown eyes twinkled and flashed. Took on mysterious shadows even when she batted her eyelashes.

Kyle looked away and entered the executive suites. There was also something else about Molly that screamed trouble. He couldn't place it, but he knew he was dealing with enough trouble.

Okay, that wasn't true. There were times when he welcomed trouble. Courted it. And when he got the better of the problem, he felt a buzz that was better than sex.

Now put trouble and sex together, Kyle considered as he strode into his office, and that would be a potent combination.

Molly and sex . . . He thought about it as he sat down at his desk. Damn dangerous. And tempting.

He wondered what it would be like, the two of them. Would it be hard and fast, or seductively slow? He admitted he'd spent too much time over the past few months thinking about the problem and never came up with a conclusive answer.

He knew what he would prefer. He would like nothing better than to have Molly come into his office—right this very minute—and close the door. Lock it. Have her sashay to his desk with the soft sway of her hips and a gleam in her brown eyes.

Kyle wanted Molly to nudge her way in and stand between him and his desk. Fall to her knees in front of him and unzip his pants.

Okay, if this was his fantasy, he also wanted her to gasp at the size of his cock, cupping it reverently with both hands, before taking him into her mouth.

She would deep-throat him—of course—and know just what to do. Nibble the length and lick him with sure, sweeping strokes of her tongue. Draw him inside her warm, tight mouth and suck hard.

Kyle shook away the daydream and shifted in his chair, his pulse pounding hard. But the images wouldn't go away. They grew stronger. Almost real.

He could see Molly as if she were right there, feel her soft hair under his hand. Watch her rise from the floor and perch on the edge of his desk. He'd run his fingers along her silk-clad legs and discovered she wore the sexiest garters that he had yet to see a woman wear.

He would glide his hands under that peach dress she was wearing today. He'd push her legs apart and reveal the fragile panties as his only barrier.

Kyle could easily imagine tearing the scrap of lace away before dipping his head and tasting her. He closed his eyes as his mouth flooded with anticipation.

His scalp tingled, as if her hands were already bunching in his hair. Her knees would be hooked over his arms as he drove his tongue into her core.

She'd go crazy, of course. Her responses would clearly show that no man had made her feel this way, and no man ever would. It was his fantasy, after all.

And in his fantasy she would be sprawled on his desk, naked and panting for his next touch. His hands would possess her breasts, pinching her hard nipples as his tongue teased her clitoris.

She'd be screaming his name and incapable of hiding anything, unable to lie, unwilling to cause trouble.

"Here's your speech for the next annual meeting . . ."

Kyle flinched violently as Sara walked into his office. His heart stopped and he felt like he was going to jump out of his skin. "I have to stop doing this," he muttered to himself.

He turned to his computer and punched in his password as Sara continued listing status reports on various projects. He listened while scanning through the voicemail saved on his computer, silently willing his cock to lie down. Damn the glass desktop.

He frowned when he saw a recent call and clicked play. The audio streamed through his state-of-the-art speakers.

"Hi, Kyle. This is Laurie, the caretaker of your island cottage. The redecorating is almost complete, although I still question the butt-ugly wallpaper in the bedroom."

"What?" He looked at the computer screen and then at Sara.

"Anyway," Laurie continued, as she was known to do,

"the reason I'm calling is because my daughter is expecting a baby soon and when she goes into labor—"

"Kyle, I'm sorry." Sara stepped closer to his desk. "I don't know why Molly forwarded that call to you. She knows I take care of those issues."

"It's not a big deal." He clicked off the audio. He wasn't aware that Laurie was about to become a grandmother. And he'd forgotten about the redecoration. It had been his first getaway and he hadn't been there in a year.

"I'll follow up with Laurie," Sara offered.

"Okay." He started to scroll down the other messages and paused. "What does she mean about butt-ugly wallpaper?"

"I'll ask the interior decorator." Sara shrugged. "And I'll talk to Molly and remind her which calls go to me."

"I'll do that." Kyle rose from his seat before he thought about it, ignoring Sara's bewildered look.

It probably wasn't a good idea to be anywhere near Molly after one of his inconvenient daydreams. What could he say? He liked trouble. He liked pushing his luck to the limit, testing his control of his environment and himself.

But he didn't know why he felt this way about Molly. Or why he had to constantly keep himself in check around her. He hadn't felt the need to around any other woman.

But maybe that was because he couldn't act on his desires. Kyle considered the possibility as he pushed the security glass door open. The other women knew the score. They were experienced and they were his sexual equals.

And he'd tamed every one of them. With ease, he remembered as he walked up to the reception desk where he saw Molly alone, but on the phone. He wasn't sure if he wanted to tame the trouble out of Molly Connors.

"Yes, I know, but—" She looked up and froze before a very professional and very fake smile spread across her face. "How may I direct your call? Thank you."

Kyle watched her push a button before replacing the handheld instrument. He glanced at the switchboard. "You hung up on them."

Her eyelashes fluttered. "No, I didn't."

A bald-faced lie. She didn't even pretend to check. He'd have to watch out for this one.

Molly primly folded her hands and rested them on her desk. "How may I help you?"

Why did he find that ladylike pose more threatening than if she went into a kung fu position? "I'm reminding you which of my personal calls go to Sara," he began, noticing the confusion flit through her eyes. "Sara said she gave you a list."

"Yes, that's right." She amped up her smile a notch. "She did."

No, she didn't. He didn't know why Sara didn't, or why Molly was perpetuating the lie. He guessed she was protecting her boss, which was admirable. Sorta.

"I must have misplaced the list. I'll ask Sara to give me another copy."

Which was worse? That Sara lied, trying to look good in his eyes, or that Molly lied to take the blame? He considered calling them both on it, but what purpose did it serve? The matter seemed trivial, but he sensed it was the tip of an iceberg.

Molly grabbed a pen and a rainbow-colored notepad in the shape of an M. "Which calls do you want to go to Sara?"

"All family." They had never been close and the only time they called was to ask for money.

She raised her eyebrows but silently wrote it down.

He squashed back the need to explain himself. He had no problems giving out the cash to his relatives. Especially if it meant he didn't have to hear from them until they needed more money.

"And anything that has to do with my houses," he added.

That got her. "Hou*es*?"

"I probably should get a personal assistant, shouldn't I?" He scratched his jaw as he thought about it.

Her gaze followed his hand. "Sounds like you should."

Kyle looked into her eyes and held her gaze. The air hummed and crackled. "Know anyone who'd like to apply for the job?" he asked.

He saw her throat working. "That would depend on the job description," she said hoarsely.

"Someone who takes care of me personally?"

Her mouth twitched. "Too broad of a description."

"Caters to all of my personal needs?"

Her eyes gleamed and she crooked her finger at him.

The blood in his veins started to zing. This was the first time she'd acted playful to him. He liked it. Wanted more. Kyle leaned over the high desk wall.

Molly tilted her head, the faint scent of perfume reaching him. "Sounds like a job for an army," she said in a low, husky voice. "You might want to rethink the personal assistant idea."

"Yeah." He straightened and stepped away. "It would really depend on the person."

"And the boss," she muttered under her breath.

Oh, yeah. She was trouble.

Molly stepped off the bus and hurried toward her apartment. The night seemed murky, the cold November moisture seeping through her coat. Her breath was trapped in her lungs. Her heart pounded in her ears.

She had no idea what she was going to do. Her landlord had given her a few days of grace to get him the money. She needed to come up with something and talk fast. Molly had a horrible feeling that she'd use every extra second and still come up short.

She'd already called in every favor, begged and bartered with every friend and acquaintance outside of the office. No one at the office could know about her problem. No one. And she'd do whatever necessary to keep it that way.

When she had finally got a hold of the landlord who had been avoiding her calls—wasn't that ironic!—she had to make up a story on the spot. She wasn't even sure what all she said. Something about a hospital stay. It was like she opened her mouth and some inner storyteller fed her the lines.

Whatever she had said must have been brilliant because her landlord became sympathetic and ready to call off the dogs. Man, she wished she had written the story down. She might need to use it again the next time a persistent bill collector got a hold of her.

Now all Molly had to do was get all the money she had on hand to her landlord, find a job she could do on the weekends, and not eat for the foreseeable future. No problem.

Molly turned the corner to her apartment. She noticed the cluttered front yard under the weak glow of the streetlights. Who was moving out? Oh, please let it be the workaholic prostitute.

Wait a second . . . Molly tripped as she stared at the sofa. That was hers! She'd recognize the atrocious orange stripe design anywhere, even in the dark. The hand-me-down was an eyesore.

She stumbled to a complete stop as it sunk in. Her landlord had kicked her out of her apartment. He'd tossed out her stuff. So many emotions slammed against each other, she was surprised she didn't collapse on the ground.

Molly stared dumbfounded at the jumble of furniture

and clothes and clutter. Her underwear was tangled with silverware. The rickety chair looked suspiciously broken. A mud puddle seeped underneath her mattress.

Whoever dumped her stuff on the wet lawn didn't care if they scratched her table or walked on her bed sheets. The carelessness, the intentional disregard for her things, dug at her like a splinter.

There wasn't a whole lot of stuff. That was the first coherent thought that floated over the multiple layers of pain. Her life was strewn before her, and this was all she had accumulated? Could this really be all of it? Molly was about to race inside when she saw her friend Bonita.

"Molly, what happened?" Bonita asked as she hurried up the sidewalk.

"I was . . ." The word zapped the strength right out of her. Molly sagged against the back of the sofa. She looked forlornly at her basement apartment. There was no going back. She never liked the place, but leaving it like this—abruptly and unwillingly—made her feel lost. Confused. Scared. "I was evicted."

"No way." Bonita looked at the furniture and clothes dumped in the yard. "I thought you were going to sweet-talk your landlord."

"I did. He said he was going to stop the process."

"Maybe the marshals got here before he could reach them?"

"No, I bet he lied to me." Molly pushed off the sofa as the indignation washed over her. "I went through this whole story of being hospitalized for leprosy and the guy lies to me!"

Bonita's eyes widened. "Are you sick?"

"No, but that's beside the point." Molly covered her face with her hands. "What am I going to do?"

"You can stay with me."

Molly dragged her fingers down her cheeks. "Oh, thank you."

"But only for tonight," Bonita clarified. "*My* landlord could kick me out on the street any moment as it is, having that many kids living in a one-bedroom apartment."

Molly nodded with understanding. She inhaled sharply, but couldn't clear the fog that numbed her mind. "What am I going to do with all my stuff?"

"Take what you can and leave the rest," Bonita suggested as she picked up a towel and folded it. "Let your landlord clean up the mess."

She couldn't leave anything behind. It was more than being sentimental. She didn't know what she was going to need right away, or what would take her forever to replace.

Her friend set the towel on the sofa cushion. "Better come up with a plan fast because it looks like rain."

Molly held out her hand and felt the fine winter mist. Not quite a drizzle, but more like the gods pumping a spray bottle at her.

Frick. Molly dropped her hand. She couldn't even think of anything right now.

"I'm going to make some dinner. It's leftovers but you come over and have some," Bonita offered. "I'll send one of the kids over when dinner's ready."

She shot a grateful look at her friend. "Thanks."

"You're going to get through this." She gave an encouraging pat on Molly's shoulder. "Everything is going to work out."

Molly nodded, but she wasn't so sure. She watched Bonita walk back to her own apartment building, fighting the urge to collapse on the sofa and have a good cry. Instead, she made herself right the upturned chair in front of her.

She shouldn't be in this mess. Okay, maybe a little, but nothing of this magnitude, Molly decided as she picked up the pillow at her feet. It wouldn't have been so bad if her good-for-nothing ex-boyfriend didn't leave her hanging with all the unpaid bills.

She would really love to curse and blame him, Molly thought as she savagely tossed the pillow onto the mattress, but she knew she was ultimately responsible for her decisions. At the time she thought some of her choices were smart. There was something to be said about protecting herself and putting all the finances in her name. Quite another to cancel that smart move by living with a loser.

Here she thought they had been working together toward a future. Instead, he took what he could get, and when there was nothing worth taking, he left. Leaving her with no home, a mountain of debt, and no future.

It could be worse, Molly decided as she bent down to retrieve what looked like a book. She could still be with the loser.

Molly stepped under the front door light and read the title off the spine. Heh. It was the library book. She could have sworn she had returned it.

Molly rolled her eyes and tossed the book on the sofa. What was she even doing checking out a book on creating a beautiful home? She knew better than to dream for that.

But that's what she wanted. She wasn't looking to make millions or dominate the world. She didn't want a career on the fast track or a showcase home or a fancy car.

What she wanted was a small corner of the world that was safe. She wanted to have money to pay her bills and not worry about how she was going to afford the basic necessities.

She wanted comfort. To her, that meant a cozy home. Warm and bright. It would have a clean and sparkling kitchen overflowing with food.

The kitchen would be big enough to hold a round table.

She didn't know why, but that's what she always envisioned. It could be large or small, but it had to be made of wood. A pine table, but oak or maple would work, too.

But most importantly, she saw people around that table, laughing and talking. They might be friends, family. Whoever they were, they loved and cared for her. Watched out for her as much as she watched over them.

Why was that so hard to get? Why couldn't she achieve that dream? She tried to play by the rules—she really did—but it only kept her further from what she wanted.

"Hey, you don't have any prices on anything."

Molly whirled around. She saw a young woman in a beige trench coat. She was standing by Molly's wash basket, which was filled with her porcelain trinkets. "Excuse me?"

"You're having a yard sale, aren't you?"

Molly stilled. "Yes . . ." She set the muddy plate down and stepped toward the woman. "Yes, I am. I'm setting up, but I don't have price tags on yet. I guess that means you get first pick."

"Really?" The woman quickly masked her interest and held up a small ceramic box. "How much for this?"

Man, why go for the small stuff? Molly tried to hide her disappointment. She needed people to take the big-ticket items, not something she got at the dollar store.

"I'll give you a quarter for this," the woman offered.

A quarter? Molly didn't know whether she should be offended or grab the quarter before the woman changed her mind. Yes, she'd rather have a quarter than nothing at all, but . . .

"I just don't know," Molly said, and tsked. "That . . . that box has been in my family for generations."

"Really?" The woman turned it over to look at it closely. Molly hoped it didn't have something printed on it, like commemorating the millennium.

"Yes," Molly continued when she didn't see any markings. "My great"—she paused and thought fast—"great grandmother brought it over on the boat to America."

"Yeah?"

She saw the gleam in the woman's eye. One dollar for sure. Molly knew she should close the deal, but she might be able to get five and make a profit.

"Yeah," Molly replied. "It held the family savings. All ten gold coins. Great-great-grandma Connors had it sewn in the hem of her dress"—*ka-ching, ka-ching!*—"determined to keep it from thieves . . ."

Chapter 3

Kyle walked into the fitness center located on his corporate campus and came to a screeching halt when he saw Molly Connors on one of the treadmills.

What was she doing here? What was going on? He glanced around the near empty room as if searching for answers. He looked back at where Molly was exercising.

His gaze wandered down her body. Chunks of her brunette hair escaped her bouncy ponytail. Her pert breasts were clearly outlined against the damp, shapeless T-shirt. The bright red shorts hugged the full curves of her hips. He watched the muscles bunch and strain in her toned legs.

The sheen of perspiration on her flushed skin did something to his imagination. He wanted to see her like this, sweaty, panting for her next breath, in his bed. Her fists bunching into the sheets—

Whoa. Rewind. What was she doing here? He was working out every morning, exhausting his body, clearing his mind until he didn't think about her. This room was his sanctuary from Molly.

Until now.

He found himself walking toward her, breaking his routine, and doing the treadmill first. He chose the one next to her.

She glanced over and tripped. Her palms slammed onto the handrails and she hung on until she could regain her pace.

"Molly," he said by way of greeting.

"Hi, Kyle." She gave him the once-over and abruptly turned her head to stare straight ahead.

"I don't remember seeing you here before."

"I thought I'd try it out," she said in between breaths. "Or is this an executive-only thing?"

Kyle frowned. What was she talking about? "No."

Her smile expressed her relief. "Good."

He entered the speed on his treadmill and started running. Kyle wanted to relieve his stress. Or catch up on the news from the TV across the room. But he couldn't stop focusing on Molly.

Even though he wasn't looking directly at her, he was aware of her every movement. The way her long hair clung to the back of her neck. The way she squirted the sports bottle in her mouth and how the dribble of water trailed down her chin and neck. He was acutely aware of the way she kept glancing at him.

And then he saw the flicker of her eyelashes as she glanced at his speedometer. She casually brushed her fingers along the control panel and moved her speedometer to meet his.

Hmm . . . So it was like that, was it? "Do you run a lot?"

"No, why do you ask?" She cast a quick look at him. For a second he thought she'd look guilty, but he didn't know why.

" 'Cause you're in very good shape." His gaze ran over her body again. If he wanted to maintain his self-control, he'd keep his eyes on her chunky running shoes.

"Thank you," Molly said. "But I prefer other . . . activities."

Yeah, his imagination was going to get the best of him. "Like?" he asked and felt her mind racing.

"Yoga," she finally answered.

The vision of an incredibly flexible Molly was not what he wanted right now. He increased the speed on his treadmill.

"What about you?" she asked, her breathing labored.

"Running. Nothing better."

"Hmm. You struck me as a golfer."

That surprised him. Golf was okay, but it required more time than he could give it. "Why'd you think that?"

She shrugged, the move messing up her balance, but she quickly regrouped. "It's the game for CEOs."

"I'm not like most CEOs."

"No kidding." She slid her hand against the control panel and upped him one.

"Running is great," Kyle said. "There's nothing like the buzz, the rush you get."

"I wouldn't say that."

"It gets the heart pumping. Throbbing."

Molly looked straight ahead.

"The muscles stretch. Burn."

She ran like she was trying to get away.

"The adrenaline rush." He upped his speed. "The sudden kick in your veins."

Molly matched him and was not the least bit coy about it. Kyle smiled. Just for that he went up another level.

She went up two.

Kyle let her get away with it for a minute. When he saw her flagging, he increased his speed by five.

She glanced at him in surprise. He wagged his eyebrows back at her.

She matched his pace and went for it.

Molly's legs were a blur, her arms pumping. Her skin

held a rosy glow, her lips parted as she breathed in deeply. She was giving him everything she got.

Kyle couldn't take his eyes off of her. There was no pretence or strategy. Just in-your-face power and energy to meet a goal. It was sexier than stiletto heels and made him hotter than hell.

Molly suddenly slammed the cool-down button.

"Had enough?" he asked with a tinge of disappointment.

"For . . . the moment," she said in a gasp.

"Don't you love the burn?"

"Not when nausea accompanies it." She hit the stop button and her treadmill turned off.

"Hey, you're going to cramp up."

Molly wasn't listening. "I need a shower. A hot one."

Thanks for the image.

She hopped off the machine and winced. She immediately lifted her leg and rubbed her calf.

"Told you." Kyle knew he should sound more sympathetic and tried again. "Let me take a look at that."

"No! No! I'm fine." She slanted her injured leg away from him. "I'll walk it off."

"I can massage it for you."

"That's okay." She raised her hand to block him. "Thanks anyway."

"Or you can lie down and I—"

"No!" She scurried out of his reach. "I better get ready for work. I don't want to be late."

He watched her hobble off. It was probably a good thing she rejected his offer. But how would he ever get his fantasies to happen if she couldn't stand the idea of his touch?

Kyle frowned and punched in the maximum speed.

* * *

Molly powered through to the bottom of her inbox, determined to have a pristine, clean desk—minus one intricate project on her desk to showcase her hard work.

She tilted the sheet of paper to the side. Perfect. She glanced at the clock. Two-fifteen. Hmm. How long did it take for a performance review around here? A couple of minutes? An hour?

She knew the review paperwork was horrendous. That sucker took hours! Trick questions and everything. Like, "How do you rate your performance?" Hello! Perfect score!

Of course, she couldn't say that. She had a feeling they were testing for her modesty level or any superiority complex.

So she knocked a few points off, but would be sure to gain those in the next review. Nothing like showing some improvement, she thought with a sly smile.

Molly tiredly rubbed her forehead as she checked her desk one more time. Her job required lots of sporadic activity interspersed with mind-numbing boredom. During those moments it seemed like everyone walked by her desk and she had to look busy. Ugh. That was more exhausting than actually working.

Of course, her exhaustion level had increased ever since she'd been waking up at the crack of dawn and exercising the life out of her body. She was stiff and sore all over.

"I can massage it for you."

Molly shivered with secret pleasure over the memory from this morning. No, thank you! Not a good idea. At all.

Okay, maybe a little bit, but it wouldn't stop at a little bit. Oh, no. The minute she allowed Kyle close to her, he would see everything. The lies, the front. Everything.

And then she'd lose everything. It wasn't a heck of a lot, but it was all she had right now.

Maybe that's why she was feeling stiff and sore. She didn't

quite have a bed these days. If she ever got it on with Kyle, it would never be a matter of his place/her place. His place, hands down. Unless he wanted the unusual experience of doing it in the back of a stuffed, do-it-yourself moving truck.

Yeah, home sweet home. Molly cricked her neck, easing the tension. All the stuff she couldn't sell at her impromptu yard sale was now in her temporary living quarters. At least it kept the rain and wind at bay. Too bad it was still cold and had no bathroom.

Which was why she'd been visiting the fitness room at the crack of dawn all this week. Not so much in the interest of good health as much as a good excuse to take advantage of the hot, pulsing shower.

Fortunately, she'd be able to kick her newly acquired health kick very soon. She couldn't wait to get a place with heating. A window. A bathroom.

Of course, Molly remembered as she heard the elevator bell ding, there was something to be said about picking up and leaving if she didn't like the neighborhood. And the daily low fee . . .

The elevator slid open and Sara burst out into the reception area, urgency pulsing around her.

"Hi, Sara." Molly greeted her boss with a smile.

"Did plaza+tag get back to you?" Sara asked breathlessly.

"No, but I'll follow up on that right away."

Sara stuffed her hands in her wild red hair. "I can't believe how insane today is."

Hmm, that didn't bode well for her. Dread settled in her stomach.

"I don't think I'm going to make the deadline," her boss confided.

Which deadline? It didn't matter. "I can help."

"Oh, you can't." Sara sadly shook her head. "You don't have the security clearance."

"Okay." How could she broach the subject without looking desperate? Inconsiderate? She got nothing. "Would you like to do my review after five?"

Sara frowned, the lines on her forehead deepening. "Huh?"

"I can rearrange my schedule so I can stay." Not like she was chomping at the bit to get to her truck, but she didn't want to appear too eager.

"Shit!" Sara smacked her palm against her forehead. "I forgot about your review."

Molly felt her smile slip. Good thing she said something. "So, after work? I'll run over to the cafeteria and get us some lattes." Her budget could take the hit. She'd think of it as an early celebration.

"I can't do the review today," her boss confessed. "We're going to need to reschedule it."

What? Molly tried not to freak. Or grab Sara by her shirt collar and demand the review right here and now. Today was Friday. She'd waited long enough. She was *not* going to live in the truck any longer than necessary!

"Well, you can just tell me how I did," Molly said as the dread twisted inside her. "No need to go through all the legalese."

"I wish I could, but I'm not allowed. Human resources would kill me."

Molly leaned forward. "I won't tell if you won't," she whispered.

"I'm sorry, Molly, I can't do that. Why don't we reschedule it for next Friday?"

Molly didn't think she would survive that long. "Human resources won't yell at you for the delay?" *Because she sure would like to.*

"No," Sara said. "As long as you get the review before your next paycheck, we're fine."

What's your definition of fine?

"So next Friday at three o'clock?" her boss asked as she headed for the glass door.

Like I have a choice. "Sure, next Friday." But she might get that latte now and drown her sorrows.

Kyle looked out of his office window and watched the sun set behind a snow-streaked Cascade mountain range. Pink and lavender smeared across the darkening sky and the colors reminded him of Molly.

Why didn't Molly take him up on his offer? She didn't even want him touching her. Was it the whole employee/employer thing? He could understand that.

"Kyle?"

But was it more than that? Maybe she didn't like him. Or men. Or computer geeks. These things happened. But he could have *sworn* he saw the interest gleaming from her eyes. The want. The need.

Or was that his want and need reflecting off of her? Damned if he knew.

"Kyle!"

Oh, yeah. He was in a meeting. Kyle turned and looked at the chief financial officer. "What?"

"Our security systems have been upgraded and tightened," Glenn said, obviously annoyed. "But there's no guarantee that it will foil any attempt."

"Any progress in finding the accomplices?"

"Accomplices?"

"Come on, Glenn," Kyle said as he loosened his tie. "Even Julia at the last meeting said she bet the programmer didn't act alone. Surely you listen to every word she says."

Glenn flinched. "What?"

"Never mind." He wasn't going to pursue that line of

questioning. It wasn't top priority. "I'm not going to play cat and mouse with these thieves. Let's draw them out. Set a trap."

"But we don't know what level, or even the department the thieves are in."

"So?" Kyle unbuttoned his collar. He never was a suit and tie guy, but he liked how they conveyed a sense of power. He'd suffer through a tie just for that.

"It's going to require a trap of . . . great . . . great magnitude!" Glenn started to bluster. "A strategy that would take time we don't have!"

"Glenn, subterfuge is not your strong point."

The guy blushed. Kyle watched, almost fascinated, as the chief financial officer's face turned brick red.

"You are making it more difficult than it actually needs to be," Kyle continued. "Keep it simple."

"How?" Glenn asked as his flushed skin slowly faded.

"Add a fake spec."

When Glenn frowned, Kyle remembered once again he wasn't dealing with a programmer.

"We are going to add a fake form to our patent process. It's going to say that we want our product to include"— Kyle thought for a second—"an online image search application."

"Say what?"

Kyle didn't know how to break it down into simpler sentences, but he'd give it a shot. "You can train the program to recognize people's faces."

Glenn's forehead puckered. "Our product can do that?"

"No. It's too expensive right now, and we haven't researched how to develop this. We only know of a thousand ways that it won't work."

"But it's a great idea!"

"Wait for the upgrade. But our competition doesn't

know this. They are going to try and take this spec before we file it."

"Why are we going to throw a really good idea to our competition?"

"Stay with me, Glenn. It's *not* a good idea. Not unless we want to delay our release date by years. Or make our product too expensive for our target customer. Or lose money on our new product."

"Oh." His brow cleared as understanding dawned on him. "So it's going to be a good idea in five years."

"Right," Kyle said as he unbuttoned the cuffs of his dress shirt and started folding them. "So let it be known that this spec is going to be added to the blueprint, but it's not going to be available online. This addition will force the thief to make a grab for the blueprint."

"Okay. Got it." Glenn rose from his seat and stopped. "Where do I get this bogus spec?"

"There's not going to be one," Kyle said slowly. "We're telling people that there's one."

Glenn nodded and then hesitated. "Just out of curiosity, how far-reaching do you think this theft is?"

"I think it's on every level." Kyle leaned back in his chair and sighed. "We are going to clean house with this."

"Are you sure you want to do this? We have the best in the business working for us."

"And they are possibly working for the competition," Kyle replied as he reached for his keyboard.

"You don't trust anyone, do you?"

"I don't have any reason to," Kyle admitted. When he noticed Glenn didn't move or speak, he looked up from the computer screen.

"What about me?" Glenn's face was tight and drawn. His eyes were flat and his mouth pinched.

Kyle didn't want to get into this right now, but some

things had to be said. "You've been my friend since college."

"True."

"We've been through hell and back. Suffered crushing defeats and celebrated every major and minor achievement."

"Yeah." The guy's face softened as he remembered some of the wild parties of their past.

"I don't think you have anything to do with this property theft." And Kyle meant it. Sad to say, but Glenn was too ignorant about the technical aspects to steal his ideas.

"Okay." Glenn looked relieved and turned for the door.

"But," Kyle continued, "if I ever find out that you lied or betrayed me . . ."

Glenn froze.

"On *anything*"—Kyle made sure to emphasize that point—"then you'd better watch your back."

His friend looked sharply over his shoulder. "Same here," he said and left the room, softly closing the door behind him.

Kyle stared at the closed door, stunned. Glenn was questioning *his* loyalty? After all this time he protected the guy's job? Glenn's MBA was stretched to the limit, but he would never force his friend out. He wasn't bringing in another CFO. He wasn't giving Glenn a fancy, useless title and making him obsolete.

He instinctively looked at the framed picture on his desk. It was the only decoration he allowed in his office. The only personal item, now that he thought of it.

It was a snapshot of him with Glenn, Timothy, and Annette outside his first pathetically small office space. He remembered that moment vividly. It was the first day Ashton ImageWorks was in business.

They had worn T-shirts and jeans, the wind ruffling their hair. Their smiles were proud and big as the sun shone down on them. Turned out that they were clueless of the challenges that lay ahead.

Kyle picked up the picture. They were incredibly passionate about dominating the world together. These guys were the only family he had. A dream held them closer than blood ever could.

Or was he being nostalgic? Kyle returned the picture to its place. And was his loyalty going to destroy him? He protected what was his—his friends and his territory—but who was going to protect him?

Molly took a bite of pizza and closed her eyes. She savored the spices and thick, chewy crust, wondering if she had died and gone to heaven.

Someone belched loudly and a spate of male laughter burst the comforting silence.

Nope, not heaven, Molly reminded herself as she opened her eyes. More like one of the research and development teams late at night.

"Hey, Molly," Curtis said as he turned the corner into the miniscule workstation she claimed for her dinner spot. "This is a great idea. Why haven't we done this before?"

Molly swallowed her bite and said, "Because you don't believe in taking breaks."

"There's that," Curtis said as he opened another pizza box and pulled out a hot slice loaded with vegetables.

The spicy aroma hit her head-on. She wanted to grab the threads of the gooey mozzarella cheese and stuff them into her mouth. She had to be careful. "And you guys don't believe in having a social life."

"Waste of time," Brian, another programmer, said over the cubicle wall.

"So have a social hour at work," she said with a shrug. "Makes sense to me."

"Party girl," Brian teased.

Molly choked on her pizza. Party girl? Was that what they thought of her? Why?

She couldn't remember the last time she went to a party. Or went out for fun. It must have been after her good-for-nothing ex-boyfriend left and before she got hit with the bills he ran up.

When it came to hitting the party circuit, she was no different than these computer geeks. Well, except for the fact that they were bazillionaires in the making. And that they refrained from going out as a matter of choice rather than necessity.

Okay, scratch that idea, Molly thought as she sank her teeth into the pizza slice. She had nothing in common with these guys other than choosing to stay at the office on a Friday night.

But at least her decision made sense. It was bitterly cold outside and she wanted to stay in this warm office for as long as possible. Even if it meant dragging out this impromptu pizza party to last all night.

Now if only she could drag it to last a week. She had seven more days before she got her promotion. And she had no idea how long it would be before she found another place to live.

The wait stretched out before her and she couldn't take another moment of it. She briskly stood up and got busy. Molly surveyed the small group of guys as they sat on the floor and on desks. "Who wants more pizza?"

Everyone groaned with pain. Heh. These guys must have had big lunches. She, on the other hand, didn't think she would ever feel full again.

"Xbox!" someone yelled out. The guys bolted up from where they sat and ran for an alcove in the department.

Okay, that was strange. Molly stood up and decided to follow. "What are you talking about?" she asked.

She stepped into a shallow room that was filled with arcade games, bean bag chairs, and a big-screen TV.

"I didn't know you had this," she said as the guys dove and fought over the game controllers.

"Every department has one," Curtis said.

"Not on the executive floor." She looked around the room. "Exactly how does this relate to image processing software?"

"Research," they all said in unison.

"*Riiight.*" Now she understood why the programmers stayed late. The offices had top-of-the-line computers, games, a cafeteria, a fitness room, and all-you-can drink free soda. Why leave? Smart guy, that Kyle.

Hey . . . could *she* stay in the building? All night? Nah, too risky. They had security guards. Cameras. Probably ultraviolet rays that would set off an alarm and a really meanlooking SWAT team.

But it might be possible, if one did it right. "Wow," she said, not sure how to form the question without revealing her intentions. "You guys have all the comforts of home right here."

"No," Brian said as he turned on the Xbox console. "They don't have the premium channels."

Cable? They have free cable TV?!

"You could stay here all night," she said as she sank into one of the bean bags.

"We have."

"You work all night?" She was surprised when they all nodded. "And then you just go home, change, and come back again?"

"Nope," Brian said, his eyes glued to the screen. "There are lots of places to crash here. Couches. Recliners. I slept under my desk one week during that last deadline." He shuddered at the memory.

"And the guards don't have a problem with that?"

"No, why should they?" Curtis said, sitting down next to her on the bean bag. "They know we work here and the hours get crazy."

Yes! She wanted to pump her arm and shout. Guess who was sleeping here tonight? Heat, lighting, and a bathroom down the hall. She was set.

"You want to try?" Brian held out a controller.

"No, that's okay." She knew the offer meant something from these rabid gamers, and she was touched. "I'd rather see how you guys do it."

And maybe she could organize a gaming championship that would last all week. And she could sit here with the excuse of moderating. Sit here with her eyes closed, nestled deep in the bean bag chair.

She wasn't sure if she fell asleep, or what stirred her into realizing that something wasn't right. The heavy silence? Her sixth sense?

Whatever it was, Molly opened her eyes and saw Kyle Ashton standing at the doorway.

Her breath hitched in her throat as she stared at him. She really wished he wasn't sexy. But she liked how he wasn't wearing a jacket or tie. His appearance was still sophisticated, especially among the programmers, but he wasn't as intimidating.

Molly leaned over to Curtis. "I thought you said you're allowed to be here," she said through the side of her mouth.

"We are. But Kyle rarely drops by."

And wasn't it just her luck he paid a visit today? Were they too loud? Did security have a problem over a pizza delivery? It didn't matter. Right now she had to act natural.

"Hi, Kyle." Molly greeted him with her best hostess smile. "We have some pizza left if you want some." *Especially since, in a roundabout way, you footed the bill.*

Kyle slowly turned and ensnared her with his bold gaze. She felt pinned beneath his intensity. Her chest rose and fell rapidly as she tried to think of an escape. She couldn't come up with one. It was like her brain froze.

The programmer leaning against the wall next to the doorway jumped into action and offered him a soda. Kyle accepted it and returned his attention to Molly.

She was in trouble. She wasn't sure what kind, but her skin was tingling and her muscles were tense and ready to bolt. Whatever rules applied during office hours were null and void.

Another programmer whose name she forgot motioned for Kyle to see the action on the big screen.

"Curtis," Molly said, as an idea began to form.

"Yeah?"

"If anyone asks, we're dating." Kyle wouldn't move on another man's woman. Would he?

"We are?"

She turned and faced him. "No, we aren't, but if anyone asks, we are."

Curtis gave her a strange look. "O . . . kay."

She better explain herself before wild rumors circulated the building. "I don't . . . want Kyle wondering why I'm here."

"Why *are* you here?"

"For the pizza."

Curtis laughed. "So don't tell me. That's fine."

The one time she told the truth, no one believed her. From the corner of her eye she could see Kyle turning at the sound of Curtis's laugh.

"Does this mean we get to have sex?" Curtis asked.

Molly's mouth dropped open in shock. "No!" she whispered fiercely.

"But we're dating." Curtis leaned in closer to her.

Molly set her jaw. "I'm going to hit you."

"Oh, you're into that kind of thing." Curtis shook his head with regret. "I'm not into kink. I'm not sure if this relationship is going to work."

"I should have asked Brian," she muttered to herself.

"Hell, no." Curtis draped his arm over her shoulders and Molly did her best not to jump from the unexpected and overly familiar touch. "Brian's gay. Everyone knows that."

Then she'd made the right choice.

"Hey, Kyle," Curtis called out and motioned for him. "Come sit down with me and my girlfriend."

Or not.

Chapter 4

Curtis and Molly?

No.

Even though he saw it, his body rejected the idea. His mind tried to block the image of the two cozy with each other. His iron control stamped out the urgency to rush over and tear them apart.

He caught Molly's eye. She slowly blinked and smiled wide. Oh, yeah. Something was up with Molly. He was going to find out what. Either that or he was going to find out why she picked that guy over him.

There was no way that could happen.

Kyle made his way to the couple. "Curtis. Molly."

"Sit down." The elite programmer gestured to the other side of Molly. "There's plenty of room."

He'd rather sit between Molly and Curtis. Then shove Curtis off the bag and have Molly all to himself. But he'd be good. For now.

Kyle sat down next to Molly. He could feel her heat. Inhale her scent. Brush his arm against hers.

What the hell was he doing? He could grab Molly by the wrist and haul her against him. Carry her out of this room and show her every reason why she should be with him. In graphic detail.

No one would stop him. Might add to his legend. Why was he playing this game?

Kyle took a long sip from his soda can. "So, how long have you guys been dating?"

"Very recently," Curtis said before he pressed Molly against his side. "Isn't that right, sweetie?"

"We sort of drifted together," Molly explained as she shifted position and tried to sit up straighter.

Kyle knew Molly was lying. But why? "What about your wife, Curtis? Did you guys separate?"

Molly's body tightened and her eyes went wide. Although she kept herself very still, Kyle could feel her muscles quivering with rage. He guessed Molly didn't know about the wife.

"Oh, the missus and I have an understanding," Curtis said with an exaggerated wink.

"Uh-huh," Kyle drawled out.

"And Molly," Curtis said as he curled his hand on her knee. "She doesn't mind sharing."

Molly discreetly crossed her legs, trapping Curtis's hand between her knees. He didn't see her applying force, but Kyle saw the other man wince.

"Hey, loverboy," Brian said from in front of the TV. He held up his Xbox controller. "You're up."

"I'll be back." Curtis dove in for a kiss. Molly automatically turned her head to the side. Curtis's mouth landed on the corner of her lips.

That was too close for Kyle's comfort. He wanted to bat the guy away like a pesky insect. Smash him into the wall.

"Try not to miss me," Curtis said to Molly.

"I'll do my best," she replied with a bright smile.

Curtis made another attempt, but Molly was too fast and his mouth landed her ear. "She's such a tease," Curtis explained with a laugh.

Kyle made some noncommittal sound and nod. He watched Curtis go to the competition with a sense of good riddance.

But his mind went into overdrive as he understood something essential about the woman he craved. Molly Connors was a liar, not a tease. She lied with her mouth, not with her body.

She couldn't help it. She would smile and lie with Curtis, but reel back from the most innocent touch.

Or was she like that with every guy?

"Do you like games?" Molly asked suddenly.

Kyle turned and gave her a look. "Depends on who I'm playing with."

She swiped her tongue against her lips. His chest squeezed tight as he watched. "I meant computer games."

"I'm looking at the screen all day. It's not my idea of recreation."

"What is?"

He knew his grin was wolfish and he didn't bother to hide it.

Molly pressed her lips together. "Maybe I better not know."

"I'm sure your imagination is wilder than my experiences."

She scoffed at the idea. "I seriously doubt that."

"But then that's the best combination."

"What is?"

He looked at her mouth intently. "When imagination meets experience."

She swallowed heavily.

He slowly reached up and pressed his thumb against the corner of her mouth. Her skin was smooth and warm. Molly parted her lips and tilted her head toward his thumb.

There was nothing he wanted more right now than to

dip his finger into her mouth and watch her close her lips around his thumb. Lick the tip, swirl her tongue against his skin before she drew him in.

No. Now was not a good time. He wanted privacy so he could act on the promise.

Kyle gently brushed his thumb against her lip, as if he was removing Curtis's branding.

Molly frowned and drew back.

"Pizza sauce," he lied.

"Oh." She dazedly covered her mouth with her fingers.

He looked into her eyes, wanting to know what she was feeling, wanting, but she shielded any message with the slow shutter of her eyelashes.

Smart move.

"Um . . ." She looked around the room. "You didn't get any pizza," Molly breathlessly announced. "Let me go get you some." She jumped up and headed for the boxes, as if demons were after her.

Smart girl.

Why wasn't Kyle leaving? Molly wondered as she nervously chewed her bottom lip. He'd stayed long enough to be considered sociable. He could leave anytime he wanted.

As it was, she was running out of avoidance tactics. She had gone into manic hostess mode and talked to everyone—not an easy task when some of the guys had no social graces and talked primarily about *Star Wars* and *Halo*, both of which she knew little about.

She flitted here and there, making sure everyone had something to eat and drink. The pizza was long gone and Kyle was still here, his eyes smoldering with a dark, sensual promise that she was about one minute away from accepting.

She had to stay away from him. She needed to keep her job, not give him one. Remember?

The only option left was to sidle next to her "boyfriend" and give him a French kiss.

Curtis. She glared at the man's back. Married! She couldn't believe he didn't mention that detail. Jerk.

But Curtis was having way too much fun with the new status. The guy had a warped sense of humor. The rays from his computer screen must have baked his brain.

She took a quick glance and saw that Kyle was playing Xbox with some other players. From the sounds of it, he was winning. Annihilating the competition. Why wasn't she surprised?

But it meant that Kyle was going to be occupied for a while. Guys got that way. Must be all that testosterone. Must be wearing.

Then again, maybe not. The only person who seemed to be fading fast was her. She plopped down on the extra large bean bag and closed her eyes. Why wasn't everyone leaving? She was ready for sleep.

And she was most definitely spending the night at Ashton ImageWorks. On this bag, if she could get it. If she didn't have to move, even better. She wondered what would work as a blanket . . .

A shadow descended on her. The bag dipped at her side. She didn't need to open her eyes to know who sat down next to her. Her nerve endings were already going berserk.

"Who's winning," she asked, not opening her eyes.

"I am," Kyle said.

"Surprise, surprise. So why aren't you playing?"

"It was getting repetitive."

She felt the corner of her mouth lift up. Only Kyle Ashton would find winning boring.

"You should head home," he whispered in her ear. He was so close that her skin tingled. "Go to bed."

Will you tuck me in? The question bubbled on her tongue and she quickly pressed her mouth closed.

"Do you need a ride?" he asked softly.

"No!" Her eyes popped open. She tried to erase the image of Kyle's sports car pulling up next to her DIY truck. "I got that covered. But thanks."

Amusement danced in his light green eyes. "You don't want me to know where you live?"

How did one answer that without offending? One didn't. "Do you want *me* to know where *you* live?"

"Don't you already?"

"Yes, okay," she admitted. "I know your address—*addresses*—but it's not like you want me to drop by and say hi."

"Why not?"

Did she have to spell it out? "Because I'm your receptionist."

"What's wrong with being my receptionist?"

"Nothing!" Terrific. Now he thought she was complaining. "It's the best job I've ever had."

"Aw." Kyle groaned and looked away. "And here I thought you were different from all the other yes-men I've met tonight."

"I'm not just saying that." Sheesh, tell the truth and where did it get her?

"Sure you are. What other jobs have you had?"

That was dangerous territory. "Go look at my resumé."

"Come on, Molly." He said it so seductively that Molly's toes curled. "Tell me the ones that didn't make it on your resumé."

Oh, he was good, but nothing would induce her to share that information. "It doesn't matter. Ashton ImageWorks offers the best pay and medical insurance. I'm here to stay."

"There's not much advancement in being an executive assistant's assistant."

She wrinkled her nose. "We really need to work on that title."

"I'll get right on it." He smiled and Molly felt her heart do a flip.

"I'm not looking to advance," she said in a nervous rush. What she said was true. It was the main reason Sara hired her. Her boss didn't want to train someone every year.

A cynical smile tugged at one corner of his mouth. "Everyone is looking to get ahead."

"Not me."

His gaze connected with hers. "Even you."

"The only thing I want to get ahead on is my bills." She froze as the words left her mouth.

What had she said? Her mind frantically scanned her words. She shouldn't have said anything about the bills. Or the benefits. It totally went against the "trust fund baby" image.

Okay, bills. People could think she had an outrageous Nordstrom's bill. But the benefits? She winced. No heiress worried about insurance premiums!

"Wow." Molly stood up abruptly. "I had no idea it was this late. I should go."

Kyle moved to get up. "I can still give you a ride."

"I'm good," she said as she hurried away. No telling what she'd say as the throaty purr of a sports car lulled her to sleep. "But thanks."

It was Saturday afternoon when Kyle walked into the kitchen and almost collided into the head of security.

"Timothy?" Kyle asked as his friend jumped away from the door with amazing reflexes. "What are you doing here? I thought you were going on a weekend getaway with Jan. No, Cindy. Marsha?"

"Carol."

"Right." Kyle headed for the refrigerator. "What happened?"

"Why do you think I'm here?" Timothy made a face.

"Because someone is trying to steal our idea before it's patented. I am going to take him down and then I'll go on vacation."

"You don't have to do that," Kyle said as he reached into the refrigerator and retrieved an ice cold water bottle.

"Yeah, I do." His friend's tone took on an edge. "My sweat, blood, and tears built this place as much as yours did."

"True." Was that why he was the unnamed insider for the tell-all book? Was he not given enough credit for the sacrifices he made? Did he not receive enough credit?

"When was the last time you went on vacation?" Timothy asked. "It's been a while."

"I go to one of my weekend homes to relax."

"Yeah?" His friend folded his arms across his chest. "And when was the last time you went to one?"

Kyle rolled his eyes. "If you are trying to prove that you are better at finding a balance between work and life, then consider yourself the winner."

"Not quite." Timothy rested his hip against the kitchen counter. "After all, I'm here on a Saturday when I should be getting laid at a romantic bed and breakfast. Have you heard that most of the working population doesn't come to work on the weekends?"

"It's a myth," Kyle said as he drank the water.

"Yeah, it must be." He thumbed toward the door. "I even saw Molly wandering around here today."

Water spurted from Kyle's mouth. "Molly? Molly Connors?"

"Yeah. Isn't she an hourly?"

"Don't worry. Her overtime won't break the bank." But what *was* she doing here?

"Since when do receptionists work while the office is officially closed?"

"Since that receptionist is working hard to be Sara's assistant," Kyle informed him.

"Ah." Timothy nodded with understanding.

"And since when have you been so suspicious?"

His friend smiled. "Since my weekend of nonstop sex was interrupted by suspicious activity."

Kyle groaned. "Am I going to be hearing about your lost weekend for the rest of my life?"

"No, only until I finally get my weekend of sex. Then you get to hear about that."

"I can't wait," Kyle said dryly.

"But it turns out it was a good thing I postponed."

Timothy was glad he delayed a wild weekend? It had to be something freaking amazing. "And that would be because?"

"I got someone talking, and he wants to tell you everything he knows."

Kyle's water bottle hit the counter with a thud. "No. Way." There were actually people in this world who saw wrongdoings and didn't want to get into the action? Couldn't be true. "What does he want in return?"

"Immunity."

Kyle clenched his jaw. "I should have known."

Timothy watched and waited quietly.

"Why should I forgive someone who made a profit off of me?" Kyle asked, rubbing the back of his neck.

Timothy shrugged. "No one said you had to."

"So I don't have to forgive you, either?"

His friend's head went up as if he sniffed danger. "What are you talking about?"

"I know that you're the unnamed insider for that tell-all book." Saying it out loud made it sting more.

Timothy took a step back. "How did you know?"

"So it's true?" Kyle's voice hitched in his throat.

"Yeah." Timothy dipped his head. "It's true."

Was that a sign of regret? For doing it, or for getting caught? "Why did you betray me?"

"I didn't mean to. I thought I was protecting you." Timothy looked to the side as he remembered. "I was telling this author about what we did and how we made it against all odds. But he gave it a different slant."

How different, Kyle wondered.

"I'm sorry, Kyle. I thought I had this punk eating out of my hands . . ." Timothy looked at his outstretched palms and shook his head.

"Why didn't you tell me?"

"I was trying to fix it on my own. I was working on a way for Legal to block the sale of the book."

"You know, for the head of security, you really need to be more cynical and suspicious."

"I'm working on it," Timothy said with a wry smile. "It's not like I pursued the job. I kind of fell into it. Just like Sara became your assistant and Glenn became the financial officer when he can't figure out the spreadsheet program on his computer."

Kyle nodded as he considered what Timothy had said. Should he believe him? Did he make a mistake and was trying to fix it before he found out? It was possible.

It was also possible that Timothy could put a twist on the facts Kyle had. For all he knew, his friend could even be behind stealing the blueprint.

Kyle froze and the insidious idea took hold. He heard the plastic water bottle crinkle under his tight grasp.

No. That couldn't be right. It didn't make sense. Timothy wouldn't steal from his own company. Destroy something that was built with his sweat, tears, and blood.

Unless the deal was amazing.

But what could top what he already had? What could be better?

Great. Kyle took a deep breath and reined in his runaway emotions. He had just crossed over to full-blown paranoia. He needed to back off. Regroup. Maybe take a vacation. Get laid.

"So, who wants to talk?" Kyle asked, his voice dropping into a low growl.

Timothy frowned at the sudden change of subject but quickly followed Kyle's train of thought. "Brian Velazquez from R&D."

Brian? Anger roared through him. He was just playing Xbox with him yesterday. And the guy was in on the theft? Brian was going to learn the true meaning of annihilation.

"Who's the buyer?"

"He says he doesn't know."

"Sure he does." Bitterness filled Kyle that he could taste. "Sue him for millions on breaking the non-disclosure agreement and he'll remember."

"Brian wants a meeting with you. He says as far as he can tell, there's a web of traitors."

"Of course he says that!" Kyle caught himself yelling and struggled to control his temper. "How much does he want for every name?"

"As far as I can tell, Brian hasn't done anything wrong other than trust the wrong guy," Timothy argued. "He knows something weird is going on and he's showing his loyalty to you."

"Then he should give us the names." Kyle wanted to storm out of the kitchen, find Brian, and shake the information out of him.

"He wants protection. Security."

The very things Kyle wanted but no one could offer. Why should he guarantee something he could never have? Kyle rubbed his face with his hands. He had to keep his emotions out of it and stop taking it personally.

And he wasn't going to have any sense of security if he

didn't get some answers. Whether he liked it or not, he had to play the game.

"Fine," Kyle said suddenly. He grabbed the water bottle and threw it in the recycling bin. "Brian has immunity. And he's got my protection."

Timothy's eyebrows rose from the sudden capitulation. "Even if he's dirty?"

"Yep." Kyle marched to the kitchen door. "The price is too great if we lose the idea."

"You won't regret it," Timothy promised.

Kyle hit the door with more force than necessary and it swung open wildly. "I already do."

Molly stretched her legs and banged her bare foot against the desk leg.

Ow! She curled her legs up and grabbed her throbbing toes. Okay, whose bright idea was it to sleep under a desk?

Oh, right. Brian and Curtis. Supposedly geniuses. Molly rolled her eyes. They must have been talking about some sort of L-shaped desk. Definitely *not* U-shaped.

Molly shifted onto her back and stared at the underside of her desk. She was feeling a bit claustrophobic, but at least she was warm. And safe. Maybe too safe.

The security guards crawled all over the building throughout every hour. She barely got to sleep last night with one guard after another waking her up and asking to see her ID.

Brian and Curtis forgot to mention that, too. Hmm . . . She hoped they weren't making this all up.

But even if this was verboten, it was better than the very cold truck. And how did she manage to park in a crime-ridden street each and every night?

Molly rolled out from under her desk. The overhead security lights were set low so she had to squint at the clock. It was only midnight? Sheesh. Was she going to have a good night's sleep ever again?

Or how about a home-cooked meal? Molly sat up and stretched her back. She'd had the hardworking beta tester guys order Chinese on their petty account tonight. The food had been so good. The scent alone made her want to dive face first into the fried rice.

Molly stood up and looked around. Well, what was she going to do? She wasn't going to lie under her desk wide awake. Since she was wearing sweatpants and a matching sweatshirt, she could roam the halls, but she didn't feel like explaining her appearance to every security guard.

There was nothing to do in her inbox. The problem with being at the office all day long was that she was all caught up. She could work on some of Sara's stuff.

Molly glanced past the glass door and wrinkled her nose. Nah. But she could explore the executive suite.

She got up, clipped on her ID badge, and headed for the glass security door. Once she stepped inside she considered where to go first. She'd been everywhere on this executive floor and explored most of the offices.

Except for Kyle's.

She'd been in there, but had never walked around and explored, always worried she would get caught for trespassing. Always feeling like she was tempting danger.

But no one could catch her now.

Molly gingerly tiptoed to Kyle's door and opened it a crack. A table lamp cast a soft glow on his sleek, modern desk. She walked in and closed the door behind her.

She never liked the stark black and white color scheme, or the minimalist decor. It was boring and bare and looked worse at night.

She sat down on his black leather chair and found it huge. She spun around in it, getting a panoramic view of how Kyle saw the world every day. Luxurious. In control. Black and white.

Her gaze fell across a framed snapshot and she stopped

the chair from twirling. Molly smiled at the sight of Kyle and his three trusted advisors. Heh. He was gorgeous back then, but his sexiness didn't have that dangerous edge.

Now he was downright lethal.

She got up from the chair and padded barefoot toward a set of doors. The first one was an unbelievable stereo system. Strange, she never heard music coming from this office. Maybe the room was soundproof. She wouldn't put it past Kyle.

She opened the other door and stopped. She squeezed her eyes shut and opened them again. She flicked on the lights just to make sure she was seeing correctly.

Yep, she was right. It was an executive bathroom. CEOs really had these things? She thought it was just something only found in soap operas and movies.

It was half the size of her last apartment. And about one hundred times nicer. All marble and chrome. Lots of glass and all the amenities. Was that a bidet? She was tempted to see how it worked, but was afraid she'd break it.

Molly caught the reflection of the shower system in the mirror. She turned and sighed when she saw the multiple jet heads staggered at different heights and angles.

If she had something like that, she would never leave. Maybe tomorrow she could take a shower in there. No one would know.

Then again, maybe not. She instinctively knew that particular shower would ruin her for all other showers. It was better not to know.

She reluctantly turned her attention elsewhere. Molly searched the cabinets and found them as empty as the kitchen. She opened the medicine cabinet, hoping it would reveal something about Kyle Ashton, the man.

Razors, toothbrush, toothpaste. Nothing unusual. Darn.

She opened a door that probably led to a linen closet. Uh, no. Make that a closet. A *walk-in* closet.

She turned on the closet light and saw the three-way mirror and the built-in drawers and bins. She staggered into the closet, filled with envy.

What man needed a walk-in closet?

Apparently a man who needed three hundred black suits. Okay, so she was exaggerating. There were also white shirts.

She stroked the heavy fabric of a suit sleeve and looked around. The floor-to-ceiling mirrors were a nice touch, but once she thought about it, a walk-in closet wasn't all that. Bummer.

Molly turned off the lights and stepped back into the bathroom. She would've liked to say the same about the bathroom, but she couldn't. This bathroom should grace those fancy schmancy bathroom magazines.

It made her wonder how grand the one at his home looked like. *Homes*, she reminded herself.

It wasn't like she was ever going to find out, even if it graced those fancy schmancy magazines. Like she had the money for a subscription. Or a mailing address, for that matter.

She turned off the light and headed out of the bathroom when she heard a familiar ding.

It was the elevator.

Wow, these security guards got their exercise. Molly was eternally thankful that she was in the bathroom and not under her desk. She didn't think she would be noticed, but she didn't want to take the chance. She'd stay in the bathroom until the guard left.

She peeked through the opening of the bathroom door as a male figure crossed the office threshold. He reached out and turned on the lights.

Frick! Her heart leapt and pounded against her ribs. It was Kyle.

Didn't that guy *ever* go home?

He walked across the room and the panic zoomed inside

her. How was she going to get out of this situation? Would she ever learn? *Don't go where you aren't allowed!*

She would follow the rule for the rest of her life if she got out undetected. But it didn't look like her wish was going to happen as she saw Kyle head straight toward her!

Chapter 5

She scurried back into the closet, begging—absolutely begging—for him not to enter the closet. It was midnight, after all. On a Saturday.

But time meant nothing to Kyle.

She heard him enter the bathroom and hit the lights. Molly dove for the very back rack in the closet and squatted down.

Her heart pounded. Her tongue felt huge and she couldn't swallow. She kept her eyes glued on the door, but she didn't want to look.

This was why she could never play hide-and-seek as a kid. She couldn't handle the idea of being found. Couldn't tolerate the wait.

She knew she was going to get caught. She couldn't shake off the feeling. Or bravely meet the inevitable.

No, instead she was huddling in the corner, images of her work record flashing in her head. *Terminated because she was hiding in her boss's closet.*

Yeah, let's see how long it would take her to get another job with that kind of reference.

She drew in a shaky breath, ready to have that door swing open. For Kyle to find her. The interrogation that would follow. She'd have come up with a good reason why she was here. Something brilliant. Irrefutable. Logical.

So far, she had nothing.

And why wasn't he opening the door? She couldn't take much more of this.

Molly craned her neck and cocked her head to the side. All she heard was the shower.

The shower! Molly sat up straight as a plan began to form. The bathroom would get all hot and steamy. The glass would fog and she could sneak out. Perfect!

But that would mean getting out of her hiding place. Maybe she should wait until he left.

So that he could what? Go to his desk and spend the rest of the night working on the computer? Leaving her stuck here?

This was her only chance to escape. She needed to take advantage of it. Now.

Molly reluctantly crept to the door. She winced and cringed as she slowly opened it a crack. She was so nervous that Kyle might see the movement. Or that he would spot her. Look right at her. Eye to eye.

Instead she got an eyeful.

Kyle grabbed the collar of his white rugby shirt and pulled it over his head. The bright lights bounced against the dips and swells of his toned arms.

Molly ignored the tingle deep in her belly as she stared. She already knew that guy was fit, but oh . . . my . . . *goodness* . . .

Kyle's lean body rippled with strength. He was solid muscle. Defined and restrained.

She memorized everything from the whorls of dark hair dusting his tanned chest to the jutting hip bone. Her heart skittered to a stop as his hands went to the snap at his waistband.

Oh . . . The tingling grew hotter. Brighter. She shouldn't look. No. She really shouldn't. Not even a peek.

He drew the zipper down.

She should turn her head away.

Her neck muscles weren't cooperating as the zipper parted.

Okay, at least close your eyes! She forced herself to obey and her eyelids started to lower.

Until the jeans dropped to his ankles.

Molly's eyes widened. *Oh . . . wow.*

He was long, thick and heavy. There was nothing elegant or refined about his penis. It looked rough. Wild. And this was before he was aroused?

She could imagine how it would feel to have him inside her. Before he even thrust. Molly pressed her legs together as the tingling blazed into an all-out ache.

Kyle turned around and she stared at his tight buttocks. *Oh, yeah.* She could go for one of those, too. She could imagine exactly how it would feel to hold onto him as he claimed her.

He stepped out of her field of vision. A shot of panic cleared her head. Where did he go? She caught a movement in the mirror and saw Kyle step into that sinfully decadent shower. She watched the reflection as he stepped under the water.

Great. Just what she needed. A hot, naked, and *wet* Kyle Ashton.

The shower stall didn't hide a thing from her. Water pulsed against body. It sluiced down his chest and ran down Kyle's powerful thighs. She wanted to lick every droplet from his sculpted muscle.

Molly pulled at the neck of her sweatshirt. How hot was that shower? It was getting really warm in here.

The scent of Kyle's soap invaded her senses. Sophisticated. Expensive. It usually made her knees knock on everyday occasions, but this was concentrated stuff. It knocked her off her feet.

The steam wafted from the shower stall and began to

cloud the glass. Molly had to squint as the fog slowly streaked across the shower glass. She was half tempted to wipe the condensation from her view when she remembered this was what she was waiting for.

Sure she was.

She glanced at the door. It was closed, but not all the way. That was her escape. She'd better get moving before he was finished. Molly glanced back at the mirror.

His head was tilted back and water streamed down the harsh angles of his face. She fought the fierce urge to join him and press her mouth against the strong column of his neck. To run her hands along his body as his hands remained in his drenched hair.

That was never going to happen. She could fantasize about that later. Right now, she had to get away from Kyle.

She slowly opened the closet door, thankful it didn't creak. Hoping Kyle was like the rest of the world and closed his eyes when rinsing out the shampoo, Molly got on her hands and knees. She gathered up the last of her courage and began crawling along the bathroom floor.

Her heart was banging against her chest. Nerves bounced around inside her. She couldn't breathe. When she had to pass by the shower, she got down on her elbows and shimmied her way to the door.

Almost there . . . She wasn't going to look at Kyle, no matter how tempting. Her focus was solely on the door, and once she got it open, she was making a run for it.

Molly reached out and grabbed the edge of the door and slowly, oh so slowly, opened it enough that she could squeeze through. She could feel the cool air wafting in from the other room.

Home free! Molly exhaled shakily.

"Hey, Molly," Kyle called out from the shower, his tone clipped with anger. "Could you grab me a towel while you're at it?"

* * *

Kyle shut off the water as he studied Molly sprawled on the floor, frozen. Did she really think she would have gotten away?

Her arms were stretched out in front of her. One leg was straight and tense, the other curled just underneath her bottom.

Her long brown hair was pulled back in a messy ponytail. Molly wore a pale pink sweat suit, and the chunky shirt had ridden up, allowing him a glimpse of her smooth, silky back. Her feet were bare.

He slicked back his hair, trying to rein in the dark swirling emotions. He wanted to know why she was here. What she had hoped to gain.

Molly slowly got to her knees and shakily turned around. "Hi, Kyle," she said brightly. "How's it going?"

She kept her eyes firmly above his shoulders.

"I could use a towel right about now." He unlatched the shower door.

"Right." She jumped up and hurried over to the towels folded on the sink. He saw her shoulders tense when his feet slapped against the tile floor.

Her fingers clamped onto the soft terry as he approached her. He shook his head to dry his hair. Water flecked on Molly's shirt.

She met his eyes in the reflection. Her gaze drifted down. She blushed and her lips parted before she dragged her attention up.

"What are you doing here, Molly?" he asked. The soft bite seemed to echo in the small room.

"I . . ." She glanced at the door.

Kyle took the towel from her tense fingers and scrubbed his hair. He decided against wrapping it around his waist. Being naked should put him at a disadvantage, but for some reason, it didn't. The way Molly was looking—and not looking—at him made him feel invincible.

He needed all the power he could get to deal with her. He had to make her answer him. Make her tell the truth for once.

"I didn't catch that," Kyle said as she stuttered into silence. "Why are you here?"

She looked down and swallowed visibly. "I'm working."

Kyle's laugh was sharp. "In my bathroom? At midnight?"

"Yes." She met his gaze and slowly blinked. That blink always happened right before she had her story in place. "When does time or location mean anything to you? When it comes to work, that is?"

"You're a receptionist."

"I'm working at becoming an assistant." Her gaze appeared level with his chest.

"Molly, cut the crap. What are you doing here?"

"I already told you." She seemed hypnotized by his damp towel. Her head moved with every stroke. "I'm working."

"Fine." He tossed the towel onto the floor. "You're working. On what?"

Her gaze went from his feet and slowly moved up to his face. He felt his cock stirring.

"I'm here to make sure you have everything you need. Towels are here. Change of clothes in the closet. Yep, you're all set." She moved for the door.

Kyle blocked her. "I don't remember Sara tending to all my needs this way."

"She's more discreet," Molly said to his shoulder. "Years of practice."

"Maybe I should ask her how she does it. Give you a few pointers."

Pure anxiety flitted in her eyes. "That's not necessary."

"Then again," Kyle said as he took a step toward her, "Sara doesn't take care of *all* my needs."

Molly bumped up against the counter. "I'm sure you have a full-time staff taking care of the rest."

What did she think? That he had a mistress? That he paid for his sex? "For the record, I have no one taking care of me."

"My condolences."

He liked her sassy mouth. He wondered what her lips tasted like. Would her kisses be uncontrolled? What mischievous things could she do with her mouth? His cock twitched with anticipation.

Kyle rested his hand on the counter next to her hip. "The position is open."

The pulse in her neck beat wildly. "I'm sure I'm not qualified."

He seriously doubted that. She had him in knots and she hadn't even kissed him.

"There's on-site training." He placed his other hand on the opposite of her. "Excellent benefits. Not to mention job satisfaction."

He leaned in, his hips connecting with hers. Kyle knew his wet body made an imprint on her sweat suit. Temporarily branding her.

Her hips bucked against his hard cock. Victory raced through his veins. She was going to say yes. Three months of intense wanting was about to end.

"Thanks for the offer," she said hoarsely, "but I'm going to have to refuse."

The words amplified in his head. "Refuse?"

She tilted her chin. "As in no."

He stepped away and his hands fell to his sides. Why was she refusing? He could feel her caving.

Molly took another step toward the door. "You better dry off before you get cold."

He grabbed her wrist before she could get away. "Why are you saying no?"

She wouldn't look at him. "I don't have to explain myself to you."

"Wanna bet?"

"If you must know," she said, sliding her hand through his fingers, "it's because I'm already in a relationship. Curtis Puckett, from Research & Development. Remember?"

Kyle smiled. "Molly Connors, you are a liar."

"What?!" She whirled around and stared at him. She looked horrified. A blush swept her face.

"Whatever is going on between you and Curtis, it ain't sex."

His words galvanized her. Molly inched closer to the door. "You don't know what you're talking about."

He placed his hands on his hips. "Yeah, I do."

Molly tried to look offended. "I don't lie."

Kyle's bark of laughter ricocheted against the walls. "Are you kidding? You can't stop yourself."

"Then why ask me anything?"

"Because I want to know what you're hiding." Molly was probably the most fascinating woman he'd met. Was it the lies that intrigued him, or the hint of the true woman underneath the image? "One of these days I will know all of your secrets."

Her flushed skin went pale. She turned on her bare heel and bolted from the room.

Kyle knew he had to let her go. This time.

He knows . . .

"Good morning, Annette," Molly said with a smile bright and early Monday morning. Her stomach was in knots and her mind kept whirling, but she was determined to keep her game face on.

He knows I lied to him.

Lied? Ha. Even that was a lie. He knew she lied constantly. Fluently. Without even thinking about it.

How long had he known? Molly wondered as the phone rang. Since the beginning? Had he been testing her? "Good morning," she greeted the caller serenely. "How may I direct your call?"

Worse, was he the only one who knew? Molly's skin went clammy at the thought. Or did everyone else know and they were too polite to call her on it?

Kyle was never accused of being polite.

She didn't mean to lie, Molly reminded herself as she grabbed the thick stack of mail waiting for her on her desk. She didn't want to start out with the intention of lying.

Okay, that wasn't true. Molly rolled her eyes with self-disgust. She started the first time she didn't have the money to cover a bill. She quickly made up for it, but she found that lying bought her time.

Now it seemed like it only bought her trouble. Embarrassment.

She felt someone standing up in front of her. Warning prickled along her skin. She glanced up and her heart tumbled.

Kyle Ashton.

Looking right at her. Past the smooth professionalism she projected. Past the expensive clothes and makeup. He saw her for what she truly was. It made her feel naked.

Molly immediately conjured up the image of Kyle in shower. She remembered with startling clarity how he looked naked. Smooth skin, sculpted muscle. Hard—

Yeah, probably not a good time to remember him in all his glory.

Molly cleared her throat. "Good morning, Kyle."

"Morning, Molly. How are you?"

Was this a test? Did he want her to tell him the truth? That she was tired and hungry? That she should have gone to the Laundromat this weekend and the clothes she was wearing passed the sniff test, or that she couldn't sleep in that horrible truck one more night?

"I'm fine," she said with her smile firmly in place. "And you?"

"I'm out of towels in my bathroom."

She felt her skin heat as her pulse quickened. His voice was low, husky, and seductive. He might as well have said "I want to have sex with you in my bathroom."

Molly nervously swiped her tongue along her lip. "You must have taken a lot of showers since I saw you last."

Kyle caught her gaze with his own and held it. "Lots of cold showers."

The heat crawled up her neck. She couldn't maintain eye contact and focused directly between his dark, straight eyebrows. But that wasn't helping because even his eyebrows looked sexy. Since when did eyebrows become sexy? She must be really losing it.

"You want me to . . ." Molly's voice trailed off and she tried again. "You want me to check the water heater while I'm chasing after the towels?"

"Towels?" Sara appeared at the desk, causing Molly to jump. "What's this about towels?"

Panic hit Molly in the gut. She flashed a look at Kyle. He raised one of the sexy eyebrows right back at her.

What did that mean? Why was she panicking? She had to take control.

"Kyle is out of towels in his bathroom," Molly said in a rush. "And I'm going to follow up on that."

Molly gave him a look. *See? No lying there.* Kyle didn't deny it. He didn't say anything. Why? That wasn't like him.

"That's housekeeping," Sara said as she placed a folder in Molly's inbox. "The same department that takes care of the meals and cleaning on the executive floor. Why are you doing it?"

Kyle turned and looked at her, waiting. He was toying with her. Waiting for her to get tangled in her own words.

Molly's heart pounded in her ears. She opened her mouth and the first thought that popped in her mind came spilling out. "I'm not one to say it's not my department. If someone tells me they need more towels, I go find more towels."

Great. Now I sound like a liar and a brown-noser. I have no dignity at all.

"See, Kyle," Sara said with pride. She placed her hand on Molly's tense shoulder. "This is why I hired her."

"Mm-hmm." Kyle gave her a look. Molly couldn't tell if it was a "good save" or an "I'll catch you one of these days" look.

"And what are you doing here," Sara asked him. "You're late for your meeting with Timothy."

"I am? Where is it?"

"Conference Room One."

Kyle nodded, turned, and walked away. "And when I get back," he called out without looking back, "there'd better be towels in my bathroom and nothing else."

Sara and Molly watched him saunter off. "What's with him?" Sara asked.

"I was going to ask you," Molly replied. "You've worked here longer."

"And Kyle is still unpredictable," her boss said with a sigh.

Terrific. Something to look forward to.

Sara turned and hesitated. She tilted her head as she studied Molly. Her forehead furrowed as she frowned.

Oh, what? *What?* Molly tensed up. She could have sworn she hadn't lied to the woman in the past five minutes. Okay, maybe she withheld information, but did Sara *really* need to know that Kyle caught her hiding in his bathroom?

"Your outfit," Sara finally said.

Molly quickly looked at her pink sweater and black wool pants. The ensemble looked fine. Professional. Not to mention the pants and sweater didn't require ironing. Which would require electricity!

But what was wrong with it? A stain? A rip? A big bright sign that screamed, *I've been balled up in the corner of a DIY moving truck for the past week*?

"What about it?" Molly slowly asked, not sure if she wanted to know the answer.

"I've seen you wear it before. That's so not you."

Molly opened and closed her mouth, at a loss. "It's my favorite."

"Oh." Sara turned and walked away. "Looks nice."

"Thank you," she answered weakly. Great. Tomorrow she had better come up with something new. Why did maintaining the trust fund baby image have to be so difficult?

Conference Room One was quiet. Tense. Kyle waited impatiently as Brian Velazquez guzzled down the soda before setting down the can with a bang.

"Curtis Puckett," Brian announced.

Kyle and Timothy glanced at each other before they returned their attention back to Brian.

"Curtis?" Kyle asked. "From your department?"

"Yep, that's the one." Brian wiped his mouth with the back of his hand.

Huh. Brian coughed up the name without any runaround. No hesitation. Nothing. Something wasn't right. It was too easy. Or he was too paranoid.

Or both.

"What about Curtis?" Timothy prodded.

"He's the guy you're looking for," Brian explained. "He's been wanting to know what I'm working on."

"And you told him?" Timothy asked, horrified.

Brian shrugged. "We're the same clearance level, and everyone is curious what the other one is doing. We're always talking to each other about our projects."

Kyle stayed perfectly still as he struggled to remain calm. He looked across the table at Timothy, who had turned pale. Kyle knew what the head of security was thinking. All those procedures and measures ignored. All the money spent to protect their secrets wasted because the programmers blabbed to the guy in the next cubicle.

"What made you realize something was going on?" Kyle asked quietly as the anger rushed through him.

"He knew about my latest spec before I did."

Kyle tensed. "Which one?"

"The online image search application."

"We're doing that?" Timothy gave Kyle a quick look for confirmation.

"I know!" Brian slapped his hand on the conference table. "That's what I said. I haven't seen it yet."

"And that's the only evidence you have suggesting Curtis is the culprit?" Kyle asked.

"Yeah." Brian looked at them. "Isn't that enough?"

"It does make him suspicious," Kyle conceded. "The spec had been added to the blueprint this weekend, and only the program managers know about it."

"But it's more than that," Brian said, and took another gulp of his soda. "Curtis is acting weird, man. Like at the pizza party. He was all in your face, Kyle. Aggressive."

"I assumed that was his normal behavior." Programmers weren't known for their social graces. Him included.

"No. I mean, he can be really annoying, but this was different. And the way he was all over Molly? What's up with that?"

"Molly?" Timothy asked, looking at Kyle. "The receptionist on the executive floor?"

"Isn't she dating Curtis?"

"No way." Brian snorted at the idea. "Molly is not rich enough or powerful enough for Curtis."

So she wasn't telling the truth. He was right about that. Dark satisfaction seeped into his chest. But why did she lie?

Kyle rose from his seat. "That's not enough evidence against Curtis."

"What?" Brian said in a squawk. "You don't believe me?"

Kyle stopped at the door. "We have nothing."

"I still get my immunity, right?" Brian looked panicked. "You're not going to sue me for talking about the specs with Curtis?"

"Yeah, a deal is a deal," Kyle said as he walked out of the conference room. "But from now on, keep quiet about your work. Consider yourself warned."

As Kyle returned to the executive suite, he made the automatic, instinctive look at the reception desk. Molly wasn't there. He truly hated the mixed feelings of relief and disappointment. He wanted to feel indifferent about Molly's absence.

Storming into his office, Kyle went straight to his desk, sat down, and stared out the window at the Cascade mountain range.

"So . . ." Timothy said as he sat down on one of the guest chairs next to his desk. "What now?"

"I don't know." And he hated that feeling. It was foreign and weakening.

"Curtis sounds like our man."

"Sounds like it." And he was ready to go in for the kill. It didn't matter if the guy had been heralded as one of the most innovative computer programmers. Kyle didn't trust him and wanted him out.

"Are you thinking what I'm thinking?"

Kyle reluctantly turned around.

Timothy looked him straight in the eye. "Molly Connors's name keeps popping up."

The muscle in Kyle's jaw twitched. "She's a receptionist." *Who keeps showing up where she's not supposed to be.*

"Yeah," the head of security said with a nod. "And that might be the problem. She's in a prime position in the office. She's the gatekeeper who is in contact with a lot of people and has access to a lot of information."

"True."

Timothy leaned back in his chair and steepled his fingers as he considered the problem. "What do we know about her?"

"Not much." *Other than she lies. A lot.* She also drove him wild, made him want things he shouldn't want. Distracted him. Turned his world inside out.

"She could be working for our competition," his friend suggested. "Or a free agent."

Kyle stood up abruptly. He didn't want to hear this. But he couldn't ignore the possibility. "We'll keep an eye on her. I'll tell Sara to keep highly sensitive documents from Molly," Kyle decided.

"That's it?"

Even to his ears the plan sounded more like keeping her away from temptation. Protecting her more than him. "We'll go from there. See if she starts hunting for it."

"And Curtis?"

"Track him." Kyle strolled past his bathroom door and paused. There was a curious white glow under the bathroom door. He reached for the handle and turned, but the door didn't budge. Kyle pushed harder.

"What are you doing?" Timothy was right next to him.

"Hold on." He rested his shoulder against the door and pushed. Something soft flopped against his face. He looked up as a waterfall of folded towels cascaded on top of him.

"What the—"

Folded white towels crammed every inch of the bathroom as far as he could tell. It was like a linen closet out of control. "Molly." He felt the corners of his mouth twitching.

Timothy stepped over the pile and peered inside the bathroom. "Are you sure?"

"I asked for towels." *And anything else . . .*

"Next time ask for a bodacious blonde."

Chapter 6

Kyle wasn't going to say a word to Molly about the towels. He knew Molly expected it, and decided to do the opposite. He wanted to see her squirm. Watch her wait, anticipate his next move. Anticipate him.

He strolled by her desk later in the day and noticed how she watched his every move. "It's five o'clock, Molly."

"Yes, it is," she replied with a cheerful smile.

"Isn't that quitting time for you?"

Her smile stiffened. "Is it quitting time for you?"

"Didn't Sara tell you the work hours? She should have. I better talk to her." He moved for the glass door.

"Five o'clock is quitting time," she answered dutifully. "Thank you so much for reminding me."

She made no move to leave. "I think you're working too much overtime," Kyle said.

"No, I'm not," Molly quickly denied. "And since when is that problem for a boss?"

"Since I don't want my employees to burn out." *Or wander around where they aren't supposed to be.*

"That won't happen."

"I'd rather not risk it. Come on, Molly." He walked around to her side of the desk. "Time for you to go."

"But, but—" She gestured at the work on her desk.

He reached for the chair. Kyle noticed how she straightened her spine as his hand landed on the backrest. "Is there anything urgent?"

Her jaw slid to the side. "No."

"Then it will be there tomorrow. You know what they say. All work and no play."

"Shouldn't you take your own advice?" she muttered as she scooped up the papers and put them in a file.

He leaned down until his mouth was level with her ear. "Ah, but that's different."

"Because you're the boss?"

Kyle saw the shiver she tried to suppress. "Because the one I want to play with refuses."

Molly pressed her lips together and steadfastly ignored him. She shut down her computer with brisk moves. Kyle realized how unusual the sight was. The woman never shut down early.

Come to think of it, the woman never shut down. Why was that?

She made a quick call to inform Sara she was leaving for the day. "Well, I'm done here," Molly said as she hung up the phone. "I'll see you tomorrow, Kyle."

Kyle pushed the call button for the elevator. "Where's your coat?"

"I didn't bring one," she said with a slow and leisurely blink.

She lied. About wearing a coat? What was up with that? Why would she lie about something unimportant?

The elevator doors opened and Kyle glanced inside. He saw that most of the people leaving were administrative employees. Kyle nodded his acknowledgement and held the door open. " 'Bye, Molly."

She flashed a polite smile, but he could have sworn her eyes said, "Whatever."

He waited until the door was closed and ran to the stairwell. He was curious to see if Molly left the building. If she headed for another department.

If she followed orders.

He knew he had other things to do. Pressing matters. High priority situations. But from the moment Timothy questioned Molly's action, it had bugged Kyle. He needed to know.

He arrived on the main floor well before the elevator doors opened. He hung back as everyone got off, not wanting Molly to see him. He saw that she was chatting with someone he vaguely recognized.

Molly was always talking with someone, now that he thought about it. It was a good trait for a receptionist.

And a corporate spy.

He shook the thought away and tried to place where he knew the woman she was talking to. Human resources, if he wasn't mistaken. Nothing potentially dangerous about that.

Molly stepped out of the building and satisfaction filled him. He wouldn't have to worry about her sneaking around today. Kyle was on the verge of returning to his office when he noticed something was off.

Everyone turned right and headed for the bus stop or car park. Molly turned left, which led to absolutely nothing. And she was being weird about it.

His instincts went on high alert. Maybe he did need to worry. Kyle decided to follow.

By the time he followed through a maze of parking lots and small office campuses, Kyle came to a few conclusions. First, Molly was going to a great extent to hide something. Second, she should be wearing a coat. They both should, he decided as he hunched his shoulders against the cold wind.

Third, she had no self-preservation, walking around in the dark. Not that there was a lot of crime on this side of the Puget Sound, but that didn't mean it was nonexistent. Molly should know better.

And his final conclusion was that he had crossed the level from following to stalking. He hoped no one ever found about it. It would be hard to live down.

Molly turned the corner of a nondescript office building and approached a parked DIY moving truck. She stopped and looked around. Kyle ducked behind the corner. When he peeked around, he saw Molly squatting at one of the wheels.

It looked like she was erasing a yellow-orange mark from the tire with her fingers. She then opened the back of the truck and climbed up. Rolling through the opening, she disappeared and the door rolled down.

What the hell?

He looked around, but it was quiet and peaceful in the parking lot. Nothing seemed out of the ordinary. Other than his suspicious receptionist entering a parked DIY.

He waited, wondering if someone was going to join her. If she was going to leave. And what was in the truck?

But nothing happened.

Kyle approached the truck. He placed his hand on the hood and found it cold. Walking around the side, he didn't hear anything going on inside the vehicle.

Okay, this was getting really weird.

He looked at the back door and noticed she'd left it open an inch. Kyle peeked underneath but didn't see anything. Not even a movement.

Okay, enough was enough. Kyle banged on the door. "Hello?"

No answer.

He knocked harder. "Hello?" He waited and heard some scurrying. Kyle grabbed the handle and tossed the door open.

And saw Molly clutching a sweatshirt against her naked body.

* * *

"Kyle?" She stared at him as he hoisted himself into her truck. "Get the heck out!"

"What are you doing here?" His eyes wandered down her body, missing nothing.

"Shouldn't I be asking you that?" She frantically searched for a place to dive and hide. The truck was filled with stuff, but there was no place to squeeze in and disappear.

He looked around the truck and grabbed hold of the flashlight next to her door. The only source of light, and she had left it upright to cast a glow that would reach most of the dark, shadowy corners. Now he had control of it. Figured.

"What is all this stuff?" Kyle asked as he closed the door behind him.

"You need to leave." She would point her finger at the door, but she was afraid the sweatshirt would slip. "Right now."

He ignored her demand and sat down on the orange sofa. "Not until I get some answers."

Molly turned around, praying that the cardboard box on the floor was hiding her from the waist down. She had a feeling it didn't. She tossed on the sweatshirt, giving up on the idea of a bra.

She grabbed the change of underwear and paused. Molly looked over her shoulder and discovered that he'd directed the flashlight right at her. "Did you follow me?"

Kyle shrugged. "Yeah, so?"

"Okay, you have crossed the line." She hopped into her panties and snatched a pair of jeans from her pile of clean clothes.

"Oh?" he asked as he stretched one arm along the back of the sofa. "And hiding in my bathroom is model behavior?"

"That wasn't intentional." She dragged the denim up her legs.

"Doesn't matter." He pointed the flashlight from one end of the truck to the other. "Are you a kleptomaniac?"

Molly scoffed at the idea. "No!"

He looked at the sofa. "You *bought* this?"

She zipped up her jeans. "No."

He seemed relieved and continued to direct the light around the small truck. Kyle paused as he spotlighted her work clothes. "Molly, do you live here?"

"This is my hometown."

"The truck, Molly." He pointed the light directly at her neck. She was sure it was unflattering and gave her a double chin. "Are you living out of this truck?"

She placed her hands on her hips. "No, of course not."

Kyle stared at her and a smile slowly appeared on his face. It would have made him drop-dead gorgeous if it hadn't been so arrogant.

"What is so funny?"

"I got you now."

Panic hit her square in the chest. "What?" What did he know? How did he find out?

"You blinked."

Molly stared at him. That was it? She shrugged. "It's been known to happen."

Kyle rested more comfortably on the sofa. "So how long have you been living here?"

Okay, don't explain yourself. He was probably bluffing anyway. "I just told you, I wasn't." She grabbed a pair of socks. They didn't match, but she didn't care at this point.

"Kind of chilly in here," Kyle observed.

"You can leave anytime." Molly stepped over a box of books and hopped to the side before she fell against the end table.

"Dark, too."

"No one is stopping you." She sat on the sofa arm.

"And your security system sucks." He aimed the flash-light at the door handle.

"Be sure to close the door firmly on your way out then." She didn't look at him as she put on a sock.

The light was back on her. It traveled slowly up her foot to her mouth.

"Buh-bye." Molly waved and picked up her other sock.

Kyle didn't move, but the atmosphere crackled. "Have you been camping out at the office?"

She jerked her head up before she could stop. "No."

The arrogant smile was back.

She wanted to throw him out, but that was impossible. The least she could do was grab the light away from him. Maybe take a chance and clock him over the head with it. "Go away, Kyle."

"Or what?" He moved the light away from her. "You'll call the cops?"

Her hands curled into fists at her sides.

"All I want is to go to dinner with you." He held his fingers up and made a bunny rabbit shadow on the opposite wall. "And you think that is reason for an arrest?"

Her stomach grumbled. "Dinner?" She looked at him suspiciously. "You followed me across town to see if I'll go to dinner."

"No, actually I worked up an appetite following you."

"Then why did you follow me?" She wasn't sure if she was ready for the answer.

"I'll tell you over appetizers."

A meal with more than one course. Oooh . . . He was ruthless. More reason to keep away from him, despite what her stomach was saying. "I don't date the boss."

He tilted his head and pinned her with a look. "You don't follow the rules, so why bother making any?"

"I mean it, Kyle."

"It's dinner," he said with a trace of impatience. "Not foreplay. Not a commitment."

She glared at him. There was nothing more she wanted than to get out of this truck. To eat something. Anything. And he knew it.

"I have plans," Molly said suddenly. Where were her shoes? She couldn't find them without her flashlight. "And . . . and you're making me late."

"Oh, yeah, right."

"You don't believe me?"

"No, not particularly."

"Fine. You are more than welcome to tag along," she said, hoping he didn't call her bluff.

She took pleasure in his hesitation. *Not so sure of yourself now, are you? That makes two of us.* But at least that leveled the playing field.

"Sure." He stood up and held his hand out to her. "I'm in."

Darn it. Now she had to come up with a night he'd never forget—or want to repeat.

Kyle leaned back on the cracked plastic chair and sprawled his feet in front of him. "Molly Connors, you sure know how to give a guy a good time."

Molly rolled her eyes and sank her teeth into the sub sandwich. Her groans were almost orgasmic. Kyle did a quick glance, but no one seemed to notice. He couldn't be the only one affected. But then, these people were in a hurry to get their clothes washed and dried before the Laundromat closed.

He admitted it had been a while since he'd been in a Laudromat. Not much had changed. The uncomfortable seats. More washers available than dryers. The eclectic mix of people. Oh, yeah. It was all coming back to him.

But he preferred the place over some of the girly boutiques she visited earlier in the evening. Kyle kept a close eye on her transactions, and if he wasn't mistaken, she had a very complicated exchange system going on there.

Kyle didn't know if he should be impressed or alarmed. If anything, he should be careful around this one. She was a lot craftier than he had originally given her credit for.

"And to think you passed up the chance for crab bisque and Caesar salad." He loosened his tie.

She stopped chewing. "Shut up."

"Grilled steaks . . ."

Molly speared him a look. "I'm warning you."

"Chocolate raspberry cake . . ."

"You are living on borrowed time."

"All to run errands." Kyle sighed and shook his head with mock sorrow.

"Unlike a lot of your dates," Molly said as she grabbed for the soda bottle, "I don't have three hours a night to hang out at a restaurant."

He looked out of the corner of his eye. "I thought all trust fund babies did."

She froze for just a second, but Kyle caught it. He hid his smile as she continued to remove her soda bottle cap. "I'm not independently wealthy."

"I figured that one out." He looked around the Laundromat.

"I never said I was."

"Strangely enough, I believe you." He didn't know why, and he hoped it was based on gut instinct and not that he was enamored of her charisma.

"My truck tipped you off?" she asked, her mouth pressed against the plastic bottle.

"So it is your truck?"

Molly groaned, obviously realizing her error. "Technically, no."

"Is it your temporary home?"

She braced her shoulders and faced him directly. "Why do you want to know?"

Kyle raised his hand. "Let's get something straight. I can't fire you because of a lack of address. It's against the law."

"Doesn't mean you won't find something else to fire me for," Molly said as she capped the bottle and set it down. "I might be late for work one day and boom! You decide to fire me. Or maybe I didn't supply you with enough towels."

"Or something like insubordination?"

Her jaw tightened. "Exactly."

Okay, when she put it like that, he could see why she didn't trust him with the facts. "Just tell me the truth about one thing."

"*One* thing?" She shrugged. "Go for it."

He didn't expect her to agree that quickly. Was she going to lie? Sidestep the answer? She was good at that.

And there were a lot of questions he wanted to ask. Deeply personal ones. Questions that would get him closer to her and get her in his bed.

But he had to get one question out of the way, and then he could pursue her single-mindedly. "What's your relationship with Curtis?"

Molly made a face. "Curtis was a big mistake."

Hmm. That could mean anything. "So, you two . . . ?"

"No. No way!" She shuddered with disgust, but the idea didn't seem to ruin her appetite as she picked up her half-eaten sandwich. "I didn't want you asking questions about what I was doing at the office after hours. So I told Curtis to just act like we're together."

"And he went with it? Just like that?" It didn't make sense. Why would Curtis do that and receive nothing in return?

"Yeah, he was totally up for it. I didn't know he was married!" She took a ferocious chomp out of the sandwich.

"Do you see him outside the office?"

She held her hand over her full mouth. "I'm always at the office."

He raised his eyebrow at her. "You know what I mean." Kyle had finally got her to open up. It wasn't a lot, but he wasn't going to backtrack.

She took her time chewing before she swallowed. "No."

Good. He didn't want Molly involved in this intellectual property mess. He wanted to pursue the woman without having to watch his back.

She gave him a shrewd look. "Does this have anything to do with why you're following me?"

"Sorry, I can't tell you," he answered, surprised that she picked up on that. "You don't have security clearance."

"In other words, you don't want to tell me and you're hiding behind corporate bureaucracy."

He smiled, knowing he was caught. "Yeah, basically."

"Mm-hmm." She took another bite of the sandwich.

Kyle watched her. She seemed to be softening up to him. Not a lot, but she wasn't dodging him, either. "By the way, where are you going to sleep tonight?"

She coughed and slapped her hand over her mouth. "Not with you."

"I wasn't extending an invitation."

"*Suuure.*" She grabbed for her soda bottle.

"I wasn't." He looked up as an older woman walked by with a metal laundry cart. He moved his feet out of the way before she ran him over.

Molly chugged down the drink. "Then why are you asking? Worried about my well-being?"

"As a matter of fact, I am." Which wasn't good. Molly was a distraction he couldn't afford. He couldn't trust her, was trying hard not to like her, so why did he care?

Molly didn't bother to hide her disbelief. "I'll be okay, but thanks for asking."

Kyle shifted his chair and studied her. "Let me see if I get this straight. You would rather sleep in a cold truck alone than in my warm bed with me?"

She considered what he said. "Yep, that pretty much sums it up."

He saw her slow blink. *Yes!* He had been getting worried there for a second.

"Okay." He shifted back and stared at the clothes flopping in the dryer. "I get it."

He watched her reflection on the machines. Her eyes narrowed into slits. "Get what?"

"Don't worry about it." He folded his arms across his chest. "I understand."

The eyebrows went up. "I seriously doubt it."

He shrugged one shoulder. "It's obvious."

She shook her head and took another bite of her sandwich. "Not to me."

"You're a virgin."

Molly choked. Spluttered. "I'm a what?!"

"It's okay." Kyle looked back at her. "There's no shame in being one."

She pounded her fist against her sternum. "What makes you think that?"

"Though maybe there's something wrong." He tapped his finger against his chin as if he was deep in thought. "Considering your advanced age and all."

Her mouth dropped open. "Now I'm an old maid?"

Kyle tilted his head to the side. "How old are you?"

Her mouth snapped shut and she gave him another warning look. "Old enough to know not to get tangled up with you."

"Molly, Molly, Molly . . ."

She slouched in her seat. "I don't want to hear it."

"You need to learn a few more things. You know, that's the problem with virgins."

"Would you shut up?" she said in a hiss and quickly looked around for eavesdroppers.

"Once they get to a certain age, they make some stupid decisions all based on their first time. They make complicated plans because they feel like they need to make it perfect after waiting so long."

"You're an expert on virgins?" She held up both hands and leaned away from him. "That bit of info isn't warming me up on the idea of sleeping with you."

"Virgins would rather sleep in a truck than share a bed." He had no idea where this stuff was coming from, but he was having fun. "Because it's not the bed in their plans."

She closed her eyes. "Here we go."

"Virgins will go through great lengths to avoid temptation. They can't have anything ruin their plans for that First Time."

"Wouldn't know about that." She opened her eyes and picked at her sandwich.

"Like gaining fake and unattainable boyfriends." He nudged her with his elbow.

"Really? Fascinating." She removed a pickle from her sandwich and stuffed it in her mouth. "Did you do a focus group?"

"Or watch a guy showering but bolt at the first offer."

Her jaw tightened.

"Or sleep in an unsecured truck rather than a bed a guy offered."

The muscle in her cheek twitched.

"And in no way did the guy offer to share," Kyle was quick to point out.

"All right! All right!" Molly interrupted. "I am not a virgin. Sheesh." She flopped back into her seat.

The Laundromat fell silent. All he could hear was the hum of the machines and the tinny voice on the television. Kyle struggled not to smile.

"Oh, come on." Molly looked around and splayed her arms in the air. "Like y'all are pure and innocent."

An infant wailed on the other side of the large room and everyone looked away. The buzz of conversation resumed.

She glared at Kyle. "Thanks a lot. I'll never be able to use this place again."

"So . . ."

She pointed her finger at him. "Don't say it."

"Where are you sleeping tonight?"

Molly exhaled hard and long. "Kyle, there are three reasons why I won't be going home with you."

His eyebrows shot up. "Only three? I'm closer than I thought."

"Number one," she said through clenched teeth. "I don't sleep with every guy who buys me dinner, does me a favor, or simply asks."

"Good to know."

"Number two"—she held up two fingers—"I don't sleep with my boss. Ever."

Kyle sighed with relief. "I'm glad to hear it."

His answer distracted her from her list. "You are?"

"Yes, because technically Sara is your boss, and that would bring a weird dynamic to this relationship."

Molly's eyes glazed over. Shook her head and pressed her lips together. She turned and stared at the dryer.

"What's number three?" he couldn't resist asking.

She hesitated before she looked at him, her eyelids half open. "You're not my type."

Blink.

Kyle tried not to smile. "What's your type?"

"I like the quiet, silent type." *Blink.* "Blue collar worker." She looked up at his dark hair. "Blond." *Blink, blink.*

"Anything else?"

She thought for a minute. "A homebody."

He nodded and leaned over to whisper, "You forgot boring in bed."

"Oh, shut up."

"Good night, Kyle," Molly said cheerfully as she pulled up to the entrance of Ashton ImageWorks. "See you tomorrow."

He leaned back in the passenger seat and studied her. "You really would rather sleep in a truck." He couldn't believe it. He really thought he was going to get his way by the end of the night.

"I'm not sleeping in the truck," she admitted.

Relief flooded through him. "Yeah?"

"No. Why should I when there's this nice cardboard box with my name on it by the Seattle Aquarium?"

"Molly," he groaned and closed his eyes, but the image was clear and disturbing.

"Why are you so concerned about my sleeping arrangements? Are you worried that I will be sneaking around work? Using up the office supplies to make a bed?"

"Something like that." He was stuck. He didn't want her to sleep in a truck, vulnerable and alone.

But he couldn't allow her to sleep in his office. She might be embroiled in this theft. She had the means and motive. No reason to give her plenty of opportunity.

He didn't trust her, but he also wanted to protect her. It didn't make sense. If anything, it should cool any thoughts of taking her to his bed. That was more dangerous. It would bring her closer than he should allow.

"Don't worry, Kyle," she said, her tone suddenly serious. "I have no intentions of sleeping in your office."

"Yeah, how do I know you're telling the truth?"

"Have you tried sleeping in your office?" She scrunched up her nose. "The carpeting is too hard."

"And a sidewalk isn't?" Why was he worried? She was an adult. She made her choices. She made it clear she didn't want him looking after her. Fine. She could look after him.

He hopped out of the van and strolled around to her side. Kyle knocked on the driver's window and waited for her to roll it down.

"Are you going to escort me to the door?" he asked.

Molly smiled. "You're funny. A load of laughs."

"That's why you want me."

Her smile quickly disappeared. "I don't." *Blink*.

Kyle was tired of the lies. There was only one way he knew how to stop them from coming. He cupped his hand around her head and sank his fingers in her soft hair. Pulling her closer, Kyle pressed his mouth against hers.

Molly's lips parted as she gasped. He took advantage of it and slid his tongue inside. She tasted hot and spicy. Hunger rolled through him, fierce and wild.

He pulled back, but he wanted more. Lots more. "Yeah, you do. You want me bad." Kyle turned and walked away. " 'Night, Molly."

Chapter 7

Sitting at one of the tables in Ashton ImageWorks' extensive courtyard, Molly enjoyed the rare sunshine. The break from the dreary weather was a good sign. She knew it.

She tilted her head up to meet the rays before returning her attention to the Cascade mountain range. Molly listened to the gurgling fountains that splashed into zigzagging waterfalls. The plants and bushes were asleep for the winter, but everything seemed brighter, more colorful.

"There you are," Kyle said as he approached her.

Molly sat up straight. Her heart did a funny little flip when she saw him in the sleek black pinstripe suit and crisp white shirt. Even the bold red tie gave her a few naughty thoughts. "Did you need me for something?"

The look he gave her was hot and suggestive.

Molly felt the excitement fizzing inside her, but offered him a wry smile. "Forget I asked."

"So what did you do last night?"

"Sleep." Barely, but she did manage a few hours.

"Where?"

It was best not to give too many details. "Around."

"Oh, so you do sleep around."

She groaned and rolled her eyes.

"But you won't sleep with me."

She rose from the bench and started down the steps that

followed the waterfall. "You're sounding like a broken record."

"You wouldn't know what to do if I stopped asking you."

"Sure, I would." She liked the playful side of him. She wished she saw it more often. Then again, maybe not. Too dangerous. "I'd get on my knees and thank my lucky stars."

"There are better things to do on your knees."

"Like crawl away from you?"

Kyle was right beside her on the steps. "You're being very feisty today."

"Don't you mean insubordinate?" She waggled her eyebrows.

"Yeah, there's definitely something different about you." Kyle's gaze traveled down her pale pink coat to her black heels.

"Today is Friday." She skipped down a few steps.

"And you can't wait for the weekend? Is this something you should say in front of your boss?"

"You're not my boss," she said, tilting her head toward him. "According to you, Sara is."

"And I'm her boss."

"Details." She decided to take the small bridge over the waterfall. "You can't change your story to fit your argument."

"Because you have a monopoly on that?"

She stuck her tongue out at him.

"Okay, come on." He reached out and took hold of her arm. "Tell me why it's so good that today is Friday?"

"I get my review." She couldn't stop her smile.

"Oh, yeah. I forgot about that. So, how are you going to celebrate?"

"I haven't figured it out yet." She reluctantly stepped out of his grasp. She was trying her best to act professional, but one touch from Kyle and it all went out the window.

"I was thinking of taking my friend Bonita out with her kids," Molly continued. "But she can't this weekend. So tonight, I'm thinking a huge dinner for myself."

"Good plan. And then what?"

"Maybe check into a nice hotel for the weekend." She'd been thinking, planning, dreaming about it ever since she was evicted. "With a bed."

He winced.

"A huge bed where I can lie there spread-eagled." She stretched her arms wide.

Kyle looked like he was in pain.

"With a gigantic bathtub. Or a hot tub."

"All by yourself?" he asked hoarsely.

"Say what?" She dropped her arms.

"You're going to enjoy all that by yourself?"

"Kyle, are you trying to get yourself invited to my hotel room?"

His smile was hopeful. "Is it working?"

Molly chuckled. "No."

"But what about promotion sex? You're going to miss out on that."

"What?" She'd never heard of such a thing. "You're making that up."

"Nope. Doesn't everyone have it?"

She couldn't say. She'd never been promoted. "And you have to have it with the CEO?" she asked with suspicion.

Kyle smiled. "Now you see why the job review process is so rigorous." His cell phone buzzed. Kyle sighed as he grabbed it and read the text.

"How do you know I'm getting a promotion?" Molly asked, hope stirring in her chest. "Did you sign off on the paperwork?"

"Maybe." He frowned as he returned his phone back into his pocket. "I don't remember seeing your file."

She poked him in the chest with her finger. "You're a tease."

"Nah." He captured her hand and pressed it against his heart. "I always make good on my promises."

An idea burst into her mind and she followed the impulse. "So what are you doing tonight?" she asked.

"Why are you asking?" Kyle asked as he lifted her hand to his mouth and pressed his lips against her fingers.

"I'd like to take you out to dinner." She suddenly felt nervous and shy.

His hand tightened around hers. "Huh?"

He couldn't mask his surprise. Molly didn't know if it was because she took the initiative, or because a receptionist just asked the CEO to dinner. Now she felt stupid.

"I have a few things to do first," she said, giving him time to back out, but really hoping he didn't. "I can call you on your cell. I have your number."

"Molly, are you asking your boss out on a date?" The arch of his eyebrow was downright wicked. "Breaking your own rules? I'm touched."

"No, I'm asking you to dinner." She retrieved her hand. "I'm not interested in a date."

Kyle smiled. "Liar."

"Tease." She smiled back.

"Keep calling me that I will be required to follow up."

"Yeah, right." A heavy warmth nestled low on her hips. How would he follow up?

"Call me," he said as he stepped off the bridge. "I'm driving."

And that meant he would take control. She hadn't planned on that. "My truck cramps your style?"

"It doesn't set the proper mood."

"No mood is going to be set." She hurried after him, determined to make that clear.

"Wanna bet?" He stopped and faced her. "Who drives is going to be the deal-breaker for me."

Oh, gee. A choice between a DIY truck and a sports car. Hmm . . . Let me think. "Okay, you win. You drive a tough bargain."

Kyle was openly suspicious of her easy capitulation. "You're not going to bail on me now, are you?"

That question was a surprise. Kyle needed to know one important thing about her. "I don't bail."

"Good to know." He leaned forward, his voice low. "But I want to seal this bargain. Let me know that you mean it. Kiss me."

She found herself about to do just that and reeled back. "What? No." She frantically looked around to make sure there were no witnesses. "How many times do I need to tell you? This is not a date."

"Come on, Molly." He leaned closer. "You know you want to."

Was it that obvious? "Kyle, you're sounding desperate."

"I am desperate."

"Aw, poor baby."

"Come on, Molly." He circled his arm around her waist. "One kiss."

She stared at his mouth. Her own lips stung with need. She wanted to kiss Kyle, but where would that lead? Eventually, the unemployment line, that was where.

Molly wasn't sure what she was doing with him, but it felt something like playing with fire. She was mesmerized by the flames and wanted to explore the magic. But she had to be careful because it was almost guaranteed that she would get burned.

"Kyle," she said as she smoothly stepped out of his loose hold. "No guy is worth risking a job." She hurried up the steps before he caught her again. "And you can't convince me otherwise."

"You can say that now, Molly," he called after her. "But you haven't seen me try."

Molly swept the mountain of empty envelopes to the side of her desk as she looked for her calendar. Yep, it was Friday. She hadn't been wrong about that.

But where was Sara? Molly looked around, wondering where her boss was. She hadn't seen much of her today. Sure, it was busy, but not *insanely* busy. About as hectic as last Friday.

Molly's throat got tight and dry. Maybe that wasn't a good thing, considering that she couldn't see the top of her desk. She might be able to get it clean before Sara wanted to do her performance review. If she found the time today.

No, Sara couldn't push her review back. Molly sat straighter and kept stuffing envelopes. Her boss *had* to meet with her today or human resources would get on her case.

Supposedly.

The phone rang and she quickly picked it up. "Ashton ImageWorks. Molly speaking."

"This is Laurie, the caretaker for Kyle's island cottage."

"Hi, how—"

"Can I talk to him?"

Molly paused, noting the urgency in the woman's voice. "He's not in, but I can transfer you to Sara."

"Eh." That one sound gave Molly a clear understanding that the two butted heads in the past. "I'd rather leave a message on his voicemail."

"It's temporarily out of order," Molly said, doing her best to keep the woman away from the voicemail. "Some sort of . . . computer virus. I can take a message."

"Tell him I'm sorry for the short notice, but I have to catch the only ferry out or I'll be too late."

"Understandable." What was she talking about?

"My kid is in labor and is on her way to the hospital in Seattle."

"Oh . . . uh . . . that's great." *Does she want me to write this down?* Molly quickly grabbed a pen.

"Her water broke—"

Molly paused in her search for the message pad. *Uh, too much information.*

"And she lost her mucus plug—"

Mucus plug?! Waaay too much information. She grabbed for her scratch pad, wishing Laurie would stop before she was traumatized for life.

"Well, it sounds like she definitely needs her mom with her," Molly interrupted, as chirpy as possible. "What would you like me to tell Kyle?" Although she would love to see his face at the mention of a mucus plug.

"Oh, right. That's why I'm calling," Laurie said with a laugh. "I feel like I'm running around like a chicken with her head cut off."

I think I'd rather stay with the mucus plug imagery.

"Tell him that the redecorating is done. I gave his neighbors the spare key in case there were any problems."

"Okay."

"It might be a while before I get back. I didn't have time to clean out the refrigerator, which I apologize for, but the freezer and cabinets are full of nonperishables in case he drops by the cottage."

Molly doubted if Kyle would care, but jotted down the key words. "Got it."

"Although that's unlikely since he hasn't been to the cottage for at least a year. I have a feeling he's going to put it up for sale. But that's okay, because then I can be there for my grandkid—"

"Okay." *Is there an off button for this woman?*

"Not that I don't like my job," Laurie quickly assured her. "Love it—"

"Okay." *Get off the phone.*

"Oops!" Laurie exclaimed. "I'm getting another call."

"It might be the hospital." Molly was quick to point out the possibility.

"I better take it."

Yes, good idea. Please do. "And I'll give the message to Kyle. Good luck."

"Thank you," Laurie said as she immediately terminated the call. Molly hung up the phone with some relief and saw Sara standing in front of her. She was frowning.

Molly glanced at her desk and felt the growing horror. Her desk looked like a tornado wreck. She felt her shoulders dip. Well, maybe she wasn't party pretty like last week, but it shouldn't wreck her review.

"Where is Kyle?" Sara asked, looking worn out and overworked.

Molly felt her nerves flaring up again. "I think he's in a meeting about security with Glenn and Timothy."

"Are you sure?" Sara paused from sweeping her red hair from her eyes. "There's no meeting on his schedule."

"That's what I heard him say," Molly answered with a shrug. "He was in a rush."

"And Annette?"

Molly had no idea. "I think she's in her office."

"No, I was just there." Sara slowly walked back to the glass doors, and then turned around. "Molly . . ."

"Yeah?"

"Since they're gone for who knows how long, we can do your review now. Could you run down to human resources and get the paperwork?"

Yes-s-s-s! Molly wanted to bolt from her chair, arch her back, and crow. Instead she tilted her head and said, "Yes, I have time to do that. Are you sure they'll give it to me? Is that allowed?"

"I don't see why not."

Molly regally rose from her chair and strolled to the elevator. *Pay raise. I'm getting a pay raise.* She caught Sara's bemused look. Oops, had she been doing a little be-bop while she waited for the elevator? *I will continue the pay raise happy dance later.*

She waited until she stepped into the empty elevator and the door closed. Molly thrust her arms out in victory. Yes! She made it! She survived!

She would never have to live in a truck again. Or sleep in one.

No more eating garnishes from the executive kitchen and calling it lunch. No more expired stuff from the vending machine for breakfast.

Getting an apartment . . . getting a bed! Molly sighed contentedly at the thought.

My own bathroom. She would celebrate by buying bubble bath. No more of this medicinal-smelling body wash from the showers at the fitness center.

That dream was so close. She could feel it. It warmed her up better than a state-of-the-art heating system. Which she would also get. She'd make sure of it.

Molly did a hop, skip, and a jump through the hallway to the human resources department. She couldn't wait to get her grubby hands on that file. Maybe peek at it while she was at it, on her way back to the executive floor.

She walked in and saw the general assistant, who glanced up from her paperwork and smiled. "What's up, Molly?"

"Sara asked me to pick up a job performance review." Molly leaned her hip against the desk.

"Who's it for?"

"Me," Molly said proudly. *Hmm, take the good vibes down a notch.* She needed to pace her party mood or she'd be too exhausted to celebrate tonight.

"Really? I didn't see that one. Let me check." Crystal looked through the files. "Maybe it's on my boss's desk."

Molly watched the assistant leave the room and started humming. She wondered what kind of raise she would get. She heard three percent was standard.

She also heard some employees received bonuses. Good bonuses. Not the take-the-family-to-a-nice-dinner bonuses, but the take-the-family-to-Disneyland kind.

"Uh, Molly?"

Molly realized she was humming "It's a Small World" and stopped. Trust fund babies probably hummed symphonies. She needed to play it cool. "Yes?"

"Are you sure she doesn't have it?"

"She just sent me down." Foreboding pricked at her. "Why?"

The general assistant winced. "I can't find it."

"You *lost* it?"

"Wow," Curtis Puckett said as he sat at the conference table, facing Kyle and his top executives. "Bringing out the big guns. I'm honored."

No one else smiled. Kyle and his friends were going into this meeting as a united front. Facing and overcoming obstacles together. They'd done it before, but Kyle didn't feel the same bloodthirsty aggression. He wasn't going in for the kill.

Because for the first time on the corporate battleground, Kyle didn't feel like anyone had his back.

The elite programmer gave another cursory look at the other occupants in the conference room and tsked. "But don't you think this is inefficient?"

"We're suing you," Glenn said, his expression grim.

Curtis chuckled and leaned back in his chair, his legs sprawled in front of him. "No, you're not."

Glenn's expression darkened. "Do you want to bet?"

"You want all of that as court evidence?" Curtis's eyebrow rose. "I'm going to say . . . no."

"By the time you get into court," Annette said, "we will be making the upgraded version."

Curtis slowly turned to face her. He gave a slow appraisal, but if it was meant to rattle Annette, he failed. "The case will never get that far," the programmer finally said.

"Yes, it will," she replied. "I will personally see to it."

"Going to make an example out of me?" His expression was hopeful.

"You," Annette emphasized, "and the person you're working for."

Curtis made an exaggerated pout. "What makes you think I'm not the ringleader?"

"You're not smart enough," Annette answered.

"Funny."

"If you were smart," Timothy said, easing into the interrogation, "you would have known that we would be conducting more security checks after the last attempt."

Curtis shrugged as if he was bored.

"According to the log, you're supposed to have the blueprint," Glenn pointed out. "And you don't. Where is it?"

"I lost it?" Curtis asked cheekily.

"The guy needs an attitude adjustment," Annette said. "Give me five minutes with him, Kyle."

"Are you supposed to be playing the bad cop?"

Annette glared at him. "Make it three minutes."

"Where is the blueprint?"

He lifted his arms. "Search me."

"No, thanks," Kyle said. "Because we know that catching you is a detour. How does it feel knowing that you're disposable to the plan?"

Curtis's eyes flickered. "More like pivotal. Anything to distract you. For all you know, the person who has the blueprint could be in the mail room or"—he met Kyle's steady gaze—"on the executive floor."

He knows my weak spot. Kyle masked his surprise and

tapped down the grudging respect. His opponent did his homework, and he was going to go on the offensive. Curtis was going for breaking the united front. And he just might be successful.

"In fact," Curtis continued, swiveling his chair from side to side. "My boss could be in this very room."

"You're grasping," Kyle said, noting the programmer had confessed to having a boss. "That's the first sign of loss of control."

"Don't talk to me about control," Curtis said sharply. "You've lost it."

Kyle said nothing, waiting for the guy to slip up. To reveal too much.

"You can't even get your friends to do what you ask of them," Curtis went on, his eyes taking on a sly gleam. "Everyone knows you told Glenn to knock off the office romances. But he hasn't stopped and gets laid right at work."

Kyle felt Glenn's tension. He bet his friend was turning bright red.

"He also screwed your last girlfriend," Curtis revealed. "Right in your office."

"You—" Glenn leapt out of his seat. Timothy jumped up and pushed the chief financial officer back into his seat.

Kyle didn't like the doubt flickering in his head. He cast it aside, knowing it would fester until he dealt with Glenn, but he had other priorities.

Kyle also noticed Curtis didn't move out of the way or look at Glenn. He was determined to break the united team and knew he made a hit. "What's your point?"

"How far can you trust these friends of yours?"

"Farther than I can trust you."

"Really?" Curtis glanced at the head of security. "Can you trust Timothy even though he's the source of that tell-all book?"

Kyle gave a show of impatience, although he would have liked to have seen Timothy's reaction. "Where are you getting your information?"

"You hear things. Like Annette is about ready to break with the company and start her own."

Annette jumped up. "What?"

"Sit down, Annette," Kyle ordered harshly. He hadn't heard that rumor, but he didn't question it.

He returned his attention to the programmer. "None of these accusations point the finger at someone at the executive level. None of them prove that they are thieves or implicated in taking the blueprint."

Curtis frowned and Kyle sensed the wavering confidence. The programmer's trump card didn't cause the desired effect.

"You are the only person I know who admitted to stealing something." Kyle pointed at Curtis. "I want to know where the blueprint is and who you are working for."

"What if I told you that it was someone at the executive level? Maybe in this very room?"

"I am in no mood for guessing games," Kyle warned him.

"Someone who is not very technical," Curtis continued as he swiveled on his chair, "or so you think."

That would point to Glenn—if Curtis was telling the truth. Kyle refused to look at the chief financial officer.

"Someone who doesn't have the access to all parts of the information . . ."

"That's everyone in the executive office," Timothy informed Curtis.

"Someone who doesn't have a lot of power, but she will soon."

"She?" He looked at Annette.

Annette turned to Curtis. "Don't mess with me."

"I never said it was you," Curtis said smugly. Kyle wanted to rip the superior look off of the guy's face. "I'm talking about Molly."

The room went quiet. No one moved. Kyle knew that if he did, the pain would rip him in half.

"Molly?" Glenn parroted and looked at his coworkers for confirmation. "Who the hell is Molly?"

"Your receptionist," Curtis informed him, his voice taking on an edge.

Annette started to laugh. "You want us to believe that the mastermind behind this million-dollar theft is the girl who answers the phone?"

"What do you know about her?" Curtis asked. "Huh? You give her access that you don't even give me."

"She poses no threat," Timothy said.

"Because you think she's not smart enough to understand the paperwork that crosses her desk. That she's not going to be able to put the pieces together and get the full picture." Curtis's smile widened. "Because you think what she wants you to think."

"Like what you're doing now?" Kyle asked softly.

"Don't you think it's weird that she's here at all hours?" Curtis asked. "Popping up in places she's not supposed to be?"

"Circumstantial evidence." Why had Curtis put the blame on Molly? Did the guy know how he felt about her? Was it obvious that Molly was becoming his weakness? "You have no proof."

"And you have proof of her loyalty?" the programmer asked.

"I don't need it," Kyle lied.

Curtis chuckled. "Then you're going down."

* * *

Stay calm. Molly silently repeated the mantra as she entered Sara's office. *Under no circumstance will you lose your cool.* "Sara?"

Her boss looked up and frowned with concern. "What happened?"

And here she thought she was handling her panic quite well. "Human resources says they don't have my job performance file. We have searched everywhere."

"Well, we need it to make it official."

Don't tell me that! "When I told them we were rescheduling the review for today, they said you must already have the file." *And if you lost that file I will have to kill you.*

"I would?" Suddenly her eyes widened. "I do!"

"You have the file?" *And you couldn't have remembered that before my mini nervous breakdown?*

"Not here," Sara clarified, gesturing at her cluttered desk, "but Kyle would have it. He needs to sign off."

"Okay." *I'm going to go back to my desk and expire.*

"Why don't you go see if it's on his desk?" Sara suggested. "And then come back here and we'll start the review."

"Sure." *Why not? After all, it's just the promise of more money.*

She briskly entered Kyle's office and immediately noticed there weren't a lot of papers on his desk. She quickly shuffled through one pile. What did a job review file look like? Shouldn't it have her name?

"What are you doing?"

Molly jumped at the sound of Kyle's voice and dropped the file. "You scared me." She pressed her hand against her stuttering heart.

He walked into the office, his stride powerful and ground-eating. There was something about it that made Molly nervous. She kept her head down and started looking through the next stack.

"Why are you going through my papers?"

His accusatory tone was biting. "I'm looking for my job review file."

"Look at me when you're talking."

Molly stopped, her senses on full alert, and slowly looked up. What was going on? Why was he all intense and everything?

"Do you have my job performance file?" She hated how her voice shook, but he was her last hope in finding the paperwork. "My review can't start without it."

He watched her. She felt cold. Bone-chilling cold as he stared at her as if she was an encrypted message.

"No."

Molly closed her eyes and exhaled, her breath coming out shallow and choppy. "Have you seen it at all?"

"No, I haven't." Annoyance burred his words. "Will you look—"

"Kyle, I don't have the time to make goo-goo eyes at you. If I don't have my file, I don't get my review. If I don't get my review—" The phone lines lit up. "Argh!"

She ran past him and hurried to her desk.

"We are not finished," he called out to her.

Molly chose to ignore him. And later tonight, after she regained her composure and had a celebratory drink, she would let him have it for the tone he took.

She grabbed her phone. "Ashton ImageWorks," she said as professionally as possible. "This is Molly."

The fine hair on her neck stood to attention. Kyle stood beside her. She didn't need to check to see if he was watching her. Staring. She could barely concentrate on what the caller was saying.

"I'm sorry," she said into the phone. She grabbed her *M*

notepad and turned away from Kyle. "Would you repeat that?"

Molly sat down, her legs feeling weak. She felt wrung out, actually. She scribbled down the information, fully aware of the tension growing in Kyle. It was like a storm brewing, the dark clouds rolling in.

Did she really need this right now? Molly murmured her all-rights and I-got-its into the phone. Today had started so hopeful and all of sudden everything turned worse.

"Yes, thank you," she said cheerfully as tears stung the back of her eyes. Tears? No, she wouldn't. She absolutely refused to cry. "I'll give—Hello?"

The line went dead. She quickly turned to look at the phone. Her eyes widened when she saw Kyle's finger pressed firmly against the disconnect button.

Her gaze flew to his face. "What did . . ." She puttered to a stop when she saw his ferocious anger.

"What are you," he asked with lethal softness as he held up a thick green book, "doing with this?"

Molly's stomach churned. She decided right then and there that she would take his raised voice over the low, raspy tone. She instinctively knew she'd done something horribly wrong. Can-never-take-it-back wrong. But what?

She swallowed heavily. "What is it?"

"It's the blueprint."

He acted like she should know. Was that the problem? "The blueprint? I don't know what it's for."

"Sure you don't."

"I don't." Why? Why did this have to happen on her review day? The tears were threatening to spill but she refused to cry. "I don't know what it is, where it came from, or where it's supposed to go next. I don't know why it's on my desk."

Kyle froze. The skin on his face tightened and paled. He took a step back.

"What?" She looked behind her, but there was nothing there. "What is it?"

"You blinked."

What? "I blinked?"

"Molly," he said, his voice barely a whisper, his face darkening as his eyes blazed with fury. "You're fired."

Chapter 8

"I'm fired for blinking?" She stared at him. "Ha. Ha. Not funny." She couldn't believe he would do that to her. It was mean. Cruel.

"I'm not joking. Keep your hands away from your desk."

She held her hands up. *Whoa.* "You know how important this job is to me and I find your humor in poor taste."

"Sara!" Kyle called out.

She took a quick glance at the glass security door. "What are you doing?"

She saw Sara run to the door and push it open. "Yeah, Kyle?"

He kept his eyes on Molly as he said, "Call security and have Molly escorted from the premises."

"What?" Molly jumped from her seat.

Sara stepped into the reception area. "What's going on here?"

"Molly had this." He held the book up.

"I don't even know what *that* is!" She gestured at the book as if it were poisonous.

"Kyle." Sara raised her palms, attempting to placate him. "I'm sure there is a reasonable explanation."

"It's not like someone dropped it off on her desk." His

hands gripped the book. "And any unauthorized personnel seen with this are immediately terminated."

Molly held her arms close to her body and bunched her hands into fists. "Will someone *please* tell me what is going on here? Why are you trying to fire me?"

"I'm not trying to. You *are* fired."

"Kyle, there is a procedure—"

"Sara," he said coldly. The muscle next to his eye twitched. "Call security. Call human resources. Call legal. Is that enough procedure for you?"

"Legal?" Sara and Molly asked in unison.

"For stealing trade secrets."

"Stealing!" The accusation was like a slap. "I haven't stolen anything."

"Molly, in my office. Now."

"No." She was not going in there by herself. Nuh-uh. No way.

He reached over her desk and grabbed her by the arm. Molly gasped. His touch didn't hurt, but it surprised her. Her feet shuffled and tripped as he marched her back to his office. The moment he slammed the door behind him, he dropped her arm.

"Start talking." He tossed the green book on his desk.

"I have nothing to say to you." She folded her arms across her chest. "Have you been stringing me along? Is this how you get your kicks?"

"I'm warning you—"

"No." She pointed a shaky finger at him. "I'm warning you. Don't you accuse me of stealing!"

Kyle rubbed his hand across his forehead. "You are a con artist and I can't believe I fell for it."

The tears were really burning now. "No matter how many ways you call me names, you're still wrong."

He pointed at the book. "I have proof that you are a liar and a thief."

"Once again, I don't know what that is or how it got on my desk. Have you ever considered the possibility that someone left it there?"

"Under boxes of envelopes?"

"Then someone planted it there." The idea was unnerving to say the very least.

"You've been here for three months and you've already made enemies?" Kyle tilted his head as if it was an interesting concept. "What kind of threat are you? You're a receptionist."

"My desk is out in the open," Molly pointed out. "It's not protected by your security glass."

There was a knock on the door and Timothy poked his head in. "Kyle—"

"Out!" Kyle didn't divert his attention from Molly.

"Okay." Timothy dropped back and closed the door.

Kyle stared at her with such intensity that it took every ounce of courage to meet his eyes. To stand her ground.

He shook his head. "You're good. I'll give you credit for it."

"You don't know what you're talking about," she whispered fiercely.

"I believed you were fighting the odds by yourself. I actually admired you for it." His soft laugh was filled with bitterness.

Admired her? He did? Molly didn't know what to say.

"I fell for your hoax. I wanted to help you."

"No, you wanted to bed me," she said with a flash of anger.

"Did you try to seduce me as a distraction?" he asked, circling her.

She stared straight ahead. "I did no such thing."

"Keep me occupied while you take from me?"

She refused to turn and watch him get closer and closer to her. She would stay her ground. "I didn't take anything.

Why are you even trying with the argument? I didn't sleep with you—remember?"

"Right. You don't sleep with the boss. Like you have rules of conduct." He scoffed at the idea. "More like you know the chase will distract me. It's all part of the game."

"This is not a game!" She squeezed her eyes shut. "This is my livelihood you're playing with."

"And mine. Do you think it's okay to steal from me and I wouldn't miss it?

"I am not a thief."

"You can say that all you want, but I've seen you in action. The way you get your clothes. Your food. It's all a form of theft."

"You don't know what you're talking about. You can accuse me all you want, but you're basing it all on one green book."

Kyle's pause crackled. It freaked Molly out more than his direct questions.

"That's right," he said quietly. "You don't know yet."

She felt like she didn't know about *anything* that was going on. "Know what?"

"We got Curtis." Kyle stood in front of her. Invaded her space. "You know, your boyfriend."

She glared at him. "I already told you he wasn't."

"But you didn't tell me that he's your partner in crime."

"He's not."

"Too late, Molly." Kyle dipped his head, his eyes level with hers. "He already confessed."

"To the theft?"

"And that you were the one who's behind it all."

She sat primly in the luxurious seat in Kyle's office, wishing she could curl up in a ball and hide from the world around her. She tried to block it out, staring at the panoramic view of the Cascade Mountains—but she was far too aware of the executives swarming around her like vultures.

"Come on, Molly," Annette said impatiently. "We need to know your buyer."

This couldn't be happening. Curtis had fingered her as the mastermind behind an elaborate espionage ring. And these people believed him!

What did she do to Curtis? Because she didn't take him up on his offer for sex? Or was this another form of his sick humor?

Glenn stood in front of her. Towered over her. "Curtis grabbed the deal we made him."

"By offering my name," she replied dazedly. *Who's the con artist now?*

"You're not getting one from us."

She looked up at him. "I'm not asking for one." What would she do with it? She had no information to give. No names. Nothing.

When she found Curtis . . .

And then it hit her. Hit her so hard, she wanted to gag.

Even if she proved her innocence, she'd already lost her job. There was no way—no way—they were going to let her continue working here.

She lost. Bile filled her mouth, knowing that she gave it her all and managed to lose. All that hard work, the juggling, the sacrifices—the lies. All for nothing.

"Molly?" Annette snapped her fingers right in front of Molly's eyes. "Don't you get it? You can go to prison for this."

Prison. They feed you there, don't they? You get a roof over your head. Heat in the winter. They probably have cable TV.

Wait. What was she thinking? Now was not the time to give up! She was not going to prison. She had done nothing wrong.

Molly looked up and saw four of the most powerful people she'd ever met staring back at her. They were ruthless and they had more money than she could imagine. They also had the very best legal minds working for them just one building away.

She had no job, no money for a good lawyer, and a reputation for lying.

Was this the punishment she received for all the lies she told? Was she now getting punished for telling the truth? If that was the case, she should learn to keep her mouth shut.

Her emotions were jumbled and threatened to ooze out of her, but she took a deep breath, determined to appear unflappable. "I don't know why you assume Curtis is telling the truth."

"Because he is—was," Annette quickly corrected herself, "one of the greatest minds in computer programming and you are a receptionist with a talent for lying."

"A receptionist is supposed to lie," she muttered. How many times did she say, "Oh, sorry, he's not at his desk," and other such polite ways of saying the caller wasn't important enough.

"He had everything to lose," Glenn said. "And you have nothing."

Ha. Curtis was now known as a renegade programmer. Thumbed his nose at the establishment. By the end of the year he would have a cult following.

The phone rang. No one moved. No one took their eyes off of her. It rang again.

"Are you guys expecting me to get that?" she asked.

Kyle answered it. It was the first time he'd moved or said anything since his advisors took over. She allowed herself to look at him, greedily taking in every detail of his gorgeous face and sleek, masculine body.

She lost something with Kyle, too. Something that could

have reminded her that life didn't have to be always worrying or hardship. That life could be fun.

Kyle looked at her and their eyes met. The pain dragged against her like claws. It was a good thing she didn't get involved with Kyle. Thank goodness she listened to her instincts.

"You can leave, Molly," Kyle said as he hung up the phone.

"What?" Glenn whirled around. "You can't let her walk out."

"There's nothing on her computer or in her belongings that corroborates Curtis's story."

"She had the blueprint!" Glenn shouted.

"It's not enough to press charges," Kyle explained coolly. "Only enough to fire her."

Kyle turned his attention on her. His eyes were wintry, and his gorgeous face held no hint of kindness. Molly knew she couldn't reach him or plead her case. His decision had been made and it was final.

"Molly, there are two security guards outside those doors. They will be with you at all times as you clean out your desk and they will escort you from the premises."

So, that's that. Could he be any more dismissive?

"Your ID, please."

Molly slowly rose from her seat and walked over to him. She felt like she was walking through thick sludge as she made her way to him. With fumbling fingers, she unclipped the ID from her dress. She dropped the piece of plastic in his outstretched hands, careful not to brush her skin against his.

"You can so forget about dinner," she said in a hiss.

She saw his muscle bunch in his jaw. Molly pivoted on her heel and walked to the door, doing her best not to look over her shoulder. Not to expect him to come to his senses and call her back.

Why did she say that? Molly knew that for exit lines, it sucked. Like he was going to care. Or remember.

Yep, it a good thing she hadn't slept with him.

"You let her go?" Glenn shoved his hands in his hair and paced the floor. "You fucking let her go!"

"I didn't have enough evidence," Kyle said, wondering why he felt the need to explain his actions.

Glenn motioned at the door where Molly had just left. "We could have gotten it out of her."

"Which would have been intimidation and illegal," Kyle pointed out coolly.

"Then why did you pull her before you had enough?" Glenn yelled.

Good question. Why did he? Why didn't he act with strategy, instead of following his anger? "I messed up. I saw the blueprint on her desk and I snapped."

"You messed up?" Glenn paced faster. "This woman may have taken all of our ideas, which will bring in millions, and all you can say is that you messed up?"

Kyle locked eyes with the other man.

Glenn viciously threw his hands in the air and stormed off. He ripped the door open, the wood panel slamming against the hinges as he walked out.

Timothy watched Glenn leave and slowly turned to face Kyle. "I'm going to put an investigator on Molly. That could give us some good leads."

"Okay." So much for getting the con artist out of his mind and out of his life. Now he'd get daily reports on what she was doing.

"I'll get on that now."

Kyle watched Timothy leave and his mind started to drift off into space. He stared at the door, feeling numb. Shutting off. Shutting down. He was definitely in survivor mode.

He remembered that Annette was still sitting there. Kyle slowly became aware of her watching him. Studying him.

"What?" He was in no mood for company.

Annette chewed on her bottom lip. "Something doesn't fit."

"You think Molly is innocent?" He felt the flicker of hope and was disgusted from it. He didn't look for excuses or explanations with his other employees. He should treat Molly the same way.

"Innocent is such a vague word. Either she knows something or she's . . ." Annette trailed off. "She's not mastermind material."

Kyle forced himself to turn to his computer and reach for his keyboard. "Believe me, she's a lot more devious than she looks."

Annette's eyebrow arched and Kyle ignored it.

"You believe Curtis over Molly?" she asked.

"Don't you?" Kyle punched in his password.

"Curtis got something for turning over Molly. She didn't ask for anything."

"There could be a lot of reasons why she didn't ask. Maybe the competitor can beat our offer. Maybe there's something she wants that we can't give." The possibility jabbed him in the gut.

"Maybe." Annette paused. "About the other thing Curtis said . . ."

Oh, God, he didn't want to hear anymore lies and excuses. "Annette, I don't have time to deal with—"

"I didn't mean to hide it from you."

That lie annoyed him. "You don't hide a start-up company by accident. You did mean to hide it."

She had the grace to blush. "Only because the terms of my contract—"

"To hell with the contract. You want to leave? Then

leave." He focused on his computer screen and pretended to find great interest in his e-mails.

"I spent ten years putting this company together." Annette's voice trembled with anger. "It's not easy walking away."

Kyle glanced up from his computer. "Then why are you?"

"Because I want something of my own." She pressed her hands to her chest. "I want something with my name on it. My own territory."

As much as he hated to admit it, he understood that need. It was the same quest that drove him every day.

"I'm not going into competition against you," Annette promised. "I want to work with image processing for the math and science fields. This is going to fill a niche."

Considering she was a math geek when he first met her, he wasn't too surprised by this passion. Annette always tried to get Ashton ImageWorks involved in the fields, but he thought the target consumer was too small.

"I'm not taking your employees or proprietary info," she was quick to point out. "I would never do that."

Annette was leaving him and not looking back. She was ready to move on. He knew why she needed to, but the way she did felt like a betrayal.

"And if you have a need for the best mathematical and scientific image processing," Annette said as she rose from her seat and headed for the door, "then we can form an alliance."

Kyle's eyes widened at his friend's moxie. "Are you already trying to do a deal?"

"Softening you up." He heard the smile in her voice.

"Just for that, I'm going to snatch up your company in a hostile takeover."

Annette chuckled. "I'd like to see you try." She looked over her shoulder. "Are we still friends?"

"Yeah," he said, but he wasn't sure if that was a lie. Friends trusted each other no matter what. Didn't they?

Molly walked slowly down the sidewalk, carrying a small cardboard box against her hip. If that didn't tell everyone on the street what she happened to her! She felt like a walking advertisement for losers.

The muted clanks and dings were getting on her nerves. She peered inside the box and kept noticing that her belongings were a few trinkets and scraps of paper, and pathetically few at that. She had tossed her purse inside so she didn't hear all the rattling around.

Fired. The word swirled around her mind. She couldn't believe she'd been fired. For something she didn't even do!

Don't dwell on that. You've got bigger problems. Like where do you go from here?

She'd have to take whatever job she could get. Two jobs. Three. She'd done it before. It nearly killed her, but she'd do it again if she had to.

Housing. Molly winced. She didn't know what she was going to do about that. Her credit blown. And now that she was unemployed . . .

Attitude. *Come on, it's all about attitude. I will get through this. Before the end of the year, I'll have a cozy place and a job.*

Riiight.

It could happen. Her luck boomeranged from bad to good. Like how it did today. Everything was looking up and then—bam! Someone lost her file.

She would have really liked to have seen what bonus she would have gotten. Molly's feet shuffled against the pavement as she imagined the dollar amount scrolling up. Ooh, maybe some stock options. Not like she had any use for them unless she could have treated them like green stamps, but it would have been a nice touch.

It was probably for the best that she didn't know. Molly sighed and felt it all the way to her toes. It was going to be difficult knowing all that money had been taken away from her. That she almost got out of living in a truck.

Speaking of which . . . Molly stopped and looked around. Where was her truck? Did she pass it?

She didn't see a truck anywhere. She parked it in this busy parking lot today, didn't she? That was one of the disadvantages of a mobile living space. Routine went out the window.

It was this parking lot. She remembered going behind the building where the other trucks were. Which would mean that her truck would be right . . .

Where that empty space was.

Molly stared at the pavement. She saw it, but didn't understand it. Then it all hit her at once.

Panic hit her in the chest. The truck was gone. The truck was . . . *gone*! And all of her stuff with it.

Oh, no. No! She pressed her lips together. The box she was carrying suddenly felt too heavy and she placed it on the curb. She whirled around and searched the parking lot, as if her truck would miraculously appear.

Where was her truck? Was it stolen? Towed? When did this happen? She looked around wildly, but no one was around. No one would have the answers.

Molly shakily walked back to the empty parking space. She sat down, clumsy and tired, and stared at the gray pavement.

She had no idea how long she sat there, hugging her knees against her chest, but it dawned on her that she needed to get up. Move. Take action. Get her stuff back. Get a job. Get a place to live.

But she couldn't move. She wasn't strong enough to fight back. And even if she were, she'd use her strength to run away.

I don't bail.

What she said to Kyle had been the truth. She always stayed the course. Finished the job. Paid the bill.

Molly rested her head on her knees. And where did that get her? Nowhere with nothing.

Maybe her good-for-nothing ex-boyfriend had the right idea. Just get up and go. Who cared what mess you left behind? Someone would have to clean it up.

That sounded so good right now.

But what about the truck? About her bills? What about her work record?

No one was going to clean that up for her. She had to fix that herself.

The weight of it all pulled her down. She felt like she was suffocating. She couldn't breathe.

She had to concentrate on the more important things. Food. Clothes. Shelter. Get her stuff and get a job.

Molly's stomach grumbled at the thought of food. When was the last time she ate? Did she throw the packet of chips in her box while the security guards watched her?

She looked through her box, knowing that she would think better on a full stomach. At least with something in her stomach.

Chips . . . chips . . . She could have sworn she had some potato chips. She pulled out the *M* notepad Bonita gave her when she got the job and saw one sheet curled backward.

What was that? She couldn't remember. Molly folded it over and saw a jumble of words among the doodling.

Laurie. Family emergency. Food in refrigerator. Coming back? Key at neighbor.

She winced. How could she have forgotten to give that note to Sara? Oh, well. Molly tossed the notepad back into the box. It made no difference. Kyle wouldn't know the house was empty.

Molly shuffled through her lucky pencil container and

her framed photos. She froze. *Kyle's cottage was empty. The one that he never used!*

No. No. Bad idea. She couldn't go over there. Live there. Even temporarily until she got back on her feet. That was breaking and entering.

Unless she got the key from the neighbors . . .

Diving her hand into the box, she retrieved the M-shaped paper. The rolled up bag of chips came up with the notepad, clinging to the sticky strip.

Molly smiled. Things were looking up already.

Chapter 9

As the ferry docked next to the island, Molly's heart pounded harder. Her stomach twisted as sweat appeared on her cold, clammy skin. At first she thought it might have been motion sickness. Then she realized it for what it was.

She was going somewhere she'd never laid eyes on. In a place she couldn't easily leave. To live in a house that wasn't hers.

"You are going to get caught," Bonita had predicted the night before. "Do me a favor and plead insanity."

"No one will find out," Molly had said as she stuffed jeans and sweaters she had bought from yard sales that morning into a bag. "Kyle doesn't use the house. I'm going to go in, find a job on the island, and then get a place of my own."

"Never going to work," Bonita had muttered.

"What I've been doing hasn't worked, so let's try it in reverse. Get the home first and then everything else will fall into place."

"And if you don't find a job?"

Molly had shrugged, although she desperately hoped that wouldn't be the case. "Then I leave and no one will ever know I had been there."

This is the craziest idea I've ever had, Molly decided as

she stepped onto the island and looked around. *And it just might work.*

She walked along the first street she found. There were lots of evergreen trees and rolling hills. The island was much bigger than she expected. That had to be good.

Molly found what looked like a quaint general store. As she walked inside, a small brass bell on top of the door announced her presence. She glanced around the small, crowded, one-room store. It was like she had entered a slower, more gracious time.

The man behind the counter stood up. "Hi, can I help you with anything?"

"Um, yeah. Could you direct me to Main Street?"

His smile was broad. "You're on it."

Huh. Maybe the action was more toward the coastline. "Where are the shops?" she asked. "The restaurants? The Starbucks?"

"There aren't any, but I do have an espresso machine."

"Really?" No Starbucks? Was she still in the Pacific Northwest?

"People live here to get away from it all." The man rested his elbow on the cash register. "How long are you staying?"

"I'm not quite sure," she hedged. This plan might not work.

The man eyed her beat-up backpack. "You don't have any camping equipment."

Molly's eyes widened. "Why would I need that?" *Oh, please tell me these people have running water and electricity.*

"The island doesn't have a hotel."

"Oh, that's okay," she said with some relief. Molly then realized what that meant. The job market on this island was much smaller than she'd anticipated. "I'm staying over at Kyle Ashton's cottage."

"You are?" He looked at her carefully. "Are they expecting you?"

Okay, that was her cue to establish her story. She worked on this on the ferry ride over. Not too much information, but just a few clues that she belonged here. "I know Laurie isn't there," Molly said, "but she told me where to get the key. Oh, did you hear any news about the baby?"

The suspicion cleared from the man's brow. "Yeah, it's a boy."

"Oh, good. I'm sure I'll hear all about it." Molly gave the shopkeeper a wink.

The older man gave a knowing smile in return. "What did you say your name was?"

"Molly. Molly Connors." She held out her hand, although she was reluctant to give out her real name. But if she was going to find a job here, she had to be truthful up front. "And you are?"

"Nice to meet you, I'm Jerry." He then proceeded to give her directions to Kyle's place. "If you have any questions, give me a call."

"Thanks." Molly stepped outside and headed off in the direction of the cottage.

The job search was going to be harder than she anticipated. No restaurants? No hotels? No businesses? How was she going to survive?

She looked in the direction of the ferry. Stopped in her tracks. Wavered.

No. She wasn't going to give up just yet. She had to think outside the box. There were other types of jobs available. Molly knew that she needed to be on the lookout.

She walked along the unpaved roads, catching glimpses of Puget Sound between the evergreen trees. She tried to remember the address and went completely blank for a minute.

Don't panic. You wrote it down somewhere. She opened

her backpack and scanned the address. The last thing she wanted to do was break into the wrong house!

She followed along the path until she found the address advertised. She looked around, surprised that there was no fence. No gates. Nothing.

Whew. One less thing to worry about.

She walked down the sloping yard. The lawn was lush and green, but by no means controlled. Plants were grouped together, flaring out and soaking in the weak sunlight.

Molly abruptly stopped when she saw the cottage. Her mouth fell open. This was *not* a cottage. Where she came from, the proper term was a freaking mansion!

Nooo . . . She looked at the address she had written down. It was the right house. Molly slowly returned her gaze to the place.

The "cottage" was freshly painted a pale yellow. It rose majestically from the ground about two stories and stretched across the wide yard. The driveway meandered to the stone steps.

The low slanted roof gave a gracious look to the sturdy house. The window balconies made her think of those movies set in Italy. Tuscany or something.

She slowly walked along the meandering driveway to the stone steps. Now might be a time to rethink her plan, Molly considered as she approached the massive front door. Taking advantage of an empty beachside cottage was one thing . . . Molly turned around and found a woman standing right behind her. She screamed and reeled back, colliding into the front door.

"Sorry, didn't mean to sneak up on you. Jerry at the store called and said you were coming."

Molly pressed her hand against her chest and took in a few gulps of air. "Hi, I'm Molly," she said shakily and stretched out her hand. "And you are?"

The woman eyed her and didn't accept the handshake. "The next-door neighbor."

Hmm . . . That doesn't sound promising. Molly quickly dropped her hand and studied the older woman. She was thin, wrinkled, and looked like she had seen a lot of life. The woman was going to be a hard nut to crack.

"Laurie didn't say you were coming."

"She didn't know."

"Uh-huh." She studied Molly with open suspicion. The woman folded her arms across her chest. "You better start talking."

Molly eyed the next-door neighbor. Okay. She had better be convincing if she wanted the key. And she really needed the key. The ferry was gone, and she had no truck or office building to sleep at. No way was she going camping in the wild tonight.

"Well, I'm so glad to meet you," Molly said with her friendliest smile. "How's Laurie doing with her grandson?"

"How do you know Laurie?"

"Well, I don't," Molly admitted. "I've only talked to her on the phone on a couple of occasions."

The neighbor gave her the evil eye. Molly's nerves skittered up and down her spine.

"It sounded awful what her daughter went through," Molly said in a rush, determined to prove a familiarity with Kyle's life.

The neighbor's eyes narrowed.

"With the water breaking and the . . ."

Her eyes went steely.

"Mucus plug." Hmm, normal people usually would have tried to stop her and change the subject. "Anyway, Laurie said you would have the key."

The woman wasn't warming up at all. "Like I said, Laurie didn't tell me you were coming."

"I didn't know myself until this weekend."

"Are you a relative of Kyle's?"

"Not exactly." She could lie, but she remembered Kyle's distance with his family. This woman might know that.

"Not exactly?" The woman frowned. "Either you are or you aren't. How do you know Kyle?"

"I'm a"—Acquaintance? Employee?—"friend."

"Friend?" The woman appeared unconvinced.

"A *close* friend," Molly added.

"How close?"

Molly's mouth opened and closed. "Excuse me?"

"Because I don't know how a close friend is not exactly related to him."

Well, she walked into that one, didn't she? Molly knew she should give up and leave. She had no idea why she was arguing with this woman on the doorstep of a house that was neither hers nor this woman's.

So why wasn't she leaving? Why was she risking getting caught? Had she passed the point of recognizing a lost cause, or was she willing to do anything to live in this house? She didn't want to think about that right now. "Okay, here's the deal, Miss . . ."

Nothing.

Molly tried again. "Mrs. . . . ?"

Still nothing. If she said sir, would she get a reaction? Molly decided not to chance it.

"Ma'am, I'm not really allowed to say anything because"—because why?—"it's not . . . official."

"Uh-huh."

"But Kyle and I are . . . engaged." Molly reviewed what she just said. That story might work.

"Uh-huh." The woman made a point to look at Molly's hand.

"I don't have a ring yet," Molly explained, fighting the

urge to curl her hands and hide them behind her back. "Because it's not official."

"When did this happen?"

"This week." That sounded good. She'd go with that.

"So why are you here?" The woman shifted back on her heels. "Alone?"

Hmm. Molly hadn't considered that a just-engaged couple would stick to each other like glue. "Kyle is talking about selling this house, but I told him I wanted to see it before he decided."

The neighbor looked at the house and back at Molly. "Why didn't he come down with you?"

Gosh, this woman was nosy! "He's been so busy at work," Molly said as if she was confiding something with the neighbor. "I told him he needed to get out more and get some fresh air, but no. The guy is fine with his treadmill. He's a good runner."

"Yes, I know," the woman said. She glanced at the unpaved road. "He used to run these hills every morning."

Aha! She was getting somewhere. Molly tried not to show her relief.

"Is he coming down soon?" the neighbor asked.

Oh, don't wish that on me! "He wants to," Molly said. "It depends on work."

"How long are you going to be here?"

This line of questioning was beginning to sound promising. "I'm not sure. I really like this place," Molly said in all honesty. "I guess I can wait until Laurie gets back. Did she say when she'll be back?"

"No, but her daughter has maternity leave and needed her help."

That was probably a couple of weeks at least. She should be able to find a job, break the pretend engagement, and find a place to live by that time.

"So," the older woman said, interrupting Molly's thoughts. "You and Kyle are engaged?"

Molly nodded. "But no one is supposed to know, so keep it between us."

"Why is it a secret?"

Good question. Why would they keep it secret? Why wouldn't they announce it right away? Molly leaned forward. "We're still negotiating the pre-nup."

"Really?" She gave Molly another searching glance. "He's making you sign a prenuptial agreement?"

Oh, darn it! She walked into that one. She just made herself sound untrustworthy. "No . . . I'm making him sign one."

"You are?" The older woman's eyelashes fluttered with surprise. "Why?"

Molly spread her arms out wide and admitted, "I'm a trust fund baby."

Kyle stepped out of the elevator onto the executive floor and stopped at the sight of the new receptionist.

The chic woman was very different from Molly. Sleek, urban, businesslike. Which didn't explain his crashing disappointment.

"Good afternoon, Mr. Ashton."

He went blank on the woman's name and gave a nod of recognition as she took another call, her voice elegant and hushed.

He walked into his office and found Sara following him in. "Your meeting with marketing has been rescheduled. Check your computer. Nothing urgent in your e-mails, and here are the summaries about Darrell and Bridget." She placed a file on his glass desk.

"Who?" he asked as he sat down.

"The owners of plaza+tag that you invited over the last week of November?"

"Right." To show they had nothing to worry about with his company. What a joke.

"Anything else?"

"Did you find Molly Connors's job review file?" Okay, he had no idea why he just asked that.

Sara seemed equally surprised. She drew her head back. "Excuse me?"

"It never showed up. I never saw it."

"I found it and returned it to human resources," Sara informed him. "Why do you need it now? Is there a legal matter?" Her expression tightened. "Is there something wrong with Joy?"

Joy. That was her name. "How's she doing?"

"She transitioned into the job smoothly," Sara said carefully. "Do you have a concern?"

"No." How could he? Joy didn't make any glaring mistakes. Worked independently. No drama.

And yet he missed seeing Molly. Who wasn't perfect, but worked hard. Only her presence was a disturbing force of nature.

Kyle heard a knock and saw Timothy standing at the open door of his office. "Do you have a minute?"

"Sure." Kyle nodded at Sara, indicating that they were done. "What's up?"

Timothy waited for Sara to leave and shut the door behind her. He silently walked to the desk. Kyle could tell he wasn't going to like what he was going to hear.

"Molly is missing."

Kyle felt the kick in his stomach. At first he thought it was anger, but then he recognized it for what it was. Panic. Worry.

He turned and stared at his computer screen as the emotions swirled and crashed inside him. He didn't want to worry about Molly. This was the woman who *stole* from him. *Lied* to him.

"When did you last see her?" Kyle asked.

"That's the problem." Timothy gripped the edge of the desk with his hands. "The investigators never got a lead on her."

Kyle glanced up. "At all?"

"She no longer lives at the apartment she rented. She hasn't used any credit cards, and her truck rental has been abandoned."

"Abandoned," Kyle repeated. That didn't sound right. If she could have left that stuff, she would have done so before she got fired. "Abandoned where? Was there anything in the truck?"

"Nothing but an orange sofa," Timothy said. "The trail is cold."

Kyle felt cold, too.

"It's like the moment she stepped out of this building, she vanished." Timothy motioned at the window.

Ice filled his veins.

"How much do you want to bet Molly isn't her real name?" His friend shook his head, obviously considering the possibility that they all had been duped so easily.

Could Molly have lied about something that basic, yet so important?

"Don't we have background checks for that?"

Timothy shrugged. "You can get around that if you know what you're doing."

Which meant Molly might have been one hell of a pro. And he turned out to have been a very easy mark.

"I'm going to keep the investigators going," Timothy said as he walked back to the door. "No one hides without a reason."

"Good idea," Kyle agreed. And he definitely wanted the reason.

*   *   *

Sara all but ran into his office Friday afternoon. "Kyle, big problem."

He looked up from the computer screen. "Lay it on me."

"We don't have reservations for Darrell and Bridget." The executive assistant thrust her hands into her curly red hair and groaned.

"What are you talking about?"

"You invited the plaza+tag owners to come visit our office," she reminded him.

"I did?" He forgot about that.

"Yes. To show them you have everything under control." She studied his blank expression. "Strong, united front? Any of this ringing a bell?"

"It's coming back to me." That was before he found out just how little control he had over his empire. Bringing over the people with whom he wanted to align forces was not a good idea at this time. But it was too late to call off the plans.

"I gave Molly the task of making the arrangements," Sara went on. "I mean, how hard could it be? In fact, Molly volunteered to do it. And guess what?"

He made a guess. "She didn't do it."

Sara tossed her hands in the air. "She didn't do it!"

"We'll come up with something." He shrugged a shoulder, ready to return to his computer.

"I've tried everything." Sara put her hands on her hips. "I've called in favors. I looked into rental apartments. We have nothing."

"Nothing?" That couldn't be possible.

Sara rolled her eyes. "Nothing that would make a good impression. Next time, don't invite clients over for Thanksgiving week."

"It's going to be Thanksgiving next week?" Wow, the year went by fast.

"The holiday falls on the fourth Thursday of every November. No reason to change it this year."

Kyle felt his eyebrow rise. It wasn't like Sara to talk back like this. She must be really rattled by the turn of events. "These guys accepted on Thanksgiving?"

"Maybe they are just like you and don't keep track."

He recalled what he knew about the guests. "The summaries you gave me said they were a married couple. Outdoorsy."

"Are you suggesting I go buy a tent for them?" Sara rubbed her hand across her forehead. "Maybe a kerosene lamp?"

Kyle ignored her as he tried to remember the guests' interests. "Hiking, kayaking, rock climbing . . ."

"What about it?"

"I bet that's why they accepted," he said as he leaned back in his chair. "They want a taste of the Pacific Northwest."

Sara considered what he said. "Possible."

"And we are going to give it to them."

"Okay, let me repeat myself." She put her hands on the glass desktop and leaned in to gain his full attention. "We have no hotel room for them."

"We don't need one. I'll take them to my place."

She looked at him as if he had lost his mind. "You don't even know them and they're going to stay with you?"

"Well, if they try to steal the family silver then I'll know I don't want to business with them."

Sara rose to her full height. "And which place are you talking about?"

Wasn't it obvious? "My island cottage."

"That's a little out of the way."

Which was why it would work. "I'll give them a tour of the company and then take them there. No interruptions, no distractions."

Sara's hand went back to her forehead. "I thought the whole point was to show them around."

"The whole point is to get the deal. And we'll get it done there."

"You're going, too?" Sara took a step back from the desk. "You're leaving the office?"

He slid a sideways glance at her. "It's been known to happen."

"Not lately."

Kyle couldn't argue with that. "Then I'll do my best to make the most out of it."

"How long are you going to be gone?"

"For the week. Think you can manage without me?" he asked with a big grin.

"I'll try."

"You better call Laurie and let her know I'm coming with two guests," Kyle said, returning his attention to the computer. "She'll be ecstatic."

Sara whirled on her heel and stopped. "The redecorating!" she exclaimed and smacked her hand on her forehead.

"What?"

She turned around. "You're redecorating. I have no idea if it's done."

"Not a big deal. From the sounds of it, we will be mostly outside." He looked out his window and felt the lick of anticipation. "You know, I'm kind of looking forward to it."

Chapter 10

Kyle pulled his car off of the ferry and looked around the island. It was unchanged from the last time he visited. Untamed. Serene. Private.

Taking this break might just be what he needed. Clear his head. Get Molly Connors—or whoever she really was— out of his mind.

"Wow," Darrell said under his breath as he looked out the car window.

Kyle nodded in silent agreement and knew it was a good choice to bring them to the island. Darrell and Bridget seemed to be full of ideas and bursting with positive energy, but if he had tried to contain them in his corporate offices, they would have been miserable.

"Hey, can we go in there for a sec?" Bridget motioned at the store.

"Sure," Kyle said as he pulled up in front. "I should warn you that this is the only store on the island." He saw the panic flash in Bridget's eyes at the news and hid his smile. He realized she might be outdoorsy, but only when modern conveniences were at arm's reach.

He got out of the car and looked around as Bridget dragged her husband into the store. The evergreen trees and hills did something to him. Comforted him.

Kyle was about to follow his guests when he saw a familiar figure step out of the store. He smiled at the farmer who had property on the other side of the island.

"Michael," Kyle greeted. "How's it going?"

"Good." The elderly man tipped his baseball cap. "Long time, no see, huh?"

"It has."

"Congratulations, by the way." The farmer gave him a sly wink and walked away.

"Uh . . ." He watched the man leave. "Thanks?" What was all that about? Michael didn't strike him as the type to read the tech and business section of the newspaper. And it had been a while since he struck a major coup. Kyle shrugged it off and stepped into the store.

"This place is like a hidden treasure," Bridget whispered to Kyle as she picked up a wooden carving made from a local artisan. "I hope this place takes credit cards."

"Kyle!"

"Mrs. Whitley." He stepped away from his guest to meet with the island's teacher who taught at the one-room school. "It's good to see you here."

She gave him a knowing smile, her eyes gleaming with delight. "I'm not surprised to see you."

"You're not?" He looked around the store, feeling lost. Bridget and Darrell were wandering around the cramped and cluttered aisles as if nothing was amiss.

"Of course not," the teacher responded. "Not when you have such a pretty woman waiting for you here."

"Uh . . ." Was she talking about Laurie? Kyle thought with growing horror. Laurie was his caretaker. He wasn't sure if the woman was pretty—he hadn't really noticed—because she was old enough to be his mother!

Mrs. Whitley patted his cheek. "I told her you wouldn't be able to stay away. She didn't believe me, but I was right."

"Uh, yes . . . you were right. I'm here." He had no idea what was *going on* here.

"Hi, Kyle."

"Jerry." Kyle said as he slowly walked to the counter. "You're not surprised to see me, either. I guess Laurie told everyone I was coming."

"Laurie? Naw." Jerry shook his head. "She's gone."

"Gone?"

"Her daughter had a baby boy." The older man's forehead crinkled with a frown. "Didn't you know that?"

"No," Kyle replied. He tried to remember if Sara had said anything and he hadn't been listening. "I didn't get the message. So she's a grandma now?"

"Yep, she's gone to help take care of the baby. But I'm sure she'll be back after Christmas."

He had guests and no food or help. He was supposed to concentrate on making a deal that would bring him billions. Why didn't Sara tell him? He had a cell phone and a BlackBerry. "When did this happen?"

"I dunno." Jerry shrugged and clucked his tongue as he gave it some thought. "Couple of weeks ago."

Something wasn't adding up. "Then how did you know I would be back? I only decided a few days ago."

"Kyle, I know you're a workaholic and all, but you would never leave your fiancée alone on a holiday."

"*What?!*"

"You're just not that kind of guy," Jerry decided.

"My fiancée?" Kyle repeated. The word kept slamming against his head.

"Oh, right. Right." Jerry held up his hand. "It's not official. That's what she said."

"Who said?" Laurie? But Laurie wasn't here.

"Your fian—I mean your . . ." Jerry stopped and scratched the back of his head. "Well, I don't know what she is, then. Molly."

"Molly," Kyle whispered as questions screamed through his head. Molly Connors was *here*? On the island?

She hadn't disappeared. She was still using the name. But why was she here? How did she know he would be here?

"Have you seen her? Molly." Kyle barely uttered the name through his clenched teeth. "Today?"

"Oh, yeah. She made a quick stop earlier this morning, but she's always at the house. She loves that place. Good luck on selling that." Jerry snorted with laughter.

The house? What house was Jerry talk—the noise in Kyle's head went deathly silent. "My house?"

"Well, yeah, but Kyle, a little advice." Jerry leaned closer and said in a low voice, "You're gonna have to stop referring to it as just yours once you get married."

Kyle turned his back on the older man. The crowded store closed in on him. The colors and sounds swirled like a kaleidoscope.

He curled his hands into tight fists as he battled with the hot anger coursing through is veins. Molly had gone too far this time. When he found that little con artist, she would learn to regret ever trying to make Kyle Ashton her mark.

Molly walked across the landing on the second floor with a pile of folded towels in her arms. She paused when she heard the sound of closing car doors.

Turning toward the big window in the center of the upstairs hallway, she went to check to see who had come to visit. She caught a glimpse of the unfamiliar silver luxury sedan. Which of her neighbors had that car?

Molly set the towels down on the side table and galloped halfway down the steps when she heard the key in the lock. She froze and stared at the door. *Who ...? What ...? Huh?*

No time to think! Molly bolted up the steps as the front door opened. Her heart pounded wildly against her ribs and she couldn't breathe as her feet hit the top step.

She heard a husky masculine voice drift into the house. "Yes, kayaking is very popular on the island."

Kyle? Molly squeezed her eyes shut. What was Kyle Ashton doing here? He never used this house. Everyone knew that.

That didn't matter anymore. She had to leave. Now. Sneak out before Kyle and his friends found her.

Friends. She leaned over the landing rail. How many did Kyle have with him? She didn't want them scattered around the house as she tried to make a getaway.

Molly took a few steps back and pressed her spine against the wall. She wanted to hide in the farthest room possible, but she needed to know how many she was up against. One friend, for sure. Two? Oops, was that a third set of footsteps. Or did she just add Kyle to the equation?

"This is the living room."

He was giving them the full tour? Molly covered her face with her hands. *Shoot me. Shoot. Me. Now.*

"The dining room."

Kyle wasn't taking a whole lot of time going through the rooms. He was almost racing through it. Her best bet was for them to reach the media room. That was the farthest distance downstairs from the front door.

"The kitchen . . ."

Molly took a deep breath and inched her way to the stairs. She took one step. Then another. She did *not* need this kind of stress in her life.

"Wait a minute. I forgot to show you the study. You guys can use that. Or the library, whichever works for you."

Molly scrambled for the upstairs hallway again. What was he doing backtracking? He was supposed to take the logical route and go from one side to the other.

"What kind of Internet connection?" a man asked. Molly didn't recognize his voice.

"Don't worry, Darrell." She heard the amusement in Kyle's voice. "It's T3."

"Thank God."

Molly saw the top of Kyle's head from where she stood at the landing. She tried to stand very still, but her legs shook as he escorted his two guests to the other side of the entryway.

"There's also a media room," she heard Kyle say after he showed them the library and study.

Finally.

"But you guys are probably more interested in the back-yard. Let me show you."

Yes!

"Unless you want me to show you to your room first?"

No! Molly fought the urge to wet her pants.

"I would love to see the beach," the woman said.

Thank you, whoever you are. She would wait until they opened the back door and then run like the wind out the front. It could work. It better work.

She heard the back door open and the voices trailed off into the distance. Now was her only chance.

Molly hurried down the steps, doing her best not to make noise. She was thankful she had been wearing her shoes.

Backpack. She forgot her backpack.

Molly hesitated on the stairs and glanced in the direction of the master bedroom. Her backpack had her money. Her driver's license.

No, she couldn't risk it. And if Kyle found it at the bottom of his closet, he could figure it out for himself.

Molly hurried down the remainder of the steps. She swerved for the front door and screamed when she saw Kyle resting his shoulder against the doorway to the formal living room.

"Going somewhere?" he asked.

* * *

"Goodness," Molly said, placing her hand over her heart. "You scared me."

If she was looking for sympathy, she better find it somewhere else. Somewhere far, far away from him. "Imagine how I felt finding out that a stranger has been living in my home."

"What are you doing here, anyway?" she asked, unable to look him directly in the eye. "You don't use this house."

"Aw, so sorry I ruined your plans." He took a step toward her. "Get out of here right now."

"Okay, okay." She took a step back. "Calm down."

"Calm down?" The suggestion riled him further. "Not only are you a liar and a thief, but you also can add breaking and entering."

"First of all"—she held up a finger—"I didn't break in."

"I didn't invite you in," he reminded her coldly.

"No, but Diana, your neighbor, gave me the key. Secondly, I don't steal."

"Really?" He motioned to the kitchen with the nod of his head. "Who paid for the food?"

She closed her eyes and exhaled. "Okay, I don't take expensive stuff."

"That reminds me," he said as he took another step. "Am I going to need to go through my itemized insurance list?"

Molly gasped. Her shoes squeaked on the hardwood floor as she stopped abruptly. "Take that back."

"Take that back?" Was she serious? "You break into my home and I'm supposed to assume you didn't take anything?"

"I'll have you know that I took care of this house," she answered, bristling with indignation. "I treated the place as if it were my own—"

"Obviously."

Her jaw slid to the side as she obviously held on to her anger. "You know, you should really be thanking me."

His eyes widened at her audacity. "Thank you?"

She smiled. "You're welcome. I—"

"Why should I thank you for invading my house?"

"I took care of it while Laurie was gone."

Kyle rubbed his hand over his eyes. "So help me, if you ever suggest I pay for your caretaking services . . ."

"Hey, I hadn't thought of—"

"Don't." He held his hand up, noticing how it trembled with barely restrained anger. "Just . . . don't."

"Would you like a cup of coffee?" She pointed her thumb toward the kitchen. "I made a fresh pot."

"Get out." He pointed at the door.

She squinted at him as if she didn't comprehend what he was saying. "Excuse me?"

"Get out of my house," he ordered in a low growl, "and get out of my life."

"I can't do that." She stepped back and collided against the front door.

He took another step toward her, wanting to crowd her. Crowd her out. "Do it now."

Her hand fumbled against the doorknob. "There are no hotels on this island."

"Leave the island." He took another step. He was close enough to lunge and catch her.

"The ferry will have already left," Molly told him.

"I will find a boat and escort you off the island."

"Okay, that's it." She stomped her foot. "Now you have gone too far."

"*I* have?"

"You have no right to kick me off this island. It's not like you own all the land." She paused. "Do you?"

"Why do you want to stay?" Molly was up to something. He could feel it in his bones.

She swallowed roughly. "I like it here."

"What's really keeping you on the island?" He stood in front of her. "You're trying to get the blueprint, aren't you?"

Molly groaned and slumped against the door. "Are we back to that again?"

"Sorry, babe. I didn't bring the blueprint with me. You're out of luck."

"Kyle, I don't care about the stupid green book." She rolled her eyes. "Drop this obsession. Move on."

"No, you move," he told her through clenched teeth. "Move out. Now."

"But . . . but . . ." She looked wildly around the entry hall.

"On the count of three," he warned softly. "One . . ."

"What will the neighbors think?"

He could care less. "Two . . ."

"Not to mention, we have guests."

"Three."

"Ack!" Molly turned around and whipped the door open. She ran out of the house and scurried down the steps.

Kyle was right behind her, determined to get Molly off his property. His pace didn't falter when he saw his neighbor walking along the circular driveway.

"Oh, hi, Diana," Molly said breathlessly as she tried to pass the older woman. "Can't stop and chat."

"I heard Kyle was back. Kyle!" Diana smiled, the wrinkles along her cheeks deepening. "So good to see you again."

"Hello, Diana." He saw Darrell and Bridget turning the corner of the house. He had to get Molly out of here before she opened her mouth and told another whopper of a lie. "If you can excuse me for a moment, I need to see Molly off the—"

"I understand." The older woman positively beamed

and looked at his guests. "Engaged couples only have eyes for each other, you know."

"Engaged?" Kyle heard Darrell's surprised voice directly behind him.

"Oh, right." Diana snapped her fingers. "It's supposed to be a secret."

Chapter 11

Kyle grabbed a hold of Molly's arm, his mind working at rapid speed. He had hoped Darrell and Bridget wouldn't overhear. He thought he could have gotten rid of his "fiancée" before they set eyes on her. No luck. He now had two choices.

He could oust Molly Connors. In front of his guests and neighbors. Have her either arrested or thrown off the island and get her out of his life for good.

But that was the problem. He lost track of Molly last time. If she was working for his competitors, he wanted every move documented.

So that left his second choice. Go with Molly's lie. Keep her close until the week was over. Real close.

"Yes." He forced a smile. "Darrell and Bridget, this is Molly." He swallowed. "My fiancée."

"I didn't realize you were engaged," Darrell said.

"We haven't announced it yet." Was that the story Molly fed the islanders? He felt like he was playing catch-up, and he hated that feeling.

Kyle wrapped his hand around Molly's shoulder and gathered her resisting body close to him. When her heat nestled against his side, his muscles tensed.

Maybe this wasn't a good idea. But it was too late. He'd committed to this course and he'd finish it.

"Molly, this is Darrell Fields and Bridget Howell of plaza+tag." He watched Molly shake their hands, noticing the tense edges of her friendly smile. "I brought them down for the week to handle negotiations."

Bridget's eyes widened. "You didn't know we were coming?"

"Kyle gave me some notice today," Molly replied. "And I'm thrilled to have extra company."

Oh, yeah. Kyle reluctantly admired his "fiancée's" technique. *She's good.*

"And this is our neighbor, Diana," he told his guests. As he watched them exchange greetings with the older woman, he felt Molly inch away from him.

He gripped her shoulder. His arm locked. *Not so fast . . .* If she made a run for it now, it would make him look worse. Damn, he should have gone for the first choice.

Molly glanced up at him. He slowly turned and met her gaze and found her brown eyes flashing with warning.

She was warning *him*? The woman was audacious. He couldn't have that. It might be the attitude he wanted in his bed, but not when he had a major business deal on the line.

Kyle slid his hand down her arm and allowed it to rest on the curve of her hip. Molly went rigid as he patted her bottom. The others might take it as a possessive claim and not as the warning it was.

"I just made some coffee," Molly announced to the group. "Would you like some? How about you, Diana?"

She stepped away, ready to bolt into the house. Kyle knew she was trying to get some distance and a few bodies between them. He moved like lightning and clasped his hand around her wrist.

"That would be wonderful," Diana replied.

Molly gestured to the front door with one hand and jerked her other hand away from Kyle, but he wouldn't let go. He rubbed his thumb against the pulse point. It fluttered wildly under his touch.

"So, Darrell, Bridget, where are you from?" Molly asked with a touch of desperation as she made another attempt to break away.

Kyle lowered his hand and speared his fingers through hers. He worked his fingers between hers and held on tight.

"New York," Darrell said, as they moved toward the house.

"Is that right?" Molly asked as she tried to shake Kyle off, but he wouldn't let go. "I've never been there."

"I'll take you there for our honeymoon," Kyle said.

Molly went rigid. "What a *wonderful* idea," she replied sweetly as she squeezed his hand tight.

Kyle ignored the powerful grip. Nothing she threw at him was going to change his mind. She'd figure it out. Sooner or later, she'd discover that wherever she went for the next week, he was going to be right there with her.

She had to make a break for it.

Molly glanced at the double doors in the living room. It had just turned dark and she was wearing dark clothes. She could creep around the island undetected and—

"Don't you agree, Molly?"

Molly flinched and her gaze collided with Kyle's. He was too close. Way too close. She could feel his heartbeat. It was powerful, solid, and not comforting in the least.

She wanted to get away, but he had her curled up against him as they sat on a very small settee in the formal living room. Every time she tried to get up, he was able to pin her back. Every time she was reminded that he was in charge.

"Whatever you say, Kyle," she said with an overly bright smile. The guests chuckled, but they didn't know her statement had an underlying hint of truth.

Because Kyle had caught her and wasn't done with her. She felt like a field mouse being tormented by a wild cat.

She definitely had to escape.

She had tried when Diana left after coffee. It would have been so simple. She could have walked the neighbor home and kept on walking.

But Kyle had gone with Molly to the door. Worse, he held onto the back of her jeans. Her nerves had been in one messy knot, especially with Kyle's knuckles brushing against the small of her back.

How was she going to get out of here? Molly kept going over the problem at different angles. The island was very isolated and cold. Rural and hilly. Kyle knew this place better than she.

She also couldn't get off the island until the ferry arrived. Which was once a day. She *could* try and get one of the islanders to transport her to the mainland on a boat. But in the night? Would they do that? Would anyone?

"I'm going to see to dinner," she suddenly decided and made her move. He couldn't argue with that, right? And she needed to get away. For just five minutes. Or better yet, just not touch him.

Because even after all that happened, he still turned her mind to mush. She still got hot all over by his touch. And that was *not* going to work for her.

"Would you like some help?" Kyle asked, rising from the settee.

"See, Darrell?" Bridget asked, swatting her husband on the arm. "Kyle helps Molly in the kitchen."

"That's because he hasn't put the wedding ring on her yet," Darrell said as he playfully rubbed his arm. "He still has to make a good impression."

"I don't need any help, but thank you." She collected some of the coffee cups and the tray. The tray served well as a shield from Kyle. "You'd probably prefer going into your office. I can call you when dinner's ready."

The office was on the opposite side of the house from the kitchen. Kyle must have picked that up because his eyes twinkled in response. "If you like, we can all go in the kitchen."

"No!" She realized how bad that sounded and tried to soften it with a casual smile. "Stay where you are. I'm a . . . very messy and . . . noisy cook. Very noisy. I'm sure it would interrupt you."

"Molly, you know it's been so long since I've seen you," Kyle said. "I just can't keep my eyes off of you."

"Aw, that's so sweet." Bridget turned to Darrell and narrowed her eyes in a pouty glare.

Darrell moved out of swatting distance. "Kyle, try not to make me look bad."

Molly retreated, grateful for the reprieve. She was stuck for now. Maybe she could make a break for it at daylight. She glanced over her shoulder. Kyle met her gaze, his light green eyes icy and alert.

Make that before daylight.

It was only nighttime and Kyle didn't think he could last a week of this. Of watching Molly only to remind himself why he was angry with her. A week more of following her, but keeping his emotions detached. Touching her without getting intimate.

He would go crazy.

Because she was proving to be more trouble. More of a threat. She was uncontrollable. Molly was the unforeseen variable in his guarded world.

"Good night, Molly," Bridget said and yawned. "I don't know why I'm this tired."

"Good night," Molly said, pausing from unloading the

dishwasher. "You don't want to miss the sunrise. It's so beautiful."

Kyle's breath caught in his chest as he watched her face. She seemed to glow from the simple pleasure.

Oh, yeah. He would be crazy before the week was up.

"Good night, Kyle," Bridget said.

"Let's talk business tomorrow," Darrell said as he escorted his wife out of the kitchen.

Kyle gave a nod of agreement and watched the guests leave. He turned and walked out of the kitchen, through the laundry room and to the back door. He slid the deadbolt home and heard it echoing in the quiet, small room.

"What are you doing?" Molly called out to him.

He thought it was self-explanatory. "Locking up."

"Would that be locking people in, or locking them out?" he heard her muttering loudly.

"What do you think?" he asked. He wished he had a security system installed. That would be top priority when he got back to the mainland.

But for now he had to watch Molly like a hawk and forget about sleeping. Kyle turned off the lights in the laundry and walked back into the kitchen, reminding himself that he hadn't had a good night's sleep ever since he met Molly Connors. Or whatever her name was.

"There's no need to lock the doors," she said as she wiped her hands on the dish towel. "Everyone on the island is very trustworthy."

"*Everyone*?" He gave her a pointed stare.

"Everyone," she said as if she didn't hear the innuendo. "I haven't heard of any crime since I've been here."

"And how long would that have been?"

Molly shrugged and looked away. "A while." She cleared her throat, braced her shoulders, and met his gaze head-on. "Kyle, why are you here?"

"Molly, you are wearing my patience." He rested his

elbow on the kitchen counter and looked her in the eye. "Let's try this again. Why are you here in my house?"

"I needed a place to stay," she admitted. She opened her mouth to say more, but apparently thought better of it. She pressed her lips tightly together.

"What happened to your truck?"

"It was stolen or towed," she answered, her shoulders drooping. "I don't know."

"You don't know," he repeated with disbelief.

"That's right," she said, her temper flaring. "I don't know. I reported it stolen and I haven't heard anything else about it."

"Maybe if you had stuck around you would have found out it was stolen and it turned up."

"It did?" Her expression brightened at the news. "Was there anything left?"

"Just the sofa."

"Why is it no one wants that sofa? I couldn't even give it away to charity." She shook her head and paused. She tilted her head and looked at him. "How do you know about my truck?"

"It was in the report."

Her eyebrows dipped as she frowned. "Why would the police give you a report?"

"The police didn't." She could figure out the rest for herself. He wasn't surprised that it didn't take her long.

"You—" She glanced in the direction of the stairs and dropped her voice a level. "You had me followed?"

"Molly, if I had you followed, you would never have had the chance to step into this house."

"That's true," Molly said. "But then how did you know?"

"I had you investigated."

"Aha!" She jabbed a finger at him. "That's the same thing!"

"No, it's not." He noticed that her reaction wasn't what

he expected. He wanted to see guilt. Concern. Panic. Instead he saw righteous anger. Either she'd led a life of good, clean living or she was a sociopath. Either possibility did not sit well with him. "Is Molly Connors your real name?"

Her mouth dropped open with shock. "I don't believe this," she said in a daze.

"Well?" He didn't want to give her time to concoct a story. "Is it?"

She tossed the dish towel onto the counter. "I'm going to bed," she announced. "Good night."

Molly marched out of the room. Kyle made sure he was right behind her. He quietly turned off the kitchen lights, noticing that she never did explain why she chose to stay at his house.

She went up the stairs and he followed her. He found that suspicious. Did she plan to jump off the balcony? Wiggle her way out of the bathroom window? But that would ruin her plan, wouldn't it? There was a reason she was here the same week plaza+tag came for a visit. Her mission was far from accomplished.

Molly stopped on one of the steps and looked over her shoulder. She glared at him when she discovered he was one step away from her. *Too bad*, Kyle thought. *She had better get used to it.*

When she showed no signs of moving, Kyle decided it was time to share the step. His placed his foot between hers and moved up. His chest rubbed her back, one vertebrae at a time.

Molly moved. Quickly.

And, now that Kyle thought about it as he followed her up the remaining steps, she never said if Molly Connors was her real name.

She hurried to the master bedroom and got around the door as his foot crossed the threshold. "Good night," she said sweetly and swung the door shut.

Kyle grabbed the edge before she could shut the door on his foot. He pushed it open without much effort. She backed away as he silently stepped into the room and closed the door behind him.

"What do you think you're doing?" she said in a fierce whisper.

"I'm going to bed." He turned the lock on the door.

"Not here." She moved her arms wide as if blocking off the area.

"Yes, here." Kyle kicked off his shoes. "We're engaged, remember?"

"Not officially."

Kyle felt his jaw tighten. "Don't even get me started. If we're a couple, we sleep together."

Molly's expression went completely blank.

"I should warn you," he said as he pulled off his shirt. "I sleep naked."

Chapter 12

Her gaze darted all over the bedroom suite. Everywhere—anywhere—but at Kyle's bronzed, sculpted chest. "Then I'm not sleeping here."

"Yes, you are."

"I'm going into the other bedroom." She reached for the door.

"Think again." He plucked her hand off the doorknob. "I need to keep my eye on you."

"I promise I won't make a run for it tonight." And she meant it. She wanted to wait until the temperature went above the freezing level.

"Oh, well, as long as you give me your word." He rolled his eyes. "We know how much weight your word carries."

Well, he had her there. "Then I'll sleep in this sitting room. On that chair." She motioned to the cushy leather chair that had a matching ottoman.

She should be very comfortable there. Especially with Kyle staying in the next room. Naked.

Hmm. She should try to forget that last part, or she'd never get any sleep.

"Next to the door?" He pulled her toward the bedroom. "I don't think so.

"What's wrong with that?" Molly dragged her heels. She

bet she looked undignified, but that was the price to pay to get her way.

"That would mean I have to stay between you and the door." He pulled her into the bedroom. "And I'm sleeping in a bed tonight."

"Fine. Sleep there." She motioned at the huge sleigh bed. "Be my guest."

Kyle gave her a look of warning.

"I'm sleeping here." She plopped down onto the floor and crisscrossed her legs. She folded her arms across her chest, just in case he didn't get the point.

"Go ahead." He grabbed a pillow and threw it at her.

She caught it before it hit her in the face. "I prefer the other one. It's softer."

Kyle ignored her. "Sleep over there." He motioned to the other side of the room. "Away from the door."

"Fine." She got up and walked over there. She tossed the pillow onto the rug and lay down.

Crossing her arms, she looked up at the ceiling. "Just for the record, you're going to have a hard time getting me arrested. Everyone is going to know that you invited me to stay in your house after finding me here."

Kyle didn't say anything. She listened intently and heard the rustle of his clothes.

"In fact," Molly continued hurriedly, "you're inviting me into your bedroom, and don't think I won't be mentioning that in my statement."

"I can't wait to see how you'll embellish it," he said dryly.

Molly shivered as a cold draft wafted over her. Maybe it was a good idea that she had already planned to make her escape first thing in the morning.

"And I'm not going to the authorities," Kyle admitted.

"You're not?" Her muscles went stiff. Kyle could easily throw her jail and he decided against it? He must have something more diabolical in mind. "Why?" she asked suspiciously.

"Because you're of more use to me outside a jail cell." Kyle suddenly stood before her. To Molly's relief, he was still wearing his trousers. "Are you going to sleep like that?" he asked.

"Yes." She squeezed her eyes shut. "Good night."

"You know," he said almost impatiently. "Your virtue is safe with me."

Molly sighed. "Oh, for crying out loud. Let me repeat myself. I'm not a virgin."

"I'm not going to jump you."

Molly clucked her tongue. "Yeah, right."

"I mean it."

"Oh?" She peeked at him through one eye. "The attraction wore off the minute I wasn't working for you?"

"No, more like the minute I found out you stole and lied to me." The skin on his face tightened, emphasizing the harsh angles of his cheekbones. "I'm not into women who are looking for ways to hurt me."

Molly flinched and rose to a sitting position. "I'm not trying to hurt you."

"You snuck into my house."

"You have more than one house," she pointed out.

"That doesn't make it any less illegal," Kyle said as he walked away from her.

"So arrest me." She wasn't going to let him keep taunting her with the possibility.

"That doesn't fit into my plans," he repeated and looked out the window.

"What does, then?" Impatience clipped her words.

"It sure didn't include you cavorting around the island as my fiancée."

"I do not cavort. Cavort." She tried the word out on her tongue. "What kind of word is that, anyway?"

He looked away from the window. "You wanna be my fiancée?"

"Not particularly."

"Then that's what you get. You're going to be my fiancée."

"For marriage proposals, that one blew." She held up her hand. "Just saying."

"And," Kyle continued relentlessly, "you have to be the best damn fiancée this world has ever seen."

Oh, great. There was no way she could meet that kind of expectation. She could knock herself out trying, and it wouldn't be enough. Kyle would hold it over her head how she didn't fulfill her side of the bargain.

"I hate to break this to you," she told him, "but that's impossible. There's no job description for a fiancée."

"Sure there is. You have to be thoughtful and considerate to my needs."

"Uh . . ." She held up her hand. "Wait a minute."

"And be"—the look he gave her was dark and sensual—"*demonstrative* while maintaining a certain . . . decorum."

She stared at him, openmouthed.

Kyle obviously was reviewing what he said and gave a sharp nod. "Yeah, that's about it."

"Here's an idea. Why don't you save us both the aggravation and just 'fire' me?" She made quotation marks with her fingers. "You're real good at that."

"Because I have to show Darrell and Bridget that I make good decisions and that I can trust the right person." His tone took on a bitter edge. "My choice in a fiancée reflects that."

"Basically, I'm the embodiment of your good judgment." Her mouth reluctantly twitched. She could cause all sorts of trouble.

Kyle must have arrived at the same conclusion. "Mess up on this and you will regret it."

"Hey, why are you putting all the responsibility on me? You could have blown my story anytime, but you didn't."

Kyle ran his hand through his hair, the movement thick with agitation. "Because I can't afford the chance of you running away again."

"I do not run away." She was offended that he would think such a thing. "I never run away."

"What do you call this?" He gestured around him.

"A change of scenery? A fresh start? Taking control of my future? Take your pick."

Kyle scoffed at the idea.

"I don't know why you need to keep tabs on me anyway," she said as she lay back down.

She heard Kyle's hesitation. "So you could lead us to your buyer."

Buyer? What was he talking about? "What buyer?"

"For the trade secrets."

Why did he think she had stolen that information? What could she do to prove her innocence? "You are wasting your time. I didn't steal that spec."

Kyle sliced his hand through the air. "I don't want to get into it."

Molly made a face. "Oh, sure, now—"

"Go ahead and change."

"Very gentlemanly of you, but I'm fine." Molly burrowed her head deeper into the pillow. She laced her fingers together and rested them demurely on her stomach.

"You can't sleep in that."

"Thanks for the advice, but I don't have anything to sleep in." And there was no way she would sleep naked. "That bed was warm enough that it didn't matter."

Kyle stalked over to the chest of drawers, grumbling unintelligibly the whole way. He pulled open a drawer and tossed a soft white T-shirt at her.

Molly caught it. "Thanks." *Maybe he could be nice . . .*

A heavy blanket suddenly landed on her with a thump. "You better not snore."

Then again . . .

Molly's teeth chattered and she cautiously opened one eye. Oh, thank goodness! She opened the other eye and breathed a sigh of relief. For a second there she thought she was back in the DIY truck and the island cottage had been a dream.

Molly sat up and looked around the dark bedroom. She couldn't see the bedside clock from here. It looked like it was the middle of the night and far away from dawn.

She untangled her legs from the blanket. It wasn't doing much good anyway. Kyle had the good comforter. The warm bed.

She wanted to crawl into the bed.

And not just for the warmth.

Molly sighed and lay back down on the pillow. She was staying put. On this hard floor that apparently was the crossroad of two cold drafts.

It wasn't like she hadn't slept on a floor before.

And she had slept in worse places.

Molly darted a quick glance at the bed and immediately looked away. She was not going to crawl into that bed. Even though she *knew* nothing would happen. Kyle had made it perfectly clear.

"I'm not into women who are looking for ways to hurt me."

Molly winced, the words "hurt me" circling in her mind. That statement nearly destroyed her. Double over with searing pain.

Kyle had seemed so invincible. So strong. She never thought . . .

Well, maybe that was the problem. She honestly didn't

think it would harm him if she stayed at his place. If she said she was his unofficial fiancée.

Not to say that he should be proud and flattered by her declaration, she thought wryly. She didn't think her lies would affect him.

But they did. Who knew how much power her lies held, or how they would ripple into other people's lives. Well, she thought with a slow sigh, she had to make it right. Make good on every white lie and every whopper.

Where did she start?

The task was almost too overwhelming. She almost didn't want to start. But she would.

There was nothing she could do about the lies she told at work. At least, she didn't think so. It was difficult to remember what she had lied about.

Okay, she knew how to handle that problem. If one of her lies slapped her back in the face, she would own up to it and make up for it.

Molly rolled her eyes in self-disgust. That was so easy for her to think right now. What were the chances something work-related would come up this week?

What about the lies she told while on the island? Molly chewed on her bottom lip, considering the problem. If she told the truth now, it would hurt Kyle.

Or was she copping out? Was it easier for her to think it couldn't be fixed? Couldn't she find a better solution? Something that would make everyone happy.

But Kyle said he wanted her to act as the best damn fiancée. Not exactly truthful, but it would temporarily fix the lie she told. Molly rubbed her hand over her forehead. All of this virtue and ethics were confusing her.

Okay, new rule. And she had to make this one stick. She would act like the best damn fiancée for Kyle. That was the only way—as far as she could tell—to repair the damage her lie caused.

From this moment on she would only speak the truth. No matter what. Molly winced. That resolution already sounded painful.

And she was going to be honest with herself. She wanted to be in that bed. With Kyle. And the only reason she wasn't there was because she was afraid.

Not because of what might happen.

But what might *not* happen.

She had fallen from Kyle's good standing. The trade secrets fiasco wasn't her fault, but maybe it just hurried the process up. Because her world of lies would have unraveled and it would have revealed who she really was.

She denied herself a taste of Kyle, saying it was because he was her boss. And that was one of the reasons. She wasn't willing to lose her job over any reason or any guy.

But now she wondered if there had been something more than the fear of losing her job.

It didn't matter anymore. He wasn't interested in her anymore. She ruined that. It was time to stop dancing around it and move on.

Was she going sleep on the floor for the rest of the week because he didn't like her? Forget that! If he had a problem sharing a bed, he was more than welcome to the excruciatingly hard and cold floor.

Molly kicked off the blanket and rose from the floor. She grabbed her pillow and hurried to the bed.

Doing her best not to wake Kyle, Molly gently raised the corner of the comforter and slowly eased onto the mattress. She found herself holding her breath as she laid her head down on her pillow with agonizingly slowness. Only until she was fully resting on the bed did she slowly exhale.

Made it. And if she was still in bed when Kyle woke up, she'd deal with his annoyance. At least she'd have had a few hours of solid sleep.

Molly allowed her eyes to drift shut.

"Wondered how long you were going to hold out," Kyle grumbled drowsily.

Molly's mouth twitched. Nothing got by this guy.

Kyle gradually became aware of the sun streaking across the dark sky. Of the enveloping warmth. Of the curves nestled against him.

Curves?

He blearily opened one eye and saw the mass of brunette waves pillowing his face. Inhaling the scent that was familiar yet mysterious, he felt the kick in his veins and the buzz in his head.

Molly.

He flexed his hand and felt the warm, smooth skin underneath his fingers. Further exploration proved his hand was resting against her midriff. Under her T-shirt.

Raising his head, Kyle wondered what made her curl against him in the middle of the night. Then he noticed that it was *he* who gravitated toward her. Worse, his leg was entwined with hers, as his arm wrapped possessively around her waist.

Smooth move, Ashton. What was all the crap about not being interested?

Kyle reluctantly removed his hand from her, his fingertips gliding along her warm flesh. His hand trailed along the lace edge of her underwear. Kyle paused before darting his hand away.

Molly shifted and rolled onto her back. He was thankful for the heavy, thick comforter that surrounded them both. He knew the shirt had ridden up her stomach and exposed the underside of her breasts. His iron control didn't need a visual.

He needed to get out of bed. Now, before the need pulled him closer. Before he rested his hand against her and curled against her side.

His leg bumped against her. Her smooth leg against his rough one offered a teasing sample of what they would be like, skin against skin.

Don't go there. You don't want her.

That was a lie. He did want her. A lot. Even when she lied to him. Even when he saw her standing in his house, he wanted Molly Connors.

But he didn't want the trouble she carried. She was untamable. Chaos.

She didn't follow the rules.

Not that that was a bad thing, but it was something he didn't have room for in his controlled world. Once upon a time, he was like that. But things changed. Now he *had* to play by the rules. Why give his enemies an easier target? The risks were too great.

He studied her face again, finding peace and disquiet. Molly reminded him of his past. Sometimes he missed those wild days. Those were the days when he was bold and brash and nothing would get in his way. He had nothing to lose and everything to gain.

When did he lose that feeling? He was on top of his game. Could go anywhere. Do anything.

And he was playing it safe.

Except when he was with Molly. Then he felt the lick of wildfire. But it was an illusion. He felt all-powerful when he was with Molly, but it was all a lie.

And he had to remember that or lose all he fought to acquire.

Molly stirred awake. She blinked her eyes open. She paused and looked at him before smiling sleepily.

The quiet pleasure in her expression turned him inside out. His chest ached from the sight.

But it was all a lie. She was up to something. No one who could lie as fluently as Molly could look that innocent.

But who cared if it was a lie? There was something

magical about the time between being sleep and awake, between night and dawn. Between real and unreal.

He wasn't ready to pull away. To wake up.

Kyle placed his hand boldly on her stomach. He felt the muscles underneath his hand bunch.

She didn't move away. His pulse kicked.

Molly watched him between her lashes. Her chest rose and fell.

Kyle lowered his head, anticipation flooding him as his mouth touched hers.

Chapter 13

His mouth touched hers. Seeking, wanting.

So much for not being able to stand the touch of her. Not that she minded, Molly decided as a hint of a smile played on her lips.

Kyle gently pressed a small kiss on the edge of her mouth. She felt herself softening under his touch. Responding.

He deepened the kiss and she parted her lips more. She wanted to know where he'd take her. How far they would go. How much it would change her life. She was ready for a life-changing, mind-altering encounter. As long as it was with Kyle Ashton, she was ready for anything.

She turned into him. Feeling safe, feeling on the edge. Molly placed her hand on his shoulder. She paused when her hand touched warm skin. Muscle.

Molly explored the contours of his shoulder and arm. He was muscular like one of those famous stone sculptures. What those artists dreamed as the ideal, Kyle achieved with his body.

Her fingers pressed into his back. His power, his restraint flexed under her fingertips. Molly traced the length of his spine until she came to the small of his back.

She cupped the compact planes of his buttocks, pleasure sparking at her pulse points. His flesh was tight and promised strength. Stamina.

Their kisses grew frantic. Passed the edge of restraint and back again. She felt her mouth redden and swell.

His large hands cupped her rib cage. Her heart fluttered so wildly, Molly was sure he could feel it under his fingers. She felt fragile under his touch, yet ready for anything.

His hands skimmed under her breasts. Her nipples tightened and stung. She couldn't wait for his palms to cover her breasts. She was ready to grab his wrist and guide him when he finally—finally—touched her.

She arched under him, her soft breasts pressing against his hard chest. Molly sought his mouth, kissing him fiercely as her body ached with pleasure.

She moved her hands forward, teasing his hips with the brush of her fingers until she found his penis. Molly wrapped her hands around his length. He was hard and smooth and warm.

She tightened her grip and enjoyed the sound of his groan. Molly felt the violent twitch under her touch. She glided her hands up, one palm after the other.

Kyle rolled on top of her. He grabbed her hands and raised them over her head. Her knuckles hit the pillow, his hands encircling her wrists, leaving her exposed and vulnerable to his mouth.

She found it exciting but unnerving. Something wasn't right in the way he held her. In the way he overwhelmed her. Controlled her.

She entwined her legs with his. Bucked her hips. Molly wished she was as naked as he was, yet she was grateful for the cotton barrier.

Kyle trailed his mouth down her neck. She wanted to sink her fingers into his hair. Clasp her hands against his head and direct him to her breasts.

But she couldn't move her arms. She tried to pull out of Kyle's grasp, but her arms didn't budge. She tried again.

Kyle's hold tightened.

"Come on, Kyle," she pleaded.

"No," he said against her throat.

"Don't you trust me?"

His mouth hovered over her skin. It was for just a second, but it was enough for the answer to hit her upside the head.

Nothing had changed. He wanted her, but he didn't trust her. Even in bed.

It shouldn't have bothered her so much, but it did. After all, he wanted her. She had proof. It was pressed against her inner thigh.

But that was it. He was going to take her and get away as fast as he could before she hurt him again.

Just how good could it possibly be between them if he was holding her down?

Well . . .

No, no. Molly pushed the tantalizing thought to the side. She might want Kyle, but not like this.

She wanted him. Wanted him *bad*. But she wanted him to lose control. Wanted him to give her everything he had. She would accept nothing less.

"Let go, Kyle."

He hesitated. His hands flexed against her wrists as he considered his next move.

"Now."

He released her and rolled over. The silence was tense. It pulsated in the room. Matched the ache inside her.

"Can you blame me?" Kyle whispered.

Molly closed her eyes. "No." That was the problem. She understood why he didn't trust her.

She sat up and tugged at her T-shirt. Molly looked and saw Kyle lying on his back. His arm was thrown over his eyes.

"I'm sorry I broke into your house and stayed." She found it difficult to say those words out loud. She felt what she said, but it stuck in her throat.

And she found the pressing need to explain her actions. Molly fought to keep her silence. She wasn't going to ruin her apology.

Kyle must have expected to hear excuses. It took a moment before he lifted the crook on his arm and glared suspiciously at her. "Uh-huh," he said carefully.

So far, so good. "And I'm sorry I lied about being your fiancée."

The corner of his mouth lifted. "Regretting it already?"

Molly jumped out of bed and didn't look at him. "What I regret is getting you stuck in this lie. But I'm going to fix it."

"Fix it how?" Concern darkened his voice.

"I'm going to play the part of your fiancée to the hilt," she promised.

"I don't like the sound of this."

"I'm going to give you guys the best Thanksgiving week ever." She noticed she was holding her hand up as if taking a pledge. Molly hurriedly dropped her hand.

"There's no need," Kyle assured her. "We are going to be working. Just keep yourself scarce and your mouth shut while I negotiate terms with Darrell and Bridget."

"Don't worry, Kyle," Molly said as she strode into the adjoining bathroom. "You'll see. I'll be the best damn fiancée this world has ever seen," she promised and closed the door behind her.

The plan was to stay away from Molly, Kyle reminded himself as he scowled at the horizon. So why was he finding every reason to see her? Be around her?

He could have said it was because he was checking up on her. But so far she'd been doing exactly what she promised.

Maybe that's what was freaking him out.

She hadn't bolted. She'd been the perfect hostess, setting the tone for the week. What could have been a number-crunching and tense working holiday was turning into a getaway for two couples.

He watched Molly and Bridget walk along the rocky beach. Molly wasn't making a run for it. She wasn't trying to get kicked off the island—which he wouldn't put past her.

He leaned back on the deck chair, unable to keep his eyes off of Molly. It took him a few moments to realize that his cell phone was ringing. Kyle picked it up and looked at the number. He turned it on. "Hello?"

"Hey, Kyle." Glenn's voice came in loud and clear. "You were supposed to call me back yesterday."

"Glenn. Sorry, man. I—" He forgot. For the life of him he couldn't imagine how he managed that. The CFO was supposed to be here today to help him with the negotiations.

"The ferry is about to dock and I'll be there in a couple of minutes."

"There's something you need to know." He needed to Glenn up to speed fast. "Molly is here."

"Molly? Molly who?"

"Molly Connors," Kyle informed the chief financial officer. "She used to work for us."

"Wait a second. The receptionist?" Glenn yelled into the phone. "She's there? At the cottage?"

"Yep."

"So what are you going to do?"

"Hold on to her." Those words pricked at him. "Keep an eye out so she doesn't make a run for it and disappear again."

"This doesn't make any sense," Glenn said, almost to himself.

"I know." Kyle hesitated, knowing he had to tell Glenn, but really didn't feel like getting into it. "By the way, if anyone asks, Molly and I are engaged."

"Whaa . . . ?"

"I'll explain it to you later. How's everything at the office?" Glenn didn't respond. "Are you still there?"

"Yeah, sorry," Glenn replied. "I just made eye contact with this hot blonde in a red Mercedes. I'm going to see if I can score."

Kyle made a face. "Glenn, you're here to work."

"Wish me luck."

As long as it wasn't someone from work, Kyle didn't care. He disconnected the call and saw Molly and Bridget walking back up to the house. He decided to meet them halfway.

As he got closer, he was able to see the glow in Molly's face. The two women were laughing. Molly tilted her head back and laughed without restraint. The sound, the sight, the beauty of it all, hit in his chest. Slammed at him so hard that he staggered back.

Molly turned to face him. "Kyle, Bridget was telling me—" She broke off and her smile dimmed. "Is everything all right?"

No. He was in trouble. He was feeling something more than attraction for this woman. How could he feel this way about someone who—he knew *exactly* what kind of woman she was. Why was he interested in her?

"Kyle?" She moved next to him, placed her hand on his shoulder and leaned in. She looked up into his face and her expression hit him like a one-two punch.

He knew it was all for show, but damn if it didn't feel good. "Uh." He swallowed awkwardly. "Glenn is on his way."

"Glenn." Caution dulled the sparkle in her eye.

"Your CFO?" Bridget asked.

"Yeah, I forgot to tell you he was coming." He found himself wincing, waiting for the fireworks.

Molly took a step back. "Oh, that's okay. When is he coming?"

"He's on the island now." He rubbed the back of his neck. "I know this is short notice . . ."

Molly and Bridget exchanged knowing glances. "What?" Kyle asked, trying to figure out the silent communication arcing around him.

"How long is he staying?"

"Until Monday." And why did he feel the need to apologize? "He's helping with the deal."

"I better go make up his room." She took a step back. "Are there any more guests? Because there are only three bedrooms."

"No more. I promise."

"Should we believe him, Bridget?"

Bridget smiled. "I don't know, Molly. But it looks like you need to train him better."

She waggled her eyebrows. "Now there's an idea." She turned and made her way to the house.

"You need any help getting ready for Glenn?" Bridget called out.

"No, I'm good."

"Thank you!" Kyle said.

"You owe me," Molly told him without looking back.

"Huh. Did you hear that?" He turned to Bridget and found her smiling. "The woman has nerve."

"Kyle, if you were my fiancé, you wouldn't get lucky for a week from that stunt."

Was this what they meant by training? "I better go help her out then."

Bridget laughed as he walked away. "Men."

* * *

190 / Susanna Carr

Kyle rested his shoulder against the closed bedroom door and watched Molly change the sheets on the bed. "You're nervous," he said.

"I'm not—" She closed her mouth. She wasn't going to lie anymore. "I'm . . . what's the word? Apprehensive? No, that doesn't sound right."

"Why? Because of Glenn?"

"I feel like I'm being cornered." She stretched her arm to cover the mattress corner with the fitted sheet. "The last time I was in a room with the two of you, I was being accused of stealing and threatened with jail time."

"That won't happen again." Kyle paused. "Unless you do something illegal."

She flashed him a long-suffering look. "I didn't do anything wrong the last time."

He shrugged a shoulder. "So you keep saying."

And she'd keep on saying. She'd already 'fessed up to enough. Why would she hold back on the trade secrets?

"I already told Glenn that you were here and that we were 'engaged.' "

"I'm sure that went over well." She fitted the bottom corner of the sheet only to have the top corner slide off. Molly straightened to her full height, closed her eyes, and took a deep breath.

"Actually, it did," Kyle said. "He was preoccupied at the time."

Molly opened her eyes. "Platinum or strawberry blonde? Here." She gestured at the opposite mattress corners. "You're supposed to be helping. Make yourself useful."

He approached the bed. "Glenn isn't going to be the problem."

Molly let out a snort. "Unless you tell him to be one."

"Don't think of running away," he warned her as he fitted the bottom corner with ease.

"What's the point?" she asked as she stretched the fabric

over the corner closest to her. "I'll have two of you after me."

"You promised you'd stay."

"Yeah, I did." She moved to the headboard. "And I am."

"Doesn't sound like it," Kyle said as he walked to the top of the mattress.

Molly put her hands on her hips. "You know, I gave my word and I'm doing my best. You don't know what it's like having it hang over your head that in a couple of days you're going to make me regret living."

"I'm not trying to punish you."

"Kyle, you fired me because I had a book on my desk. I didn't get a chance to defend myself. You decided I was guilty. Case closed."

"It's standard procedure. As part of the non-disclosure—"

"And then you have me investigated"—she bit out the word—"thinking I'm going to lead you to whoever wants your stupid green book."

"I—"

"And now Glenn is coming over." She hurriedly fitted the sheet over the other corner. "Like having one warden isn't enough."

"Warden?"

"I already find life difficult," she told him as she walked around to his side. "Why would I want to add to it?"

"Molly, I promise you. While you're here, I won't let anything happen to you."

She fixed the corner he left undone. "Because you want to drag me back to your office, make me break down and give you all this information off record."

Kyle didn't say anything. He didn't deny his plan and his silence tugged at her.

"I didn't do anything," she muttered for the hundredth time as she grabbed the top sheet.

"I'm beginning to believe you," he said softly.

She glanced up at him. "You don't sound too happy about that."

"I don't know if it's because I want to believe you," Kyle admitted.

Her mouth tilted into a cynical smile. "You want me to be guilty."

His eyes widened. "No, I don't."

"Yeah, you do." She flipped the sheet open and watched it unfurl. "Then it would be easy to hate me. I got it."

He grabbed at the sheet. "I don't hate you."

Molly didn't want to talk about it. She tried to yank the sheet away from him.

"I don't." He pulled the sheet harder, dragging her closer.

"You don't like me," she said, unable to look him in the eye.

"I never said that."

She gave a little huff. "You don't have to."

"I like you," he said roughly. "More than I should."

"What's that supposed—" He muffled her question with a hard kiss. Her pulse leapt from his possessive touch.

Kyle tilted his head to the side, his lips still rubbing against hers. "You distract me." He dropped the sheet and cupped her face with his hands. "You make my head spin."

He kissed her again, his tongue surging in her mouth. She parted her lips, desperate for more. As he explored her mouth, he curled his arm around her waist. It was a good thing, too. She felt a little dizzy.

"I should be working," he murmured against her lips. "Making the deal of a lifetime. But what am I doing? I'm up here with you. Trying very hard not to throw you onto this bed."

Really? Excitement flickered deep inside her. "What's stopping you?" she asked.

The feral gleam in his eye was her only warning. Kyle pulled her into his arms and kissed her deeply.

She felt the fierce, hot need all the way to her toes. His hands flattened along her spine, her stomach pressed against his. She felt contained. Wild. Hot.

Her world spun and her back rested against the mattress. She lay across it and tried to find the floor, but her feet dangled from the bed.

Kyle hovered above her, his arms bracketing her head. He kissed her again, this time slow and deliberate, creating a fire inside her she didn't know existed.

Molly tasted that heat she wanted. That untamed quality lurking under the sophistication. She reached for his head, her hands tangling in his hair.

His hands drifted to her waist and found the edge of her sweatshirt. He slid his fingers up her ribs, and she wiggled under the acute pleasure of his feathery touch. He pulled her flimsy bra up and splayed his hand on her bared breasts.

She felt her heart racing as Kyle caressed her tight nipples. She desperately wanted him to taste her. Suck. Bite. Go wild.

Kyle leisurely trailed one hand down the waistband of her jeans. Molly's heart jumped into her throat. Her skin crackled with anticipation.

He unsnapped her jeans and slowly dragged the zipper down. Molly wanted to do the job for him. Kick off her jeans. Rip them down her legs.

He cupped her sex against the palm of his hand. Molly felt the steamy heat contained. When Kyle pressed the heel of his hand against her, she was ready to leap off of the bed. She arched her back, her hands grabbing the sheets, bunching them in her fists.

Kyle pulled her panties down her legs and Molly forgot to breathe. She was exposed. Nervous. Needy.

She closed her eyes as he reached down and rubbed his fingers along her wet slit. Molly all but whimpered as he dipped into her wetness.

He took her nipple into his mouth and wildfire streaked through her blood. Molly dug her nails into his shoulder as she gasped jaggedly for her next breath.

The doorbell rang.

Molly froze, the chime screeching in her ears. She looked at Kyle as he raised his head. Their gazes met, his blurry with desire.

And he continued to stroke her.

She flopped her head back on the bed. Oh, did that feel good! But they had to stop. Molly turned her head from side to side. She had to move away.

Her gaze flew to the door of the bedroom. It wasn't locked. Anyone could walk in. Anyone who was looking for them, wondering where they were . . .

"Doorbell," she whispered.

But Kyle didn't stop. He dipped his finger deep inside her and brought his other hand down on her clit.

Oh, she didn't want to stop. And he didn't understand. It could take her *forever* to come. Sometimes she didn't. She couldn't orgasm on command. She couldn't let the doorbell ring until she did.

And she couldn't take the pressure to perform. The delicious pressure building inside her. Should she fake it?

The doorbell rang again.

She was really good at faking.

"Ignore it," Kyle said against her breast, his hot breath wafting over her sensitive nipple.

She couldn't ignore it. And she couldn't fake it. That was like lying. And she'd promised she wouldn't lie.

That, and she really wanted to hold out for the real thing.

But the doorbell was right there. On the brink of her

consciousness. She wondered why Kyle didn't feel this sense of urgency. Wondered how he could dip into her core with a languor she was far from feeling.

And then she felt it. Right in the back of her knees. The white-hot tingling that threatened to grow. Burn bright. Consume.

The sheets came undone from the corners and bunched around her. She grabbed for Kyle and kissed him hard. The tingling shot down her legs and arms.

The doorbell rang again.

Oh, go away! She almost yelled. *Leave!*

She had to find out. She didn't want to stop. She was almost there. Almost . . .

Kyle seemed to sense it. His touch became more aggressive. Deeper. His kisses were slick and unrefined.

"Kyle?" Bridget called up from the stairs.

She tensed, her gaze dragging to the door. *Oh, almost . . .*

"Molly?"

She ignored Bridget, just like Kyle was. Ignored the world around her. The world stopped outside the door. Didn't exist past the edges of the mattress.

"I'll get the door," Bridget said, with a thread of laughter.

Molly didn't understand what Bridget said as the blood roared in her ears as sunbursts exploded behind her eyes. She . . . she . . .

And it crashed against her. She launched off of the mattress, anchored only by Kyle. She may have screamed, but he took that with an openmouthed kiss.

She pulsed around him. She couldn't catch her breath. She felt like she got too close to the sun and she was melting.

And once she regained her strength, she was going to take a hammer to that doorbell . . .

Chapter 14

It was past midnight and Kyle was nowhere finished with the work he had to accomplish for the day. The house was quiet, but far from peaceful. Because he knew Molly was asleep in the master bedroom. Wearing nothing more than a large, rumpled T-shirt.

Which was why he was here, and planned to work through the night. Kyle glanced across from the study and spotted Glenn staring at the flickering flames in the fireplace. He wondered when the CFO planned to turn in like the rest of the household. If he was hoping to find a nightlife on the island, Kyle thought as he returned his attention to his work, then the guy was out of luck.

Glenn took a sip of his whiskey, the ice clinking against the crystal glass. "I don't think she did it," he mused quietly.

Kyle stared at the computer screen and then looked at Glenn. "What did you say?"

His friend slowly turned his head and looked at him. "I don't think Molly took the blueprint."

Kyle sat back in his chair. He was tired, but his body suddenly went into full alert. "Why?"

"There were no leads on her computer. The forensic computer expert went all over Molly's computer and found nothing incriminating. There is no hint of her anywhere near the specs on our online database. Nothing."

"We have Curtis's statement."

Glenn squinted. "And we're believing him . . . why?"

It was always a risk to take a thief's word over a liar's, but Kyle was guided by one simple fact. "Because he already lost his standing in the computer industry and had nothing else to lose."

"I don't know about that." Glenn made a face. "He now stands out in the sea of nameless computer geniuses. I wouldn't be surprised if he gets an agent before the end of the year."

"It doesn't matter," Kyle decided. He turned his chair so he could go back to work on the computer. "We found Molly with the blueprint. End of story."

"Let me ask you something." Glenn slid his feet off of the ottoman. "If she's such a pro, and there's nothing that links her to this crime, why would she put the blueprint on her desk in clear view?"

"It wasn't in clear view," Kyle said as typed on the keyboard. "It was under a pile of papers."

"But the blueprint is in that weird green. You can spot it in a sea of white. She wouldn't hide it like that. That would be stupid."

Or brazen. Kyle paused from his work. "What are you getting at?"

Glenn's sigh was slow and uneven. "I think Molly was framed."

Kyle closed his eyes and pinched the bridge of his nose. He didn't want to rehash old business. "No one would get the blueprint only to dump it on Molly's desk."

"They would if they were about to get caught." Glenn set his glass down and rested his elbows on his knees.

"Curtis was nowhere near Molly's desk that day," Kyle pointed out.

"Okay, forget Curtis for a minute. I was talking to Molly tonight at dinner." He motioned toward the dining room.

"She knows less about computers than I do. Take my word on it, you can't fake that."

"You don't have to know how a car operates in order to steal it."

"True." Glenn acceded to that point with a nod of his head. "But you do have to know where to take the stolen car. And you need to know the market value. Plus you have to know how to drive the car so you don't get caught."

Glenn was making sense in his own way. Molly would have needed contacts in the computer industry. She would have also needed to know how to access more than her e-mail program.

"But then, why is Molly here?" Glenn splayed his hands in the air and fell back against his chair. "It doesn't make sense!"

"Have there been any security breaches since Molly left?" Kyle asked.

Glenn pressed his lips together. "No," he said reluctantly.

So there was no reason to question Molly's guilt. But he did. It nagged at him. Had been after that first wash of anger. "She probably was framed."

"Or sacrificed," Glenn suggested, gazing at the fire. "Low guy on the totem pole."

Kyle wasn't too sure about that. If she really was someone holding on to her job, she wouldn't risk it for a small cut of money. "You know what this means?"

His friend froze from retrieving his whiskey. "The thief is still in business."

"Son-of-a-bitch," Kyle whispered.

Glenn raised the glass to his lips. "My thoughts exactly."

Molly walked into the study early in the morning and almost dropped her basket of cleaning supplies when she saw Kyle at his desk.

"Uh, sorry," she said as he looked up from his computer. "I didn't mean to interrupt." She started to back out of the room.

"No, it's okay." He motioned for her to enter the room. "I'm catching up on some work."

She noticed his ruffled hair and the tired lines bracketing his mouth. "Have you been working all night?"

"Yeah." He rubbed his face with his hands.

That would explain where he'd been. He never came to bed. She thought he was avoiding her because of what happened when she was preparing Glenn's bedroom. He probably was, but using work as his excuse.

"Where's Darrell and Bridget?"

"They are still asleep." She grabbed the soft cloth from her basket and swiped at the top of the table next to the door. "I think Glenn is, too."

"What's that?"

"This?" She lifted the cloth in her hands. "It's called a dust rag."

Kyle rolled his eyes. "Yes, I figured that one out on my own. Why do you have it?"

"Do you think this house runs by itself?" Oh, great. Now she was sounding like her mother. She never thought that day would happen.

"I never expected you to do all the cleaning . . ."

Molly shrugged. "I don't mind. It's kind of fun," she said as ran the cloth over a beautiful sculpture.

"Fun?" Kyle repeated, obviously not believing a word she said. "Dusting is fun?"

"It is when you're taking care of nice things." Which was really causing her problems. She liked pretending that this place was hers. She was once again dreaming for something that was out of reach. She needed to keep her distance. Keep her heart out of it.

"Hey," she said as she picked up a framed photo. "I've seen this picture before. It's on your desk at work."

"Yep." He turned back to his computer.

It was the only truly personal thing in this room, too, Molly noticed. She was sure the other items had meaning, but this was the only window to Kyle's true self. "What happened that day?"

He paused from typing and glanced at her. "What do you mean?"

"Well, you have this picture on your desk here and at the office. It must be a special memory."

"It was the first day Ashton ImageWorks was in business. Ten years ago."

That was his most special occasion? *Wow, way to live it up, Kyle.* "Do you have a picture when you made your first million? How about when you took over the tech world?"

"No, I don't remember when that happened."

"Maybe you should." She returned the picture to the table and started dusting the leather box next to it.

"Molly, sit down."

She paused and cast a quick look at Kyle. "Am I bothering you? I can leave."

"No, I have something to say to you." He motioned for her to sit at the chair in front of his desk.

Molly froze. This did not sound good! Any news that required sitting down never was. She wanted to bolt from the room, but reluctantly found her way to the chair and slowly lowered herself onto the cushion.

Kyle exhaled sharply. "I'm sorry."

About what? Having sex? Not having sex? Sleeping together? Not sleeping together? The list was endless. "About what?" she asked, hunching her shoulders.

He met her gaze head-on. "I don't think you had anything to do with the blueprint."

She sat completely still. "Oh." She didn't know what to say. She had truly given up on making him believe her. The sudden gift made her nervous. She looked out of the corner of her eye. "What brought this on?"

"Circumstantial evidence points to you," he said, "but there are a lot of unanswered questions."

She glanced at the door. "Should I be thanking Glenn for this change of heart?"

"No, although he feels the same way." Kyle folded his hands on the edge of his desk. "Rather than assume you're guilty, I want to give you the benefit of the doubt."

"Th-thank you?" So he didn't really think she was innocent. He just knew she wasn't guilty. It was a start, she guessed. Molly moved to get up.

"And I'm going to repair the damage I've done," he promised.

She sat back down. This she wanted to hear. "How are you going to do that?"

"I'll do something about your work record," he offered. "I will make sure you won't have difficult finding another job."

Another job. Not her old one. Why?

"And I can recommend you to some businessmen I know. That would simplify the job hunt."

Another company altogether? Why not make it another state, while he was at it? "Why can't I go back to Ashton ImageWorks?"

His sexy eyebrows dipped as he frowned. "I thought you would be better off elsewhere."

Ow. He didn't want her around. He very well might be planning a transcontinental move for her.

"I thought you would rather have a change of scenery," he added. "A new start."

She stared at him. He was trying to make up for his mistakes, so why did she feel like she'd been kicked in the stomach?

"Was I wrong?"

"No. You aren't." She jerkily got up and grabbed her cleaning basket. "Thank you, Kyle. I'd appreciate any help you can give me." She headed for the door, wondering how she could fall for a guy who went to extreme measures to keep his distance!

"I've been thinking about this since he told me yesterday morning," Molly said into the phone, "and I don't know what I'm doing."

"Well—"

"I could go after any guy, so why am I hung up on him?" She drove her hand into the cavity of the thawed turkey.

"Uh . . ."

"I mean, why am I falling for him?" She grabbed the packet filled with the turkey's giblets and neck. "He doesn't want me here. Not that I blame him. And he had no problem firing me." She ripped the packet out of the ice cold carcass.

"He fired you?"

"Yeah." She tossed the packet to the side. "Didn't I tell you that?"

"I must have zoned out at that point."

"And when this week is over, we are over," Molly said as she readjusted the cordless phone between her ear and her shoulder. "*So* over."

"Uh-huh."

"So it's probably in my best interest not to have sex with him." Not that she really had a say in the matter. Kyle did not return to the bedroom last night.

"I . . . guess so."

"And I'll try to remember that before my jeans wind up

around my ankles." She tossed the turkey into the sink and turned the water on.

"Huh?"

"But there are lots of reasons why I like him. He's everything I want in a guy. He can be very protective, which I think is sexy. He's smart and he's got a weird sense of humor, but I kind of like it."

"Uh-huh."

"But he doesn't think the same way about me." Molly rested her elbow against the sink's edge. "He thinks I'm a con artist."

"He called you that?"

"Yeah. To my face." She was so glad she wasn't the only one who was appalled by that.

"Wow."

Molly sighed. "So, what do you think I should do?"

"Maggie?"

"Molly," she corrected.

"Right. Molly, do you realize that you're calling the Just Like Mom's Turkey Hotline?"

"Yeah . . ." Who else could she talk to? No one in this house, or on the island, for that matter. And Bonita was out of town visiting relatives. "Your point?"

"I'm an expert on basting and roasting turkeys," the woman said. "Nothing about love."

"Then what's your gut feeling?" she asked the woman as she rubbed water over the turkey.

"Gut feeling? Dump him and keep your distance."

"Really?" Molly grimaced. That was *not* what she wanted to hear.

"Honey, he's not going to get close to you unless he trusts you."

"And I'm working on that."

The woman tsked with regret. "I think it's too late in the relationship."

"Oh . . ."

"But you should still have the sex," the woman was quick to say.

Did she hear that correctly? Molly pressed the phone closer to her ear. "Have sex all weekend and then leave him?"

"Pretty much."

"But . . . but . . ." That wasn't what she wanted!

"Look what happened last time," the woman said. "You held out and you got nothing."

"But I wasn't in love with him then." Molly knew she was beginning to whine, but she couldn't stop herself. This was important.

"Well, then I don't know what else to tell you."

Molly sighed. "Okay. Well, thank you. I appreciate your advice."

"Any more questions about the turkey?" the woman asked, her voice indicating she was ready to wrap up the conversation.

Molly glanced at the turkey in the sink. "No, I think I got that covered."

"Alrighty, then. Thanks for calling Just Like Mom's Turkey Hotline. Happy Thanksgiving!"

"Yeah, you too." Molly slowly pushed the button to end the call. She surveyed the kitchen and winced.

Every pot and pan was out. Vegetables were in various stages of being prepared. The Thanksgiving dinner checklist she printed off of the computer was spattered with water and only a few completed checkmarks.

Molly blew at the hair falling in her face. Well, she got herself into this mess. She was going to get herself out of it. Be a stronger person because of it.

At least, that was the plan.

Chapter 15

The candles on the dining table cast a glow against the dark, rainy afternoon. The scents of cinnamon, cloves, and ginger permeated the house. Soft music and hard raindrops melded in the background. Kyle looked at the other end of the table and felt his heart swell at the sight of Molly.

Her long brown hair fell in waves past her shoulders. The red-gold flecks glimmered when she turned her head. Kyle clenched the linen napkin in his hands as he remembered how soft her hair felt under his fingers.

He greedily watched every move she made. The demure dip of her eyelashes and the hint of dimple in her left cheek. She looked beautiful in his cast-off white sweater. It might conceal her curves from his eyes, and she had to fold the sleeves so she could use her hands, but he liked seeing her wear something of his.

There was also something to be said about seeing her at his table. Now if only he could bring a blush to her skin, or make a primitive claim on her body, his holiday would be complete.

No, he would feel complete if and when she placed the same claim on him. She wanted to see how she would make him a home. Align herself to him. Creating this feast for him made him want more gestures, more gifts.

Okay, so she made the meal for him and their four dinner guests, he admitted as he watched Darrell and his neighbor Diana chuckle over something, but he could pretend it was all for him. Just this once.

"Hey, Kyle," Glenn called down from the other side of the table. "I need to talk to you about the spec we created earlier this month."

Kyle showed no expression, but he wanted to scowl at his chief financial officer. This was one moment when he didn't want to think about Ashton ImageWorks. He didn't want to return to his computer after dinner, or even talk about image processing.

All he wanted to do was sit back and watch Molly Connors preside over his dinner table. And after she charmed his guests, he wanted to whisk her away to their bedroom with the sole intent to seduce her.

"Now, Glenn," Molly said with a gracious smile, "I have a rule. No business discussions at the dinner table."

"It's bad for digestion," Diana added.

Glenn's head snapped back. "Kyle agrees to this?" He looked at Kyle for clarification.

"It's part of his training," Bridget said with a smile as she raised her wineglass to her lips.

"What happens if someone breaks the rule?" Glenn asked.

"Then he's banished to the kid's table," Molly said with a sly gleam in her eye.

"There is no kid's table," Glenn pointed out.

"We'll make one," Diana promised, bestowing a steely-eyed glare on his friend.

Kyle hid a smile. It was almost as if Molly had deciphered his mood. She had protected him, in her own way. The idea gave him a buzz.

He caught Molly's attention across the flickering candlelight. The last defense crumbled as he held her gaze. He couldn't stop looking at her. He didn't want to. He didn't want to hide what he felt or what he wanted.

And he wanted her. In his bed, at his table, in his home. In his life.

Molly shyly dipped her head, and to his amazement, Kyle saw pink stain her pale cheeks. She bit her bottom lip and looked back at him.

Yep, Kyle thought as he leaned back in his chair. Molly always looked good in pink. Now what would he have to do to make her entire body blush . . . ?

Molly squeezed her eyes and slowly opened them as she swallowed back a yawn. What had she been thinking trying to create the perfect Norman Rockwell Thanksgiving dinner? She was exhausted!

Molly rubbed the crystal wineglass dry and placed it gently in the drying rack. She had been up cooking, baking, washing pots and pans, ironing the tablecloth, and then trying to look halfway presentable at the actual meal without falling asleep face first in the mashed potatoes.

For a minute there, she thought she was hallucinating at the dinner table. Kyle looked . . . well, it didn't matter what he looked like. She was wrong. She was fantasizing again. She had to stop it.

Next year she would start a new tradition and order pizza. And if she was feeling ambitious, she'd splurge on napkins. Paper, so she didn't have to iron or be expected to fold them in some sort of origami knot.

Crash!

Molly winced as the sound of tinkling glass echoed in the kitchen. She hesitantly turned to see Glenn crouching, holding shards of a wineglass.

"Oops." He smiled sheepishly. "Slipped right out of my hand."

"Did you hurt yourself?" she asked as she carefully took the broken pieces from him.

"I'm okay," he said with a slight slur.

"Are you sure? Because you might have a cut on your hand and it will hurt like the dickens if you put it in the soap water." *Translation: give up on "helping" me wash up!*

Glenn looked at his hands. "Yeah, I'm sure."

"Let's not risk it." She had to give him a different job or they wouldn't have any glassware left. She gave him a damp towel. "Here, you dry and I'll wash."

"Sounds good to me," Glenn said, and took a step to the other side of the sink.

"Don't move!" She quickly gathered the dustpan and brush that she had kept out when she swept up the last shards.

"Why can't we use the dishwasher again?"

"Because these have a gold rim. And they're extremely fragile," she said pointedly as she swept the sharp pieces scattered at his feet. Obviously he thought all he had to do was load the machine, press a button, and call himself helpful. "Okay, you're good."

She walked to the trash can and deposited the broken bits into the bag. Why did this guy insist on helping? He was tipsy and he was all thumbs!

But she saw the mischief brewing in his eyes and decided to let him have his way before he made a scene. Kyle owed her big for this favor.

And if Glenn was going to break the crystal, could he at least do a complete set? One goblet, one champagne flute . . . ? No, of course not.

Kyle was going to have a mismatched set after this week. He better not blame her for it. And if he wanted to replace the missing pieces, he needed to harass Glenn about it. She was no expert on crystal, but what she was washing looked terribly expensive.

She heard the ring tone of a cell phone. Molly looked at Glenn as he retrieved the electronic device from his pocket. She hoped the call would distract him from his drying chore.

"Hey, Sara! Happy Thanksgiving!" Glenn tilted the phone away from his face. "It's Sara."

"Really?" Like she would never have figured that one out by herself. Molly placed the broom and pan to the side and walked back to the sink.

"I'm talking to Molly. Molly," he repeated. "Molly Connors."

Great. Molly rolled her eyes. Soon everyone was going to know that she was on this island. How she got here. Why she stayed. Yeah, she was never going to get another job in the tech industry after this week.

"No, I'm not lying," Glenn said with a wide smile. "Why would I make something up like that? Here, I'll prove it to you."

Oh, come on. She didn't want to talk to her former boss. She had nothing against Sara, but the way she had been dismissed from her job had been nothing less than humiliating.

"Say hello to Sara," Glenn urged her, handing over the phone.

Molly sighed and took it from him. "Hi, Sara," she said in her best receptionist voice.

"Molly?" Sara's voice rose as she stretched her name into several syllables. "It really is you? Why are you there?"

"It's a long story."

Glenn grabbed the phone away from Molly and put it against his ear. "She's engaged to Kyle. But, shush. It's not official." Glenn gave Molly a wink.

Okay, new rule, Molly decided as she faced the sink. Glenn was not allowed near the wine and liquor for the remainder of his stay.

"Why are you calling me?" Glenn asked Sara. "I did? I

said that? Well, yeah . . . That does sound like me. Okay . . . Talk to you later. Say 'bye, Molly."

" 'Bye," she repeated halfheartedly as she put on the yellow rubber gloves. She paused and tilted the glove over the sink, watching the water pour out of the yellow rubber. She was going to kill Glenn. Those were the last rubber gloves the island store stocked.

Glenn pocketed his phone. "Sorry about the interruption."

She looked at him and then at the glove.

He shrugged. "What?"

Molly put the glove down. "You're the one who's going to be sorry. I would like to see you explain to Kyle how all of Ashton ImageWorks found out he was engaged."

Glenn dismissed the possibility with the wave of his hand. "Sara isn't going to tell anyone."

Since he'd known the executive assistant longer, he was probably right, but Molly didn't think it was wise to chance it. Deciding it was none of her business, she pressed her lips together and carefully picked up a crystal goblet.

"Why are you worried about Kyle's reputation?" Glenn asked when she silently handed him the dripping wet glass.

Molly glanced up and saw their reflection in the kitchen window. Glenn's eyes had narrowed with suspicion. "I'm not."

"This engagement of yours isn't going to last," he said. "You know that, don't you?"

Duh! Was Glenn warning her off? About an engagement he already knew was fake? Just how much did this guy have to drink? "I appreciate your concern—"

"What you going to do once he dumps you?"

She grabbed another glass and plunged it into the soapy warm water. "He's not going to dump me." Because one had to be hooked up first to get dumped.

"Oh, yeah, he is. It's his method. I've seen it before. He'll leave you with his world intact, and where will you be? Without a job. Without a home."

"Is there a point to this?" Molly asked as she quickly scrubbed the glass. She didn't want the reminder. She especially didn't want to hear the hint of pleasure in Glenn's voice over the fact.

"Not really," he said, his voice dropping into a low, husky whisper, "but you're always welcome at my place."

Wow. That was unexpected. Maybe Glenn was one of those friendly drunks who wouldn't remember what he promised the next day. "Why would you . . . ?" Wait a second. He was not making the offer out of the goodness of his heart. "What are you saying?"

Glenn wiggled his eyebrows.

Ew! "Are you suggesting that I have sex with you in exchange for a roof over my head?" What kind of woman did he think she was? Or how desperate, for that matter.

"Yeah." He leaned closer and she could smell the wine on his breath. "How 'bout it? You and me? Once we get back to the mainland?" He reached for her.

Anger poured through her and she took a step back. "Don't touch me," she warned him.

Glenn made another attempt to catch her. "Now—"

She grabbed one of the glasses and held it up high. One more step and he was going to get clobbered. "Let me put it to you straight. I am never going to sleep with you. Ever."

"Hey," Glenn straightened his shoulders proudly. "A girl like you—"

Molly's jaw locked. "A girl like me knows better."

"You think Kyle is going to make this engagement 'official'?" He made air quotes and snorted. "You're living in a dream world."

"Glenn, I don't know how to make this any plainer." She

tilted the crystal up and down between her fingers. "I would rather starve and live on the street than sleep with you for my most basic necessities."

He squinted at her and then at the glass, as if the light catching on the crystal had a hypnotic effect. "So . . . that's a . . ."

Maybe she should just hit him with the crystal and knock some sense in him. "It's a no."

Glenn's upper lip curled. "Well, fine." He slapped the dish towel on the counter. "You can just forget about me helping you wash the dishes."

"Gee, that hurts," Molly muttered to his back as he stomped out of the kitchen. Now if only she could forget that in three days, she was going to be right back where she started. Out of a home, out of Kyle's life, and out of luck.

Kyle sat in front of the fireplace in his study, his feet propped on the ottoman. He looked over at where his computer rested on his desk and felt no urge to join it. Huh. Maybe he was coming down with something.

He heard the soft tap on the door and looked around. Kyle masked his disappointment when he saw Darrell standing at the entrance. He had no reason to hope it would be Molly.

"You have a minute?" Darrell asked.

"Yeah, sure. Take a seat." He motioned at the chair next to him. There was something about the hard edge in Darrell's voice. "What's up?"

"How important is Glenn to this deal?" Darrell asked as he sat down.

Kyle paused. It was an odd question. Glenn had his shortcomings, but negotiation wasn't one of them. "He's the chief financial officer—"

"Yeah, I know." Darrell leaned forward and perched on the edge of his chair. "But how important is he to *this* deal?"

"You have a problem with Glenn?"

"I don't trust him," Darrell said. "And I don't want to enter a deal with him."

Kyle closed his eyes as he fought back the sense of dread. If Glenn made a move on Bridget he would castrate the man himself. "What did he do?"

"He propositioned Molly."

Kyle's feet hit the floor with a thud. "What?" He felt nauseous. Acid ate at his gut. He must have been in shock because the only thing he could think of was that Molly wasn't blonde. Red-gold highlights didn't count. "When?"

"Just now." Darrell jabbed his thumb in the direction of the kitchen. "While they were doing dishes."

He had thought Glenn's offer to help with the dishes was strange. Had marked it down as a side effect of one too many drinks. "What did he say?" Kyle asked softly as his hands flexed into fists.

"He said you were never going to make the engagement official"—Darrell studied Kyle for a long moment—"and that they could get together after this week was up."

Kyle made himself lean back in his chair. He stared at the flames, wondering how he could still breathe when it felt like someone punched a hole in his chest.

He now had no doubt that Glenn screwed his ex-girlfriend in his office.

Glenn was much shrewder than he gave him credit for. He knew the right moment to swoop in for Molly and what to offer. He had a fight on his hands.

"She said no, of course."

"Who said?" Kyle asked. He felt like he was crawling through thick fog.

"Molly. She turned him down flat." Darrell sliced his hand through the air.

"She did?" Hope, fragile and weak, began to bloom inside him. "Are you sure?"

"Yeah. I just came back from walking along the shore with Bridget. She heard the same thing."

"Did Molly see you?" She could have been playing her role, knowing she was being overheard.

"No, she was too busy dodging Glenn and threatening him with a wineglass," Darrell said with a small smile. "I could have jumped in, but Molly was handling herself just fine."

Kyle felt the corner of his mouth tug up. He could picture Molly brandishing the crystal. But he was afraid to believe that Molly said no. She was offered the one thing she needed. And she turned it down without hesitation.

Darrell sighed as he rubbed his hand along his chin. "I know Glenn is one of the founding—"

"He's no longer a part of this deal," Kyle quietly assured the man. "And his days at Ashton ImageWorks are numbered."

"Whoa." Darrell reared back, holding his hands up. "Because of Molly?"

"Among other reasons," Kyle said, unwilling to discuss it. That was between Glenn and him. "But yeah. Molly is the deciding factor."

"Isn't Glenn your friend?"

Kyle shook his head. "Not if I can't trust him around my woman." He didn't know when he started to align himself with Molly, but it didn't matter. He trusted her more than his friend of over ten years.

Darrell leaned back in his chair and stared at the fire. "I'm sorry I said anything."

"I'm not." He had been loyal to the wrong person based

on history, not on facts. "Thanks for telling me. Molly
wouldn't have."

"Why not?"

"As a misguided attempt to protect me." Or because she
didn't think he would believe her. He had a feeling it was
the second choice, which bugged him. Kyle rose from his
seat. "I better go check on her."

"Are you sure—"

"I'm sure. Darrell, there's one thing you need to learn
about me. I protect what is mine. And Molly is most definitely mine."

"One more . . ." Molly muttered to herself as she filled
the sink again. "One more plate and then you're done."

She rubbed the bottom of her bare foot against her jeans-
clad leg, but the ache didn't go away. Molly knew she could
let the dishes go until tomorrow, but that was just asking
for more work.

Anyway, best damn fiancées didn't leave work undone.
Molly grabbed the soap bottle, ignored how red her hands
looked, and squirted the liquid soap into the water. Best
damn fiancées didn't let on that their feet hurt, shoulders
ached, and that they would rather sleep than have wild jungle sex with their fiancés.

She dumped the gilt-edged serving platter she had forgotten into the sink and saw a movement glinting off of the
window in front of her. Molly glanced up and saw Kyle
walk into the kitchen.

Walk? Her eyes widened as he strode toward her. More
like prowled. Dressed in jeans and a thin sweater, Kyle
looked less like a computer tycoon and more like a hunter.

The soreness of her feet disappeared, replaced by the instinct to make a run for it. But before she considered the
move, Kyle stood behind her.

The shroud of tiredness slipped away. Her body was alert. Alive.

He planted his hands on the edge of the chrome sink, his arms containing her.

You know, she thought as she looked at his big hands, the excitement popping and fizzing in her veins, *sleep is overrated . . .*

His solid chest pressed against her spine. Her bottom nestled against his hard pelvis as he trapped her.

Molly swallowed, her throat feeling tight. And she never did have wild jungle sex, so she really couldn't compare the two. Sex, yes. Maybe even wild sex. But wild jungle sex? Not even close.

"Thanks for making everything special," he said softly next to her ear.

Molly parted her lips. He thought she . . . Oh, the *dinner*. He was talking about the holiday feast and her best Betty Crocker imitation.

"You're welcome." She plunged her hands into the sink filled with bubbles. The hot water did nothing to dispel the tension swirling around her. She grabbed onto the serving platter as if her life depended on it.

Molly froze when his hands found her waist. "Uh . . ." Her gaze darted to the window. Her heartbeat skittered as she watched Kyle's dark head dip and he pressed his mouth on the curve of her throat.

"Um . . ." Her eyelashes fluttered as thick desire dripped and settled deep in her hips. His warm mouth on her neck gave a savage kick to her bloodstream. Molly couldn't resist turning her head to the side to catch his mouth with hers, but he wouldn't cooperate.

His hands dipped underneath her sweater. She shivered, her muscles contracting and twitching, as his hands spanned across her warm skin.

Molly moved to face him, her lips tingling for his mouth, but Kyle held her still. "Stay where you are."

Why? She watched him cautiously in the reflection, her hands unmoving in the water, as he caressed her body underneath the sweater. She could see the outline of his hands roam her abdomen and chest. It ignited her imagination. Intensified her need.

Kyle unclipped her flimsy bra and cupped her breasts with his big hands. Her breasts grew heavy, her nipples furling tight from his possessive touch. Her knees locked as she tried to remain standing, and found herself heaving against his chest, thrusting her breasts deeper into his hold.

He let go with one hand and bunched her sweater above her stomach. Molly's eyes widened with alarm. "Kyle, no," she whispered, scandalized. "We can't."

"Everyone is upstairs," he murmured in her ear. "Asleep."

"But . . ." She glanced up at the ceiling, wishing they had the house to themselves.

"Take your sweater off," he urged her.

Molly hesitated. She was tempted. She wanted to know what it was like to make love to him, skin upon skin, free from clothes, from hiding, but . . .

"For me."

The request did it. She didn't know why, but she weakened at those two words. Kyle sensed her submission and his hands boldly swept the sweater from her body. Molly raised her arms up, globs of soap falling from her fingers as he dragged it off of her, along with her bra.

The sweater landed on the floor with a soft thump. Molly trembled as she watched the reflection. She looked pale against him. Naked from the waist up, with nothing to shield her from his intense dark eyes.

Her skin prickled as Kyle looked at her, but she didn't want to cover up. She didn't want to hide. He lowered his mouth against her shoulder and Molly's hand slipped back into the soapy water.

Kyle covered her breasts with his hands. He caught her nipple between his fingers and squeezed.

Molly leaned her head against his shoulder as the wildfire licked her blood. She gripped the slick edge of the sink before she fell down from the intense pleasure.

Kyle captured her earlobe between his teeth. He bit down just as he pinched one of her nipples. Molly moaned and quickly pressed her lips together as her voice echoed in the kitchen.

"We should . . ." she began. Should what? Molly wondered dazedly, swiping her tongue along her lips. Stop? Get naked? Find a room with an actual door?

"Shush," Kyle whispered in her ear. She shivered as his warm breath caressed her skin. She closed her eyes and swallowed, all too aware of his hand trailing down her stomach and edging the waistband of her jeans.

With quick, sharp moves, Kyle unsnapped her jeans. The hiss of her zipper seemed loud to her ears. She forgot all about it as he wrenched her jeans and panties off her hips and allowed them to drop.

"Lift your leg."

She did without thinking. Kyle stepped on the jeans as she slid her foot from the denim.

"Now the other."

She raised her leg and felt the last of her clothes kicked away. She stood there, between Kyle and the sink, naked. Her hands were submerged in the water, her legs bracketed his.

He grasped her hips and pulled her against him. The sudden move had her sliding forward. She was up to her elbows in hot water. The tips of her breasts and the ends of her hair brushed against the tufts of bubbles. The rising steam wafted over her flushed skin.

She felt his arousal through his jeans and her muscles clenched with anticipation. But she discovered she was more interested in his hand skimming down her pelvic bone before he cupped her sex.

Molly bucked against his touch as he dipped into her core. She was surprised by her body's silky, wet welcome.

"Kyle . . ." She gasped from the mind-shattering pleasure as he thrust his fingers in and out. "Please . . . let me touch you."

He leaned over her, his thin sweater scratching her back, which glistened with sweat. She felt surrounded by him, but unable to touch him. It wasn't fair. She couldn't let it happen again.

"Don't you like this?"

Was that a rhetorical question? "Yes-s-s . . ." Her breath hitched in her throat. "But I want . . . I want you."

Kyle slowly withdrew and stepped away. Molly thought she was going to sag to her knees from the loss of his strength, his touch, when he grasped her by her hips and turned her around. She was face-to-face with him and the look he gave her was dark and challenging.

"Go ahead," he said, his voice hoarse and ragged. "Touch me."

She wasn't sure where she should start. Molly cupped his face with her wet, soap-flecked hands and kissed him. His lips were wide and firm as the stubble on his chin scratched her. Water dripped from his face, between their lips as they kissed.

Kyle broke away and shucked off his sweater. He grabbed her hands and placed them on his shoulders. "Touch me," he repeated.

She obeyed, rubbing her damp hands over his chest and stomach as he kept his hands to his side. She felt his muscles bunch and flex under her slow explorations until she reached his belt buckle.

She pulled at the strip of leather. The clink and hiss mingled with their choppy breathing and her heart pounding in her ears. She finally withdrew his penis and clamped her hand around him. Her hands shook as she followed his length from the dark pelt of hair to the weeping tip.

"Okay, enough touching." He pulled her against him and maneuvered her to the kitchen island. "I need you right now."

Molly went rigid. "No, not there," she said and shook her head. No kitchen island. Ever. She'd rather lie on the cold tile floor.

Kyle didn't question it. He swung her around and her spine came into contact with something very hard and very cold. She tried to look behind her. The refrigerator? Please let there be no magnets.

"Wrap your legs around my waist," Kyle said as his hands cupped her bottom.

She didn't know if she had the strength, feeling soft and yielding as he slid her up the cold surface. She shivered as the tip of Kyle's penis nudged her opening. Molly's breath suspended as he surged inside her.

"Kyle, I . . ." Molly's eyelids drooped as he filled her completely. Her mouth sagged open. Her toes curled as a brilliant white energy whooshed through her.

She grabbed Kyle's shoulders, her fingers biting into his skin as the power crackled and flared.

"Oh, my . . . Kyle . . ."

His thrusts grew stronger. Wilder. She bucked against each thrust as she felt him nuzzle his face against her neck. She couldn't catch what he said with her blood roaring in her ears.

"I . . . I . . ." Pulsing energy glowed hot between her hips. Sparked. Caught. She lit up, burning hot as he thrust into her, muffling his shout against her neck.

"I love you, Kyle . . ." The words escaped from her before she could call them back. She felt Kyle tense and knew she had just ruined everything.

Chapter 16

Kyle stood at the French windows in the media room and watched Darrell and Bridget kayak out of sight. He glanced at the steel gray clouds that suited his mood, as did the cold, gusty wind. He didn't know why he wasn't outdoors, battling against the grim weather, other than the fact that Molly was staying inside.

Molly. His chest pinched at the thought of her, his mind zooming to the moment he held her against the refrigerator and sank into her. Her wildness fed the primitive side of him, yet he had found a sense of peace at the same time. And then she said those four little words.

I love you, Kyle.

Shit. Why had she said that? Kyle rubbed his eyes with the heel of his hands. Did she really believe that? Or was it one of those in-the-heat-of-the-moment deals? He *had* been buried deep inside her when she said it.

But he didn't want to disregard her words. And that was what bothered him the most. Not that she declared her love, but that he wanted those words to be true.

Doubt niggled at him. What if they weren't true? What if she had an ulterior motive behind those words? Molly was, after all, an accomplished liar.

But she didn't lie with her body, Kyle reminded himself as he turned away from the window. He knew that for a fact. She didn't hide or fake anything last night as she bucked and twitched underneath him.

Kyle clenched his teeth as he banished the memory. Those words of love hadn't stopped him from pounding into her. From coming hard until he sank to his knees and took Molly with him.

Afterward he had helped her get dressed and took her to bed. He acted as if he hadn't heard her declaration, but it was all he could think about. It crowded his head.

Why had she said it?

The doorbell rang, interrupting Kyle's thoughts. He was thankful for the distraction and strode to the front door. By the time he got to the hallway, he found Molly there, un-latching the lock.

Wearing threadbare jeans and a faded gray hooded sweatshirt, Molly shouldn't look so irresistible. But all Kyle wanted to do was drag her into his bed and make her pant with need, moan with pleasure, say those four little words again . . .

Molly swung the door open and paused. "Sara?"

"Hi, Molly," Sara said as she stepped into the entry hall. Her curly bright red hair was an unexpected splash of color in the gray day. "Kyle."

The last person he expected to see was his executive assistant. "What are you doing here?"

"Say what?" Sara asked as she took off her dark green parka. "You guys asked me to come over."

"No, I didn't."

"Glenn said—" Sara closed her eyes and took a deep breath. "I'm going to kill him."

"You had to end your ski trip?" Molly asked as she took Sara's coat.

Kyle winced. He didn't know Sara had been on vacation. He tilted his head back and yelled. "Glenn!"

"I think he's taking a nap," Molly said in a hushed tone.

"A nap?" Kyle repeated, incredulous. "What is he, a toddler?"

"Well, he had better damn well wake up," Sara said, putting her hands on her hips. "I left my vacation early, found out on the ferry that I get seasick, and now I'm stuck on this island all because of him."

It was rare to see his executive assistant in a bad mood, but he figured she had good reason to be pissed off. "Molly, why don't you prepare a room for Sara?"

It was Molly's turn to grimace. "We have no more rooms."

"What?" Sara's jaw dropped. "Uh, no. There is no way I'm sleeping on the floor. No way. Uh-uh. Think again."

Kyle ignored her and kept his attention on Molly. "Then have her use Laurie's."

"You're putting me in the *maid's* room?" Sara's voice echoed in the entry hall.

"Laurie is the caretaker," Molly corrected Sara, "and her room is the only one left. I'm sure she would understand, considering the circumstances."

"Well, you can take her room," Sara decided. "And I'll take yours."

"Molly is sharing my room," Kyle said. The moment he saw Sara's sharp look, a wave of fierce protection for Molly overtook him. He raised his eyebrow as a silent warning. "She's pretending to be my fiancée for the week."

"Oh, that's right." She snapped her fingers and she remembered. "I'm curious as to how that came about."

"That's all you need to know." Kyle knew that the fewer details he shared, the better. "We already have had a few close calls and I'm not going to have anyone mess it up this late in the game."

Sara rolled her eyes. "Fine, fine. You guys are the perfect couple."

Kyle didn't look at Molly, but he knew she tensed under

those words. When did he become aware of every feeling, every move Molly made?

"Since I'm here, and will be until the ferry returns tomorrow," Sara said, "I might as well make myself useful. You have anything you want me to work on, Kyle?"

"Sure, follow me." He admired Sara's ability to stay on task. He wished he had the same focus. It had been on the fritz since he met Molly.

Maybe if he kept Sara around for the remainder of the weekend, he could reclaim his focus. Dig into the work and not get distracted by his loving fiancée. It just might work.

"Here you go, Sara," Molly said an hour later as she escorted her former boss to the caretaker's room. "I changed the linens and towels. You're all set."

"Thanks. Hey, stay with me while I unpack," Sara invited as she hefted her suitcase onto the bed.

Molly cast an uncertain look over her shoulder toward the kitchen. "Well, I need to make dinner." No easy task as the food was dwindling and the number of guests were increasing.

"That can wait," Sara assured her.

"O . . . kay." Molly reluctantly gave in. Going out of her way for her fiancé's executive assistant was probably included in the best damn fiancée job description.

"So," Sara said as she unzipped her suitcase. "How did you manage to wind up as Kyle's fiancée?"

Not that again. Molly leaned against the doorframe. "It's a long story. And like Kyle said—"

Sara waved the concern to the side with the flick of her wrist. "He didn't have the time. And I really want to know."

But Molly *really* didn't want to incriminate herself. "All that matters is that the engagement is fake and it's temporary."

"You won't tell me? Suit yourself." She grabbed one of her shirts and walked over to the closet. "You know, I really miss you at work."

"I'm sure the new receptionist is doing well." Although Molly wouldn't mind hearing that she was indispensable and that no one could ever surpass her work performance.

"She is," Sara informed her, "but I'm not considering her as potential assistant material."

That tidbit perked Molly up. "Why not?"

Sara shrugged as she hung up the shirt. "You and I would have made a better team."

Molly felt the pleasure radiate from inside her. "Thanks." She paused, undecided if it was the right time to bring up the subject. "I was wondering . . ."

"Yeah?"

"Well, I never got to see my review score and I would love to know what I would have received."

"Your score?" Sara's eyes narrowed with incomprehension.

"You know, maybe you shouldn't tell me if I got a pay raise or bonus." She didn't think she could handle the might-have-beens regarding money. "Just tell me what you would have recommended for me."

Sara frowned. "I don't remember."

"You don't remember?" Was she serious? Okay, it might not have been the most important moment of the woman's professional life, but still!

"That review process is a bitch," Sara complained with a wry smile. "All those forms to fill out."

"Tell me about it."

"Now I remember. I had agreed with you on your performance."

"You did?" Molly smiled. Well, how about that? Her hard work had been recognized.

"Yeah, I gave you a perfect score," Sara said as she walked toward her suitcase. "And let me tell you, those are hard to come by at Ashton ImageWorks."

Molly's smile stiffened. "I can imagine."

"I mean, everyone gives themselves the best score, but you earned it."

"Uh-huh. Well . . . thanks." Molly took a step back into the hallway. "Thanks for letting me know."

"No problem."

"I better start fixing dinner." She jabbed her thumb in the direction of the kitchen.

Sara looked up from her unpacking. "Okay."

Molly closed the door behind her as questions crowded her mind. Sara had lied about the performance review. Why?

It could be because she really gave a low score. Molly stood still in the hallway as she considered the possibility. She could understand why Sara wouldn't tell her that to her face. Although she would have had to explain it during the review meeting.

But why would she say she agreed with Molly and gave a perfect score? Molly purposely gave herself a lower score. Hadn't Sara read the review? Well, of course she did. She had to in order to fill out the paperwork.

But what if she hadn't? No, that was ridiculous, Molly decided as she walked into the kitchen. Sara had to because she was ready to give the review.

Molly stopped in her tracks. The review no one saw.

No, now she was getting paranoid. She was wrong. She had to be. There was probably a very good reason why Sara couldn't remember her score. It wasn't important to her. It was too long ago. She never looked at it.

Okay, the fact of the matter was Sara made her go look for the file when it was now obvious she hadn't prepared it for the review. Sure, Sara was disorganized and forgetful, but she would never have told her to go look on Kyle's desk for the completed review.

Which meant only one thing. The woman lied.

Lied on the same day the blueprint showed up on Molly's desk.

She glanced in the direction of Sara's room and glared. Highly suspicious.

Okay. The chances were good that her boss set her up and got her fired. What had she done to make an enemy out of her boss?

And what was she going to do about it now? Sara was beyond reproach in Ashton ImageWorks and was the most trusted employee in Kyle's company.

She couldn't just waltz into Kyle's study and tell him her suspicions. Against his trusted assistant? He wouldn't believe her.

Anyway, she had no proof, Molly acknowledged as she tapped her fingers on the kitchen counter. *Tap, tap, tap.*

No one else could back up her suspicions. It might be no big deal firing a receptionist without proof, but the executive assistant? Ha.

It was none of her business, and it was not going to change her work situation. She was going to keep her mouth shut. Molly pressed her lips together for good measure.

Come on! Tell the truth! Remember your promise.

Molly closed her eyes, willing away the reprimand. But it was no good. She had to admit the truth.

She didn't want to say anything because she knew Kyle wouldn't believe her. He would think she was lying. He would take sides, and she'd wind up losing everything again.

She exhaled slowly and thought it over. Yeah, that was pretty much it.

What was she thinking? She didn't have Kyle in the first

place. Did she really think she could hold on to him—hold on to this dream life—for a few more days if she kept her mouth shut?

Not even. Because she messed that up the moment she told him how she had felt. She saw how he almost flinched when she said those words. How he made a point not to mention it.

Molly's fingers tapped faster. *Taptap, taptap.* Yeah, she should have kept her mouth shut.

And she was going to do that now.

Taptaptaptaptaptaptap.

None of her business.

Oh, crud. Molly smacked her hand against the hard surface and set off to look for Kyle.

He heard the knock on the office door and didn't have a chance to turn before he heard Molly's voice.

"Kyle?" she said softly. "I need to talk to you."

Kyle closed his eyes and breathed in deeply. He knew what this was about. The *L* word. She wanted to talk about it. Either she wanted to hear it from him, or she wanted to take it back.

He wasn't ready for that conversation. She probably wanted to hear him reciprocate. He could truthfully say that he cared for her. Worried about her. Felt like his heart had been ripped out when she disappeared. But was that love? He didn't know.

"I don't know how to tell you this." Molly stepped into his office and approached his desk.

She was going to take back those words. He should have known. It was too good to be true, and he really didn't need the complication. So why didn't he feel relief?

"So, I'm going to come right out and say it." She gripped the edge of his desk. He noticed how her knuckles whitened.

"Go ahead." Should he accept her retraction or find a way to make her say those words again?

"I figured out who is behind the blueprint theft," she said in one big rush of words. "It's Sara."

Kyle went rigid. It suddenly hurt to breathe. "What?"

"Sara," Molly repeated. "I have reason to believe she's behind all this."

"Molly, I already told you that I don't think you did it." She had no right to question his most trusted employee. Stone cold anger formed inside him.

"I know that."

"So there's no reason to start pointing fingers."

Molly took a step back from his desk. "I wouldn't be saying anything if I really didn't feel this way."

"Sara has been with Ashton ImageWorks forever." The cold anger radiated throughout his body.

"I know."

"She's privy to most of the top-secret information."

"To the business deals," Molly pointed out. "Not the actual product."

"There has never been any question of her loyalty," he said through clenched teeth.

"I'm sure," she muttered. "Otherwise you would have booted her out long ago."

"Why would she do this? Now?" The coldness rolled through him like a storm and he barely kept it in check. "For this blueprint, after all the products we've made."

"I don't know," Molly said carefully. "People change."

"Why are *you* doing this?" He glared at her. "Sara has always been the one person I trusted more than anyone else."

Molly pressed her lips together and didn't reply. She glanced at the door as if she regretted starting this.

"What's your proof?" he demanded. Whatever it was, he would rip it to shreds.

She shifted from one foot to the other. "I don't really have what you would call proof."

"Uh-*huh*."

She rotated her hands in the air. "It's more like a hunch."

"It's more like slander."

Molly flinched. "Listen, Kyle. I'm trying to warn you so you can watch out."

"What's this hunch of yours?"

"Well, it's about my job performance review."

"Oh, God." When he got back to the office, he was going to abolish the system altogether.

"I was talking to Sara about it just now"—she gestured in the direction of the door—"and it became clear to me that she didn't work on it."

Kyle stared at her, waiting for more, but apparently that was it. "This is your hunch?"

"Why did she send me on a wild goose chase looking for something that she knew wasn't done?"

"You're assuming it wasn't completed."

Molly's jaw shifted to the side. "Yeah, I'm assuming, but it's an educated guess."

His eyebrow rose. "A missing file means she stole a blueprint?"

"Okay!" She held up her palm to stop him. "I know that sounds like such a leap, but it's too much of a coincidence that once I'm looking for this file—that no one ever saw—the blueprint shows up on my desk."

"You're wrong," he said with a mix of certainty and relief. "Human resources found the file."

She jerked her head back. "They did? Did you see it?"

"I didn't have to."

Molly frowned. "Then how do you know?"

"Sara told—" Kyle gritted his teeth. He abruptly stood up. "Enough. I will not have you questioning Sara's integrity."

"I'm trying—"

"Sara has been in my confidence for years," Kyle informed her as he pressed his hands on his desk. "*She* doesn't lie to me, and *she* doesn't steal."

A blush crept up Molly's neck and flooded her face. "I . . ."

"If it comes down between choosing her word over yours"—Kyle leaned forward, pinning Molly with a cold glare—"I will choose her side. Every time."

Molly looked away. He saw the way her eyelashes fluttered and the tremor that swept through her body as she fought for her composure. He realized he wanted to take her in his arms and comfort her. Make her feel better.

But he couldn't. Not this time. Because he couldn't let her poison his mind about the one person who had proven her loyalty to him over and over again.

"Do I make myself clear?" he said in a low voice.

"Yes." Molly didn't look at him and walked to the door, her movements awkward in her haste. "I understand perfectly. I won't disturb you anymore," she promised and closed the door behind her with a sharp click.

Chapter 17

On Saturday morning, Molly decided to put her plan into effect. She was going to protect Kyle whether he liked it or not.

She saw Sara walking along the beach and decided to confront her there. Braving the biting wind, Molly marched toward her former boss.

"Sara? What are you doing out here?" Molly asked, hunching deeper into the coat she borrowed from Kyle. "It's freezing."

"I love this kind of weather." The woman raised her face to the sky. "Don't you?"

"Can't say that I do."

Sara cast an odd look in her direction. "Why are you out here, then?"

Molly bit the inside of her lip as she struggled against the wave of uncertainty. "Because I want to talk to you. I want to know why you lied to me about my review."

"Say what?" The woman huffed. "I didn't lie."

"Yes, you did. You said you gave me a perfect score because you agreed with me."

Sara shrugged. "So?"

"I didn't give myself a perfect score."

"What are you talking about?" She turned to give Molly her full attention.

"I was giving myself room for improvement for the next review," Molly admitted.

Sara scoffed at the idea. "Everyone gives themselves a perfect score."

"Not me."

"Okay, so I don't remember it correctly." The woman made a face. "Whatever you gave yourself, I matched it. What's the big deal?"

"The big deal is that I don't think you looked at my review." Molly felt jittery inside. She wasn't sure where this was going to lead, but she knew it had to be said. "In fact, I think you said let's do the review that Friday because you needed time to get me away from my desk. That excuse was a surefire way of doing it."

"And why would I do that?"

Molly shivered slightly inside the voluminous coat. She wasn't sure it was from the cold wind. "Because you planted the blueprint on my desk."

"*I* did?" Sara's eyes rose with disbelief.

"Yep," Molly said with a sharp nod. "I thought about this all last night and it dawned on me. All of the top advisors were in a meeting that you didn't know about. They cornered one of your partners in crime and you needed to get rid of the evidence fast."

"I don't know what you're talking about," Sara said.

"Oh, don't worry. Your secret is safe with me." Molly turned to face the choppy water. "I could shout it from the rooftops and no one would listen."

Sara rocked back on her heels and studied Molly. "What is it that you want?"

"Why did you make me lose my job? That's all I want to know."

The woman looked at her in the eye. "Like I said, I don't know what you're talking about."

"Huh. I must scare you somehow," Molly said, trying to sound casual as her stomach did flips.

"Excuse me?" Sara's voice rose.

"Because there's no reason to frame me." Molly really hated in-your-face confrontations. She was never good at this. "And there was no reason to come running over the minute you heard I was here."

"You think I'm here because of *you*?" Sara's laugh was short and sarcastic. "Have you forgotten that Glenn told me I had to be here?"

"No, he didn't. I heard his side of the conversation. You invited yourself over here and made it sound like it was his idea."

"And once again, you don't know what you're talking about." Sara pivoted on her heel and walked back to the house.

"I guess I'm trying to figure out why you did it," Molly called after her. "You have a cushy job. Accumulated a lot of stock options."

Sara kept walking.

"For all I know, you could be secretly in love with Kyle and see me as a threat." Okay, it was a wild hypothesis, but it was all she could come up with.

"Kyle is not in love with you."

Ouch. Didn't even miss a step on that. "Are you in love with him?"

"I have worked with him for over ten years, and believe me," she said with a quick glance over her shoulder, "there is *nothing* lovable about him."

Molly wanted to disagree, but she had to keep her focus on the real issue. "Ten years?" she asked as she hurried up to the other woman. "Wow, so you've been working at Ashton ImageWorks almost from the time it started."

Sara's brisk walk slowed down to a shuffle. "Almost?"

"Yeah, because if it was on the very first day, you would have . . ." Molly smacked her forehead with her hand. "The picture."

"Picture?" Sara stood still.

"You've been with them since the beginning," Molly said as it finally dawned on her. "You were the one behind the camera."

Sara's shoulders dipped and she looked away. "I really don't want to talk about this."

"How come you're not in the picture?" she persisted. "Because you're not one of the founders?"

Sara closed her eyes in defense. "Go away, Molly."

"Because you're a woman?" she guessed, and then shook her head at her mistake. "No, that can't be right because Annette was in there."

"Because," Sara said in a low, raspy voice. "I. Was. The. Secretary."

"Huh?" That was not the answer Molly had expected. "I . . . I don't get it."

"I helped build that company," she declared. "But do they see it that way?"

Probably not, Molly admitted silently. "I'm sure those guys invested money, and . . . and . . ." Okay, she had nothing to argue with.

"You really don't get it." Sara irritably swept her red hair from her face. "I showed up for work when a regular paycheck wasn't guaranteed. I worked for them before they could offer me benefits."

"Really?" Now that was dedication. Molly wasn't sure she could do that.

"I have a college degree, too, you know." Sara's mouth twisted in a wry smile as she looked back at the water. "But guess what? They needed my office skills more in the beginning."

"And you wounded up being the secretary."

"I didn't set out to be an executive assistant. I wanted to be an executive. I still do. And I can't be that at the company I helped establish."

"Why not?"

Sara sighed with impatience. "Molly, a little career advice," she said, and looked at her. "Once you do secretarial work, the powers-that-be will never see you as anything but the girl at the front desk."

Molly clucked her tongue. "That's not true."

"Yes, it is. I'm living proof. If I want to be an executive, I have to go elsewhere. And I have to move into an executive position, otherwise those entry-level jobs are just another way of becoming a secretary."

"And for you to walk in as an executive, you need to bring something big to the negotiating table," Molly guessed. "Like a blueprint."

"Now you're catching on."

But it didn't make sense to Molly. "Why would Curtis help you with this?"

"For the money," she answered simply.

"What money? I thought this was all for an executive job with the perks."

"I wouldn't exchange a blueprint just for a job. There's money involved. Big money. I'm giving the blueprint to the one company that would give me the best price and the best executive position."

"You got the blueprint?" This was news to her. "But you gave it up when you planted it on my desk."

"That was a temporary setback," Sara said confidently. "And it all worked out in the end. Everyone thought you were behind it and then they let their guard down."

"Then why did you come running over here if you already have the blueprint?"

"Because of you!" Sara pointed at Molly. "You keep popping up, messing up my plans. You are the only factor I can't predict or control. I had to find out how much damage you could cause."

"And what did you find out?"

"You have no power at all," Sara said with a smile. "Not over my plan, and certainly not over Kyle."

Molly felt her chin tilt with defiance. "Wanna bet?"

"You could run back to Kyle or Glenn and tell them everything I said verbatim," Sara taunted, "and they won't believe you."

"It doesn't mean I'm going to sit on the sidelines quietly."

"Go ahead, Molly. Do your worst," Sara said with a jeering grin. "Because by the time you get someone to believe you, I will be long gone."

Kyle stood at the balcony and watched Molly and Sara from the shadows. Anger, cold and fierce, roared back inside him. When he first saw Molly approach Sara, he wanted to go down there and interrupt. But something stopped him. They were too far away to hear, the wind muffling their voices, but he picked up the signals and body language.

Doubt crept up again, and he couldn't shake free.

He watched Sara as she tilted her shoulders back. His skin prickled with warning as she braced her stance. And then numbness blanketed him as he took in Sara's angry, indignant gestures with her hands.

Something wasn't right.

Damn Molly for filling his head with suspicions. Kyle stepped inside the master bedroom. Just once he would like to look at someone close to him and not shield himself.

He retrieved his cell phone and punched in a familiar number. "Timothy?" he asked as he stared out the window.

"Kyle, this had better be good," the head of security said, his voice thick with sleep. "You are screwing with my wild weekend."

"Sara is behind the blueprint theft." His announcement

was met with stunned silence. "I need you to check her computer and office. Find anything that links her to Curtis."

"You are going off the deep end, Kyle. This is *Sara* we're talking about."

"I know." Kyle said as he watched the two women and noted Sara's cynical smile.

"Okay, fine, I'll do it," Timothy said. "I don't like it, but I'll do it. Sara's going to find out about this eventually. And when she does . . ."

"I'll deal with the consequences." And if he was wrong, he wouldn't forgive himself for allowing Molly Connors get under his skin and in his head.

Timothy's sigh was loud and long. "Anything else?"

"Yeah," he suddenly decided and turned away from the window. "See if human resources has Molly Connors's job performance review."

"Huh? How is this related?"

"They are. Trust me on this."

Molly lay awake that night, wondering why she left the light on for Kyle. He'd probably shared this room twice during the course of the week. What made her think he would do so today? Wishful thinking?

Anyway, she didn't need the distraction. She had other problems. Her mind buzzed with random questions, but no answers.

Why was she trying to come up with a solution for Kyle? He was going to be fine. She needed to think of what she was going to do after this weekend. As of Monday, the charade was over, and she needed a place to stay.

Why was she even thinking of Kyle? Molly rolled her eyes with self-disgust. He didn't want her help, her love—and he definitely didn't want her opinion.

"If it comes down between choosing her word over yours, I will choose her side. Every time."

Molly sniffed as the words echoed in her head. Fine. Be that way. Trust the wrong person. See if she cared.

Molly stared at the ceiling. She did care. She didn't have a whole lot of a power—okay, she didn't have *any*—but she could watch over him.

She lifted her head off the pillow when she heard the doorknob turning. Molly quickly turned to her side, tucked her hands primly under her head, and closed her eyes. She peeked through her lashes as Kyle opened the door and stepped inside.

She truly hadn't expected him. Molly closed her eyes and tried to breathe as if she was asleep. For several nights he'd worked in his office, and she suspected he fell asleep on the couch. He didn't even look in her direction last night, so angry that she should suggest Sara was less than trustworthy.

So why was he here right now?

She nearly leapt out of bed when she felt the mattress sink. She didn't know if she should pretend to sleep. That was a form of lying, though, wasn't it? And she really shouldn't break her new rule over something so trivial. Why did she come up with this new rule, anyway?

"Molly?" Kyle said in a whisper.

Molly slowly opened her eyes. "Yeah?" she asked cautiously. She saw his grave face and foreboding trickled down her spine. "What's wrong?"

"Nothing." He placed his hand on her arm. "Everything is going to be fine."

"Going to be?" She wasn't sure if she liked the sound of that.

His fingers glided up and down her forearm. "I want to tell you . . ."

Uh-oh. It wasn't like Kyle to talk in incomplete sentences. "It must be something important if you're waking me up in the middle of the night."

"I think it might be," he said with a shrug. He looked

down, not meeting her eyes. "I want to tell you that I'm sorry."

Here it was. The big brush-off. The it's-been-fun discussion. The don't-get-too-comfortable-around-here talk. Or just the I-don't-trust-you would do the trick.

But did he really need to do this in the middle of the night? Then again, time meant nothing to Kyle Ashton.

" . . . and so I followed up," Kyle said. His fingers stilled on her arm.

Followed up? On what? She was almost embarrassed to ask him to repeat himself. Then again, if he was going have a discussion in the *middle of the night*, he better expect some nodding off.

"And what did you find out?" she asked hesitantly.

"That you were right." Kyle sighed. "Sara is behind the blueprint theft."

She lay quietly, waiting for the other shoe to drop. It didn't happen. "This is your big news?" Because she already knew this. Told him about it yesterday. Got a whole lot of grief from him because of it.

"Hey," Kyle said, the corner of his mouth twitching. He looked up and met her gaze. "I was wrong and I know that now."

Apparently this was a momentous occasion. One that required getting up in the *middle of the night* to commemorate. "What are you going to do with Sara?"

"Pretend everything is okay, and when she returns to work on Monday, she'll be caught by surprise."

"This is your plan?" She thought he would devise some brain-bending strategy. "How come I got the full public humiliation and Sara gets the kid-glove treatment?"

"Because you're special?" Kyle asked with a smile. "Come on, Molly. I don't have security guards here that can escort her off the island."

"True."

He lay down beside her, his face inches away from hers. The way he looked at her made her nervous. It was like he was really *seeing* her. She closed her eyes, her only line of defense.

"I'm sorry I didn't believe you," he said quietly.

She shrugged, feeling very charitable now that she was proven correct. "You had good reason."

"And you kept at it."

She frowned, keeping her eyes closed. "What do you mean?"

"I saw you confront Sara this morning. I couldn't understand why you bothered when I swore I would believe Sara before I took your word."

"Heh. Still sounds harsh."

"Why did you pursue it?"

"I dunno." She was getting uncomfortable by this line of questioning.

"To prove to me that I was wrong?"

She fought the smile wavering on her lips. "I'm sure that had something to do with it."

"Or to protect me?"

The need to smile disappeared. "Probably." He was getting too close to the truth.

"Or because you love me?"

She opened her eyes. "Oh, so now we're not ignoring what I said almost three days ago?"

"Maybe," he said with a smile. He tilted toward her and placed a gentle kiss against her lips.

"Maybe?" she asked against his mouth.

He kissed her again, his touch soft and exploratory, but his touch still managed to sizzle right through her. "It depends if you still feel that way," he said.

Molly turned her head to the side. "Oh, gee. It has been three days. I'm sure my mood has swung entirely to the op-

posite direction. I'm flighty that way." Sheesh, was this what
he thought of her?

"Kiss me," he commanded in a whisper.

She scooted away. "Forget it."

Kyle cupped the back of her head and prevented her escape. "You know you want to."

Yeah, she wanted to, Molly silently admitted as he outlined her mouth with small kisses. Wanted him. But more
than anything, she wanted him to trust her and her feelings
for him.

That wasn't going to happen overnight. So she had two
choices. Either she grabbed this last chance to make love
with Kyle, or she ended everything right here and now.

Okay, it was kind of hard to make an unbiased decision
as his tongue darted along the seam of her mouth. And as
the heat from his body made her skin tingle. And she was
very aware that the only thing she wore was his T-shirt.

She wanted to take this last chance and make it good.
But how good could it be if he really didn't trust her?
Would he give her full access to his body? Hand over total
control? Not likely.

But she could try. Gain his trust little by little, inch by
inch. There had to be a way to convince Kyle to give her
anything and everything.

Molly gradually surrendered to his kisses, softening
under his touch. She framed his face with her hands, fan-
ning her fingers along his jaw. The bite of his whiskers
promised an uncivilized side to her lover.

She darted her tongue past his firm lips and tasted him,
but Kyle had other ideas. She teased him with the tip of her
tongue, but before she knew it, he was invading her mouth,
boldly staking his claim.

She felt his hands under her T-shirt. Molly arched and
swayed against his knowing touch. When Kyle pulled the

cotton off of her body with little effort, she knew she couldn't wrestle control from this man.

Why was she even trying? She could easily allow him to sweep her away and enjoy every delicious moment. But she wanted more. She wanted to see a glimpse of him unguarded, or a sign of trust.

One step at a time, she reminded herself. And this time, she was not going to be the only one naked. Molly struggled with his shirt. Stripping his clothes off wasn't going to strip him of his power, she decided, but it would equalize.

Kyle pulled his shirt over his head and tossed it over the edge of the bed. She stared at his sculpted muscles before he pulled her against him, the hair on his chest scratching her breasts. Okay, how was this supposed to be an equalizing maneuver?

His jeans rubbed against her bare leg. He was still overdressed. Forget equalizing, she decided, bailing on her plan. She wanted him naked. Now, if not sooner.

She hurriedly unzipped his jeans and pushed them down his lean hips. She hated how her hands shook and her muscles quivered with impatience. Her fumbling was at odds with every deliberate, sleek move Kyle made, designed to give her maximum pleasure.

She wanted to give him pleasure. Molly grasped his penis with both hands. Wrapping her fingers around him, her palms tingled and the sensations zinged through her wrists. Kyle lay back, stretching his arms above his head, welcoming her to explore.

Her pulse galloped as she watched how he twitched and hardened under her touch. How his eyes glittered and his skin flushed as she caressed him. This was where she felt powerful and weak. Dominant and submissive.

She wanted to see him go wild. Lose control from her touch. Molly scooted down the bed, intent to take him in her mouth. Kyle tried to stop her progress, but was too slow. He only managed to bunch her long hair in his hands.

Grasping him firmly with her hand at his base, Molly teased the domed tip with her tongue. She started with small, darting licks. As he flexed and bucked against her, she became bolder. She laved him with broad strokes of her tongue, pumping him with her fist.

His hands twisted in her hair. His breathing was uneven as he bit back his groans. She could tell he wanted to guide her head closer, and resisted, just barely. She wanted to break that restraint. Molly pressed his tip between her lips and drew him in.

He gasped and his hips rose from the mattress. "No, Molly," Kyle said and reached for her.

She lifted her head. "You know you want me to," she said, mimicking his earlier words.

"And it'll be over before you know it."

"Kyle," she said with a pout. She needed to know he could trust her. Maybe not with his life or with his love, but at least in bed.

"Anything but that," Kyle decided. "I want to make this last."

She crawled back up to face him. "Anything?" she asked mischievously.

His eyes narrowed. "What do you have in mind?"

She might not be the master of negotiation, but she had picked up a few tips during the week. Basically, ask for more than you hope for and you could get what you originally wanted.

"How about you lying on your back," she began, tightening her hold on his penis.

"Sounds good so far."

"Me riding you," she said, gliding her hand up. "Hard."

His muscles in his throat constricted as he swallowed. "Even better," he said hoarsely.

She met his gaze. "And you're blindfolded."

Her suggestion was met by silence. The tension in the room crackled as his green eyes darkened.

She met his gaze with bravado. Where did *that* suggestion come from? She'd never blindfolded a guy before and would probably crush his corneas if she tried. But she didn't have to worry. From Kyle's reaction, she didn't have to do any on-the-job training.

"Hmm? Not ready for that?" Molly said with a smug smile. She scooted down. "There's always . . ."

"Okay." Kyle said in a rough voice.

Molly froze. He couldn't possibly mean what she thought. "Okay to what?"

He arched his eyebrow as he called her bluff. "Blindfold me."

Chapter 18

Molly got on her knees and looked at him. Kyle wanted to smile at the shock stamped on her face. "Are you sure about this?"

He wasn't, Kyle realized as he propped himself on his elbow, but he also wasn't going to back out. He sensed that Molly needed his trust. It wasn't enough that he shared his bed. She needed proof. That was something he could understand.

And blindfolding wasn't so bad. It was a piece of fabric over his eyes. No big deal. It wasn't as if it would incapacitate him.

Anyway, how much trouble could Molly possibly cause while he had it on?

Hmm. Scratch that last question.

Kyle sat up when he noticed Molly hadn't moved. "Are you chickening out?" he teased.

His question bolted her into action. "No, of course not." Molly grabbed her T-shirt, which had been tossed and forgotten at the corner of the bed. She pleated the cotton into a wide strip. "I'm giving you a chance to chicken out."

"I don't need it." He was going to prove that he could trust Molly. Prove it to her and to himself.

"Okay, if you say so," Molly said hesitantly. She reached

over and covered his eyes. It immediately blocked out the light.

That surprised him. For some reason he had thought he would still be aware of the light. See shadows. Anything. His body went on full alert, his muscles tense, as he looked for a hint of light or movement along the edges of cotton.

Molly tied the ends firmly at the back of his head. "Is it slipping?"

"No." If anything, it was going to leave creases in his face. He twitched his nose, wondering if he could make it slide. No such luck.

"And no peeking," she warned him.

"I don't need to cheat," Kyle said. He paused when Molly didn't say anything in response. He tilted his head to the side, but didn't hear a sound.

Playing games already? He was up for that. Yeah, sure he was. He could win. He always won.

She had to still be on the bed, he decided. He hadn't felt the mattress move or heard the bedsprings creak.

But where was she, and what was she doing? A couple of wild ideas came to mind, but he would have heard her.

Was she just sitting there? Watching him? The seemingly innocent act set him on edge.

"Molly?" he asked softly, but she didn't respond. Kyle was ready to yank off the blindfold, but something stopped him. Pride? Determination?

He listened and noticed his other senses had heightened. The cotton sheets were softer than he remembered. The blindfold still held Molly's scent and warmth. He heard Molly's quiet breathing. She was close.

Kyle reached out and his fingertips collided with skin. He knew his smile was triumphant. "Gotcha," he murmured.

"Oh, you think so?" Molly moved away.

"I am not going to chase you around this room," he warned her.

"You won't have to," she promised with a teasing lilt.

Kyle turned to the sound of her voice and lunged. He had been aiming for her arm, but found soft flesh instead.

He lifted her breast into his hand. It was heavier than he remembered. Fuller.

Kyle thumbed her nipple until it beaded under his touch. He yearned to see the color, but he felt the aureole crinkle against his thumb. The simple reaction fascinated him and he circled his finger round and round until he reached the tip.

He reached for her other breast, fingers splayed, and found nothing.

Kyle bunched his fingers tight. The anticipation thrumming inside him evaporated. He was beginning to hate this blindfold.

"Stop fighting it," Molly suggested, laughter threading her voice.

"Why should I?" he asked as he rolled her nipple between his thumb and finger. He smiled when he heard her breath hitch.

"Don't think of this as a test," she said as she dodged him.

But it was a test. And he was going to pass with flying colors. "I'm—"

"Stop trying to anticipate my next move." He turned when he heard her voice behind him on his left. Predicting her next move, he swung to the right. Hearing Molly's muffled shriek, he knew his hunch had been correct.

He snagged her arm and dragged her to his lap. "Stop thinking that you can get away with anything because my eyes are closed."

"I wouldn't dream of such a thing," Molly said primly as she straddled his legs.

"Riiight."

Her legs brushed the outside of his thighs and his hands went for her hips. He felt her fingers skim from his jaw to his cheekbone. For a brief moment, he thought she would remove the blindfold. Instead Molly tilted his face up and kissed him.

He drew her in his mouth, tasting her with a fierce need. Kyle cupped the back of her head, tangling his fingers in her long hair.

He wanted to roll over and cover her body with his. Make her beg for his kisses. Tell her the game was over. He'd proved more than enough.

But he knew he hadn't. It was getting more difficult, and he didn't know if he trusted Molly enough. Damn it, he didn't want to fail. Not in front of Molly, who had already seen him at his worst. He'd keep the blindfold on for as long as he could.

Trailing his hands down the length of her spine, Kyle was aware of every dip and swell of her back. He wanted to memorize every curve. Next time, he promised himself, as he grasped her hips and moved her closer to his cock.

She murmured against his mouth and resisted his coaxing. Kyle knew how to convince her to see it his way. He slid his fingers along the slant of her hipbone before spearing through her wet, silky curls.

Molly's staggered moan sounded raw and primal to his ears. It echoed with something deep and elemental inside of him. He wanted more of that. He wanted to know that she was on the brink of control just like him.

Kyle dipped his fingers into her moist heat and she bucked against him. He found her clit, caressing her lightly, and she shuddered with pleasure. Her hands fell to his shoulders and she tried to push him down on his back.

He went willingly. Kyle knew he could display his strength

and resist. But he was going to give her his trust. Let her take charge. Just this once.

As he lay down, he struggled with a wave of disorientation. It was like his world was turned upside down. The blindfold was making matters worse.

His head hit the pillow just as Molly wrapped her hands around his length. She teased his cock with her wetness. Rubbed her slick flesh against his engorged tip. Kyle knew he would come before he entered her.

"Molly," he warned in a ragged breath.

She sheathed him in one fluid move. The pleasure was so intense, so sudden, that Kyle bucked violently against her. He hissed through his teeth as tiny starbursts bloomed in front of his eyes.

He needed to take charge. He'd been patient enough. He wanted to rip off the blindfold, flip Molly on her back and drive himself inside her to the hilt.

He could do it. Easily. Instead he grasped her soft, rounded bottom and thrust inside her. She felt too good. Slick. Tight. A sheen of sweat formed on his heated skin as his iron control slipped precariously.

Molly rocked against him in a mind-blowing slow rhythm. Her uneven breathing hitched and expelled with every languorous roll of her hips. Kyle desperately wanted to increase her pace. Have it match his rocketing pulse.

She moved against him faster. The sound of skin against skin sparked his imagination. He knew Molly was giving him everything she had. She hid nothing.

He wanted more than anything to take off the blindfold. He bet she wouldn't stop him now. But it was more important to give Molly his trust. He could do this. He wanted to do this.

Kyle dropped his hands from her hips and spread them out wide as she rocked against him in a fast, wild frenzy. He felt like he was free falling, waiting for something to catch him. Nothing did. Nothing was going to.

His fingers curled as he fought the need to hold onto her. Guide her. It was too much of a temptation to grab her. He moved his arms above his head.

Kyle felt Molly tilt forward. He jolted in surprise as her small hands encircled his wrists.

And he let her hold him in place.

The simple act didn't come easy for him. His arms slowly relaxed. His fingers uncurled. And then he knew that he could trust Molly. With anything. In his bed and in his life. With his heart and with his dreams.

Kyle jerked as he felt that sweet, satisfying kick in his blood. The white-hot energy roared through him, sweeping in front of his eyes as he shouted his release.

" 'Bye!" Molly called out from the front yard. She waved at Bridget and Darrell as Glenn drove them away in his sports car. He honked his horn and sped down the driveway. Sara followed Glenn in her car at a cautious speed.

Molly watched until the cars were out of sight. Her shoulders sagged with relief. "Whew! We did it."

"Did what?" Kyle asked beside her, his shoulder grazing her back.

"Kept up the engagement story," she explained as she did a small happy dance. "It was touch and go there a few times, but it worked!"

Kyle didn't say anything. She stopped dancing and turned to him. His solemn expression took the fizz right out of her. "Are you okay?"

"Yeah, I'm fine," He continued to look off into the distance, right where they had last seen the cars.

No, he wasn't. Molly could see that. The end of the week meant the return of the real world. Dealing with Sara's betrayal and the cutthroat high-tech business. She didn't envy him. She only wished she could carry some of the burden so he didn't have to face it alone.

"Are you sure you don't want to go back to the mainland with them? You still have time to grab your bag and catch the ferry."

Kyle looked down at her. "And leave you behind?" he asked, his eyebrow arching.

"It's not a problem."

His mouth twitched with a smile. "That's like keeping the mouse in charge of the cheese."

Molly's eyes widened. "Excuse me, are you calling me a mouse?"

Kyle grinned, but didn't reply.

She tilted her chin. "I'll have you know that if it weren't for me, this place would be a pigsty."

"Probably." He reached for her and wrapped his arms around her waist before gathering her close. "Thanks for everything."

"You're welcome." She wanted to close her eyes and lean against his chest. Hear his heartbeat and be surrounded by his heat.

"You really did make everything special," he said in a low, husky voice.

Don't read too much into this. Don't get mushy over a simple thank you. Keep it light. "That's what best damn fiancées do. It's in our job description."

His serious mood threw her off. She wanted to end this week on a high note. With some class. No regrets. No drama. And definitely no tears.

Molly disentangled herself from his embrace. "I better get started on the chores," she said with a bright smile.

"Why?" Kyle dropped his arms reluctantly. "Leave them."

"Isn't that why we stayed behind?" Molly asked as she

walked into the cottage and headed straight for the kitchen. "I heard you tell Darrell that we were closing up."

"I was lying."

"You?" She looked over her shoulder. "Lie? Shocking."

"Isn't it?" he said. "But seriously, it would look weird if we got back home and you didn't know anything about my real life and didn't fit in."

"Oh." *Didn't fit in*. She grabbed for the tea kettle as if it was her life preserver. "Good planning," she said hoarsely. "I hadn't thought of that."

Didn't fit in. That shouldn't hurt so much. What Kyle said was true. She couldn't disagree. She didn't fit in his life anymore than he fit into hers.

"Speaking of plans," Kyle said as he leaned against the kitchen counter. "What are yours?"

"Plans?" She took the kettle to the sink, not sure what she wanted to do with it. "For what?"

"Once we get back home."

"Oh, I'm not really sure. I'll think of something." She turned the faucet on. "I always do."

Kyle was silent for a moment. "Where are you going to stay?"

"I don't know," she said over the sound of the kettle filling with water. "I could always stay with my friend Bonita for a night or two."

"That's not much of a plan."

It was all she had to work with at the moment! Molly turned off the water. "I'll be able to settle down once I find a job. The recommendations you're going to give me will be a big help."

"Yeah. About that . . ."

Uh-oh. She didn't like the sound of that. Kyle wouldn't back out on his promise. Not unless there was a really good reason.

"What about it?" Molly asked, cautiously turning to look at him.

"Well"—he rubbed the back of his neck with his hand, which was never a good sign—"if you're looking for something more local, those recommendations won't work."

Wow. She set the kettle down in the sink as disappointment pulled at her from all directions. He really *was* backing out. She couldn't believe it.

"Location doesn't matter," she assured him, trying to sound cheerful. She didn't think she was successful. "There's nothing keeping me here."

He paused and met her gaze. "Nothing?"

"I have no family in this area, and I lost everything in my truck," she reminded him. She should revel in the freedom of nothing holding her back, but she couldn't.

"Except for the orange sofa," he reminded her with a wry smile.

She rolled her eyes. "Not really a reason to hang on." But he would be. If she wanted to have a real relationship with Kyle, she wouldn't think twice about staying put. In fact, if he decided to relocate to Timbuktu, she'd be right by his side.

But he gave no indication that he wanted to prolong the fantasy. And why should he? She had nothing to offer him but herself.

"What if you had a chance to stay here?" Kyle asked softly. "In this cottage? Would that be reason enough to stay?"

She gripped the sink as the questions boomeranged in her head. Stay at the cottage? Make the fantasy real? Hope cracked through the heavy disappointment. "I thought you were selling it."

He shook his head and surveyed the kitchen. "I don't think I could sell it now."

Why not? It was beautiful. Well, the funky wallpaper in the bedroom would have to go, but she didn't think it was hurting the resale value.

"Of course," Kyle continued. "I don't know if Laurie is coming back, so that could throw off the plan."

Oh. Was he offering her a job? As his caretaker? Molly's heart plummeted. She staggered from the second wave of disappointment crashing over her. For a second there . . .

How did she go from fiancée to caretaker? Well, probably the same way she went from trespasser to fiancée. She knew karma was going to come around and punish her for that.

But when she took care of the cottage, it wasn't just to meet the challenge Kyle threw her. She enjoyed it. She was living out a fantasy. Molly hadn't considered that she was applying for a job!

Molly looked away from Kyle. Why was she so upset? This would be her dream job. A place to live. Food to eat. No dress requirement. She would rarely have to deal with guests because Kyle hardly used the cottage.

And that meant she would rarely get to see him. Molly could easily imagine waiting here, impatient for a glimpse of him. Living for the brief moment she saw him.

No, she couldn't live like that. It was all or nothing. She wanted to share a life with him. She would not hang on the fringes of his world. No way. Not going to happen.

"I don't think it would be a good idea. Me being here." It hurt to refuse. She felt sick to her stomach. She couldn't believe she was saying no to the best job she had ever been offered.

"Why not?" He walked to her. "It would be ideal. It would be just you and me. You can add your personal touch to the cottage. And at night—"

Molly had to stop him. "No, that won't work. In case you have forgotten, I don't sleep with the boss." And it was going to be really hard to enforce that now that she knew exactly what she would be missing.

Kyle drew back. "Boss?"

"I appreciate the offer. I really do. But if you want to look for Laurie's replacement, you should take out an ad in the paper."

She couldn't handle this anymore. She found it difficult to stand. To breathe. She was giving up something she would have begged for a chance at a week ago. And it was all because she dreamed too big.

Molly knew she had to get out of this kitchen, get out of this cottage, before she made it worse. She turned and headed for the door when Kyle captured her wrist.

"Molly—"

"No, Kyle." She couldn't look at him as the tears burned in her eyes. She didn't want to cry. *Please, don't let them fall.* "When I told you that I loved you, I wasn't lying. I wasn't trying to con you."

"I know."

"And I'm not going to work for you." She made herself turn and look at him. He was too close. The gentle look in his eyes was too much. "I need a job, and I need a place to stay, but if that's all you can offer me, then I have to move on."

"You don't." He pulled her closer to him.

"I can find a job elsewhere," she assured him. "It's not like my skills are completely unmarketable."

Kyle wrapped his arms around her and held her snugly against him. "Molly, I want you to stay. With me."

She tried to break from his hold and wasn't having much luck. "Haven't you heard a word I said?"

"I'm not offering you a job," Kyle explained. "Although you have suggested that looking after me would require an army."

"What . . . ?" She stopped struggling. "What are you saying?"

"I want you to stay with me. As my real fiancée," he said, and suddenly looked away. "Well, to start with."

She stared at him. Fiancée? She hadn't even allowed herself to dream that far, that big. "Why?" she asked.

Kyle met her gaze directly. "I love you," he said, his voice cracking.

Her chest clenched. She couldn't accept that. She was too afraid to believe it. Too afraid that she misunderstood. "You do not."

"Uh"—his eyes narrowed—"yeah, I do."

"Kyle." She held her hands up, needing to stop him before he said something he really regretted and couldn't take back. "I know we had fun pretending to be engaged, but it wasn't for real. What you're feeling isn't for real."

"Yes, it is." He brushed his mouth against hers. "I know it, and I'm willing to prove it. Every day."

She leaned away from him. His kisses were muddling her mind. That promise sounded too good to be true. "How?"

"You'll have to stay with me to find out," he said with a sly smile. "Are you ready to take that risk?"

On him? On the future of them? Oh, yeah. She'd take that risk. Molly nodded. "Yes, are you?"

His light green eyes glowed brilliantly. "I wouldn't offer it otherwise."

"You're talking about staying here at the cottage?" That wasn't going to happen, no matter how much she wanted it. "You can't stay here. It's too far away from work."

"Okay," he reluctantly agreed as he skimmed his mouth against her forehead. "So we can't stay here all the time."

"But I like this cottage." They could create their own reality here. What if she really didn't fit in his life?

"You haven't seen my other homes," he reminded her, his lips skimming along the corner of her eye.

"True." She hesitated. *"Homes."* She shook her head with disbelief over the idea.

"Although," he mused as he placed soft kisses along her cheek, "I know you have a thing for living at the office."

"Forget that!" She dodged away from his mouth. "Now that I have lived in the lap of luxury, I have a few requirements."

"Name them."

"I need you," she told him.

"You have me." Kyle said it with a direct simplicity that it sounded like a vow to her. "What else?"

What else did she need? She remembered the list she made when she stayed in the DIY truck. "I need heat."

He pressed her against him, her breasts flattening against his chest. "I'm more than willing to share."

"Food."

Kyle nodded with agreement. "Makes sense. I'll provide and you do the cooking."

She wasn't too sure about that. After Thanksgiving dinner, she was ready to do take-out for the rest of her life. "That's up for negotiation."

"Anything else?"

She tried to remember the other items on her list. She knew it wasn't a lot, but there were a few essentials she would never live without again. "Showers."

His eyes took on a naughty gleam. "Only if I get to watch this time."

264 / Susanna Carr

Molly felt the blush creeping up her face. He was never going to let her live that down. "And a bed."

"Absolutely," he said in a low growl. "I'll make sure you have all of that."

"And what do you need?" she asked. She didn't know if she had anything to provide him, but she would find a way to give him everything he needed.

The look in his eyes softened. The lines bracketing his eyes and mouth faded. "You. Beside me."

Molly waited, but Kyle didn't add anything to that list. "That's it?"

The corner of his mouth tilted. "It's not as easy as it sounds."

As far as she was concerned, it was easier than being away from him. "I'm there for you," she promised.

"Oh, and one more thing," he said as he let her go.

Yeah, she knew that list was too short. There was no way she could provide him with everything he needed. "What?"

"This time, you get to wear the blindfold," he said as he shrugged out of his long-sleeved T-shirt.

Molly took a cautious step back and waved her finger at him. "Oh, no, no, no!"

"Hey," he said as he pulled the shirt off, revealing his lean, muscular chest. "I wore it last night."

A wicked excitement curled around her chest as she felt her breasts tingle. "But that was different."

"Come on, Molly." He twirled the edges of the shirt until it became one wide swath of cotton.

"You'll have to catch me first!" Molly ran out of the kitchen. She looked over her shoulder and screeched when she saw Kyle coming after her.

Molly skidded around the corner and bolted up the

stairs, wondering when she should let him catch her. She didn't want to make it too easy for him.

But would that be cheating, she wondered as her feet hit the second floor. Or was it a form of lying?

Nah, she decided as Kyle grabbed at her waist and hauled her against him. It was destiny.

It's the most wonderful time of the year! *Not.*
Here's an advance look at
Susanna Carr's
hilarious "Valentine Survivor," in
VALENTINE'S DAY IS KILLING ME.
A January 2006 book from Brava . . .

Shanna pulled out a sheet of paper, slightly crumpled from constant viewing. "I'm concentrating on the basics."

"Give me that." Her sister snatched it from her fingers and read it aloud.

THE LIST

1. Receive a dozen long-stemmed red roses. At work. In front of everyone.
2. Dinner at the most romantic restaurant in downtown Seattle. Champagne optional, but would gain bonus points.
3. A date with someone who knows where my G-spot is without asking for directions. And knows what to do with it.

"So?" Shanna prodded, anticipation buzzing inside her again. "What do you think? Good, huh?"

Heather pressed her lips together and shook her head slightly. She wordlessly returned the list.

"Knock it off." Shanna reverently folded the paper and slipped it back in the purse. "You have to admit that this list is fail-proof."

Heather's forehead crinkled. "Are you kidding? *Everything* will go wrong."

"You wanna bet?" She already regretted showing her sister the list.

"Sure. Let's look at your dinner requirement. What do you consider the most romantic restaurant in Seattle?"

"Swish." She hadn't actually been there, but it had topped the ten most romantic restaurants for the past three years. For all she knew, they could serve macrobiotic junk. Who cared, as long as they did it with a romantic flair?

"Oh, sure. Swish." Heather scoffed at the idea. "Like you're going to get in there. I hear that they take reservations a year in advance."

Shanna didn't say anything, but she knew she was gloating. The best kind of gloat, as long as you weren't on the receiving end. The smirk tugged at her pursed lips. She felt the pull of her eyebrows as she tried not to waggle them.

"You didn't."

"Didn't what?" she asked innocently.

"You made reservations a year in advance." The way Heather said it made it sound like an accusation. "Without even having a boyfriend on the horizon."

The smile she tried to contain broke through. "Yep. I decided I was not going to suffer through another bad Valentine's Day. On February 15 of last year, I called Swish and made reservations. I got a table for two by the window overlooking Elliot Bay."

"Lovely." Sarcasm shimmered through the single word. "Too bad the second seat in your dinner for two is going to be empty."

"Not necessarily." She felt her eyebrows waggling.

"I'm not eating dinner with you."

Shanna tilted her chin up. "You're not invited."

"Are you telling me you have a date in mind?"

Pure pleasure kicked into her veins. "I sure do."

For the first time that morning Heather showed a spark of enthusiasm. "You and Calder?"

Calder. Calder Smith. Her breath hitched in her throat as her ex-boyfriend's image slammed into her brain.

His pitch-black hair was cropped close against his skull. Tanned, weathered skin stretched over his lean, angular face. Lines fanned from his gleaming brown eyes and bracketed his stern mouth. And every once in a while, a slow, almost shy smile that made her heart tumble.

She used to think that Calder had been almost too tall for her. So tall that she felt delicate next to him. Or maybe it was his harsh masculinity that made her feel fragile and ultrafeminine. Whatever it was, Shanna still shivered at the memory of his earthy sensuality.

She swallowed roughly and tried to clear her suddenly swollen throat. "Heather, you know the rule," she reminded her in a hoarse whisper. "Do not speak his name in front of me." It was bad enough she had to see him almost every day because they worked for the same computer software company.

"Okay, fine. But He-Who-Shall-Not-Be-Named should be on that checklist." She shook a finger at Shanna. "That would be the perfect V-Day you're searching for."

Like she didn't know that already. She didn't want to think about it. Shanna tried to push the image aside, but the tingling of her skin remained. She had to forget about him and not let any what-might-have-beens get in the way of her goal.

"So who's your date?"

She wasn't too sure if she wanted to share any more information, but she knew her sister wouldn't let the topic rest until she found out. "Dominic."

"Dominic? Who's Domi—no!" She grabbed Shanna's arm and pulled her to a stop. "Not . . ."

"Yep, that's the one."

Heather's eyes widened with dismay. "He's a *slut*."

"I think the term you're looking for is 'serial dater.'" Even though she hated it, Shanna did the quote thing with her fingers. Just because she could.

"For future reference, anytime you use the word 'serial' to describe a guy, it's not going to be good."

Damn if her sister didn't use the quote move again. "I'll remember that."

Heather covered her face with her hands. "Dominic. Why-y-y?" She wailed and stomped one foot after the other. "Why him? He's not going to send you flowers."

"Yes, he is." If the subliminal messages didn't work, the full-frontal request could not have been misunderstood.

Heather dropped her hands from her face and glared with suspicion. "Shanna, tell me the truth. Did you order and pay for the flowers in advance?"

"No!" Her mouth dropped open in shock. Outrage. "I would never do that. That's pathetic! I can't believe you would even think I'd consider it."

Her sister's jaw slid to one side and she arched a knowing eyebrow. "Shanna."

"Okay, the idea crossed my mind," she admitted, as she and Heather jaywalked through a parking lot, "but I rejected it. I know the minute I did that, all my bitchy coworkers would sniff out the truth."

"Yeah, you would never live that one down." She shuddered at the possibilities.

"Anyway, the whole point of the exercise is having a *guy* send me a bouquet at work. A dozen red roses, to be exact. I will accept no substitutes."

"Why do you think Dominic is going to send you flowers?"

"He will if he wants to find my G-spot on Friday." Shanna knew the motivation didn't sound the least bit romantic, but it would all work out in the end.

"Do *you* know where it is?"

"It hasn't made itself known for the past three months," she said with a shrug, "but that doesn't mean it changed addresses on me."

"And you think it's going to head the welcome committee for Dominic?" Heather exhaled long and hard. "Of all the men you could have picked. Couldn't it have been anyone else?"

"Heather, think about it." It wasn't like she had randomly picked Dominic. He fitted her requirements for the night. "How many guys can you name who know what a G-spot is, let alone what to do with it?"

"There's me," the familiar, rough voice said from right behind her.

Shanna stumbled to a halt and forgot to breathe altogether as Calder steadied her. His fingers spanning against the curve of her hip made her knees melt. She trembled as his heat washed over her. And, if she wasn't mistaken, her G-spot just announced that the hibernation season was officially over.

Let the good times roll . . .
with JoAnn Ross's
"Cajun Heat"
from BAYOU BAD BOYS,
available now from Brava . . .

It was funny how life turned out. Who'd have thought that a girl who'd been forced to buy her clothes in the Chubbettes department of the Tots to Teens Emporium, the very same girl who'd been a wallflower at her senior prom, would grow up to have men pay to get naked with her?

It just went to show, Emma Quinlan considered, as she ran her hands down her third bare male back of the day, that the American dream was alive and well and living in Blue Bayou, Louisiana.

Not that she'd dreamed that much of naked men back when she'd been growing up.

She'd been too sheltered, too shy, and far too inhibited. Then there'd been the weight issue. Photographs showed that she'd been a cherubic infant, the very same type celebrated on greeting cards and baby food commercials.

Then she'd gone through a "baby fat" stage. Which, when she was in the fourth grade, resulted in her being sent off to a fat camp where calorie cops monitored every bite that went into her mouth and did surprise inspections of the cabins, searching out contraband. One poor calorie criminal had been caught with packages of gummy bears hidden beneath a loose floorboard beneath his bunk. Years later, the memory of his frightened eyes as he struggled to plod his way through a punishment lap of the track was vividly etched in her mind.

The camps became a yearly ritual, as predictable as the return of swallows to the Louisiana Gulf coast every August on their fall migration.

For six weeks during July and August, every bite Emma put in her mouth was monitored. Her days were spent doing calisthenics and running around the oval track and soccer field; her nights were spent dreaming of crawfish jambalaya, chicken gumbo, and bread pudding.

There were rumors of girls who'd trade sex for food, but Emma had never met a camper who'd actually admitted to sinking that low, and since she wasn't the kind of girl any of the counselors would've hit on, she'd never had to face such a moral dilemma.

By the time she was fourteen, Emma realized that she was destined to go through life as a "large girl." That was also the year that her mother—a petite blonde, whose crowning achievement in life seemed to be that she could still fit into her size zero wedding dress fifteen years after the ceremony—informed Emma that she was now old enough to shop for back to school clothes by herself.

"You are so lucky!" Emma's best friend, Roxi Dupree, had declared that memorable Saturday afternoon. "My mother is soo old-fashioned. If she had her way, I'd be wearing calico like Half-Pint in *Little House on the Prairie*!"

Roxi might have envied what she viewed as Emma's shopping freedom, but she hadn't seen the disappointment in Angela Quinlan's judicious gaze when Emma had gotten off the bus from the fat gulag, a mere two pounds thinner than when she'd been sent away.

It hadn't taken a mind reader to grasp the truth—that Emma's former beauty queen mother was ashamed to go clothes shopping with her fat teenage daughter.

"Uh, sugar?"

The deep male voice shattered the unhappy memory. *Bygones*, Emma told herself firmly.

"Yes?"

"I don't want to be tellin' you how to do your business, but maybe you're rubbing just a touch hard?"

Damn. She glanced down at the deeply tanned skin. She had such a death grip on his shoulders. "I'm so sorry, Nate."

"No harm done," he said, the south Louisiana drawl blending appealingly with his Cajun French accent. "Though maybe you could use a bit of your own medicine. You seem a tad tense."

"It's just been a busy week, what with the Jean Lafitte weekend coming up."

Liar. The reason she was tense was not due to her days, but her recent sleepless nights.

She danced her fingers down his bare spine. And felt the muscles of his back clench.

"I'm sorry," she repeated, spreading her palms outward.

"No need to apologize. That felt real good. I was going to ask you a favor, but since you're already having a tough few days—"

"Don't be silly. We're friends, Nate. Ask away."

She could feel his chuckle beneath her hands. "That's what I love about you, *chère*. You agree without even hearing what the favor is."

He turned his head and looked up at her, affection warming his Paul Newman blue eyes. "I was supposed to pick someone up at the airport this afternoon, but I got a call that these old windows I've been trying to find for a remodel job are goin' on auction in Houma this afternoon, and—"

"I'll be glad to go to the airport. Besides, I owe you for getting your brother to help me out."

If it hadn't been for Finn Callahan's detective skills, Emma's louse of an ex-husband would've gotten away with absconding with all their joint funds. Including the money she'd socked away in order to open her Every Body's Beautiful day spa. Not only had Finn—a former FBI agent—not charged her his going rate, Nate insisted on paying for the weekly massage the doctor had prescribed after he'd broken his shoulder falling off a scaffolding.

"You don't owe me a thing. Your ex is pond scum. I was glad to help put him away."

Having never been one to hold grudges, Emma had tried not to feel gleeful when the news bulletin about her former husband's arrest for embezzlement and tax fraud had come over her car radio.

"So, what time is the flight, and who's coming in?"

"It gets in at five thirty-five at Concourse D. It's a Delta flight from L.A."

"Oh?" Her heart hitched. Oh, please. She cast a quick, desperate look into the adjoining room at the voodoo altar, draped in Barbie-pink tulle, that Roxi had set up as packaging for her "Hex Appeal" love spell business. Don't let it be—

"It's Gabe."

Damn. Where the hell was voodoo power when you needed it?

"Well." She blew out a breath. "That's certainly a surprise."

That was an understatement. Gabriel Broussard had been so eager to escape Blue Bayou, he'd hightailed it out of town without so much as a good-bye.

Not that he'd owed Emma one.

The hell he didn't. Okay. Maybe she did hold a grudge. But only against men who'd kissed her silly, felt her up until she'd melted into a puddle of hot, desperate need, then disappeared from her life.

Unfortunately, Gabriel hadn't disappeared from the planet. In fact, it was impossible to go into a grocery store without seeing his midnight blue eyes smoldering from the cover of some sleazy tabloid. There was usually some barely clad female plastered to him.

Just last month, an enterprising photographer with a telescopic lens had captured him supposedly making love to his co-star on the deck of some Greek shipping tycoon's yacht. The day after that photo hit the newsstands, splashed all over the front of the *Enquirer*, the actress's producer husband had filed for divorce.

Then there'd been this latest scandal with Tamara the prairie princess . . .

"Guess you've heard what happened," Nate said.

Emma shrugged. "I may have caught something about it on *Entertainment Tonight*." And had lost sleep for the past three nights imagining what, exactly, constituted kinky sex.

"Gabe says it'll blow over."

"Most things do, I suppose." It's what people said about Hurricane Ivan, which had left a trail of destruction in its wake.

"Meanwhile, he figured Blue Bayou would be a good place to lie low."

"How lucky for all of us," she said through gritted teeth.

"You sure nothing's wrong, *chère*?"

"Positive." She forced a smile. It wasn't his fault that his best friend had the sexual morals of an alley cat. "All done."

"And feeling like a new man." He rolled his head onto his shoulders. Then he retrieved his wallet from his back pocket and handed her his Amex card. "You definitely have magic hands, Emma, darlin'."

"Thank you." Those hands were not as steady as they should have been as she ran the card. "I guess Gabe's staying at your house, then?"

"I offered. But he said he'd rather stay out at the camp."

Terrific. Not only would she be stuck in a car with the

man during rush hour traffic, she was also going to have to return to the scene of the crime.

"You sure it's no problem? He can always rent a car, but bein' a star and all, as soon as he shows up at the Hertz counter, his cover'll probably be blown."

She forced a smile she was a very long way from feeling. "Of course it's no problem."

"Then why are you frowning?"

"I've got a headache coming on." A two-hundred-and-and-ten pound Cajun one. "I'll take a couple aspirin and I'll be fine."

"You're always a damn sight better than fine, *chère*." His grin was quick and sexy, without the seductive over-tones that had always made his friend's smile so dangerous.

She could handle this, Emma assured herself as she locked up the spa for the day. An uncharacteristic forty-five minutes early, which had Cal Marchand, proprietor of Cal's Cajun Café across the street checking his watch in surprise.

The thing to do was to just pull on her big girl under-pants, drive into New Orleans and get it over with. Gabriel Broussard might be *People* magazine's sexiest man alive. He might have seduced scores of women all over the world, but the man *Cosmo* readers had voted the pirate they'd most like to be held prisoner on a desert island with was, after all, just a man. Not that different from any other.

Besides, she wasn't the same shy, tongue-tied, small-town bayou girl she'd been six years ago. She'd lived in the city; she'd gotten married only to end up publicly humiliated by a man who turned out to be slimier than swamp scum.

It hadn't been easy, but she'd picked herself up, dusted herself off, divorced the dickhead, as Roxi loyally referred to him, started her own business and was a dues paying member of Blue Bayou's Chamber of Commerce.

She'd even been elected deputy mayor, which was, ad-mittedly, an unpaid position, but it did come with the perk of riding in a snazzy convertible in the Jean Lafitte Day parade. Roxi, a former Miss Blue Bayou, had even taught her a beauty queen wave.

She'd been fired in the crucible of life. She was intelligent, tough, and had tossed off her nice girl Catholic upbringing after the dickhead dumped her for another woman. A bimbo who'd applied for a loan to buy a pair of D cup boobs so she could win a job as a cocktail waitress at New Orleans' Coyote Ugly Saloon.

Emma might not be a tomb raider like Lara Croft, or an international spy with a to-kill-for wardrobe and a trunkful of glamorous wigs like *Alias*'s Sydney Bristow, but this new, improved Emma Quinlan could take names and kick butt right along with the rest of those fictional take-charge females.

And if she were the type of woman to hold a grudge, which she wasn't, she assured herself yet again, the butt she'd most like to kick belonged to Blue Bayou bad boy Gabriel Broussard.

Take a sneak peek at
CLOSE TO PERFECT
by Tina Donahue.
Available now from Brava!

Straightening, Josh rubbed the side of his neck and looked past his own reflection to the rest of the office. Beyond it was a glass wall that separated his space from Peg's.

She was standing beside her desk as she spoke to a young woman whose back was to him.

Josh's fingers paused on his neck. The pain was forgotten as his gaze drifted down that young woman's thick, dark hair. It fell in gentle waves to her narrow shoulders, all soft and natural.

Nice.

His gaze inched lower.

She was slender and tall and dressed in a suit that Brooks Brothers never thought to design. Foolish boys. That suit was unbelievably nice. The jacket was fitted, while the slim skirt was slightly above the knee with a side slit to make walking easy and to give a man just a hint of her very nice thigh.

That thigh was currently hidden, but that didn't stop Josh from exploring what he could of her beneath that suit. The fabric appeared lightweight and silky—from here it seemed to be the color of a ripe peach—and hugged her so well that she looked both elegant and sexy.

His thoughts whispered, *Turn around.*

She did.

Without pause, Josh swiveled his chair so that he was facing his desk and her.

Alan immediately stepped into his line of sight. "Then you agree?"

"What?" Josh leaned to the right to look around Alan.

"Then you agree?"

"Sure—whatever—dammit, Alan, stand still, will you?"

The attorney finally stopped pacing. "Why?"

Why else? So he could look around the man to her.

Beneath the harsh fluorescent lights that lovely hair was glossy, the color of an expensive cognac, gently framing her face. Features that were both delicate and exotic complemented her creamy flesh and those lushly lashed eyes that were either a very light brown or hazel.

Josh imagined heat in those eyes, the kind that made a man promise all sorts of things and not regret a one of them. He imagined her in island wear—one of those sheer cotton camisoles and white skirts with a ruffled hem that hung low on her hips, baring her navel.

Something deep within him was stirred as he skimmed the outline of her breasts. Full breasts that would easily fill a man's hands.

Who was she? Why was she turning away? What were she and Peg talking about?

What was Peg doing?

Josh watched as the woman went behind her desk. Each movement caused Peg's beaded hippie dress to sparkle as wildly as the glittery scarf she had wrapped around her reddish curls. There were rings on each finger and too many bracelets dangling against her wrists as Peg reached into her wastebasket, pulled out a copy of that tabloid and showed it to the young woman.

Josh stared as Peg pointed to his buck naked pictures on

the cover—as if anyone could miss them—then pointed to the glass that separated her office from his.

The young woman's gaze lifted to where he was seated, then returned to the tabloid as if she just couldn't help herself.

Please don't keep looking at that.

She did.

A moment passed and then another, while heat rose to Josh's chest and throat.

He had to wonder what in the world that young woman was thinking and why he cared. He didn't know her. If she was some weirdo who was here to ogle him in the flesh, so to speak, he would never know her. So why did he feel so damned embarrassed?

Many women had seen him nude, really nude, his stiffened cock and tightened balls ready for action and not one bit ashamed. What was the big deal about this woman seeing his bare ass?

Josh told himself it was no big deal, but didn't believe it, because those pictures hadn't been his choice and certainly weren't something he was proud of.

Of course, try to tell that to Peg or those females who continued to call. Even better, try to explain it to this one. For some reason she seemed different than the rest. She was special, although Josh had no idea why.

He hoped to God she wouldn't laugh.

She did not. After a long moment, she simply lifted her gaze, touching his.

It was a surprise Josh had not expected.

There was understanding in her eyes, but beneath that a female wanting that was so damned honest it touched his core. As embarrassed as he had just felt, he was now as confident. Her gaze gave him that.

So, when was the last time he had needed a woman's approval—a stranger's approval, no less—to feel as if he hadn't been such a bad boy or a fool?

"Yo, Josh, remember me?"

Alan? His gaze drifted to the man. He was still here?

The door to his office opened.

Josh looked in that direction as the young woman came inside, her long legs moving fluidly, like a dancer.

Peg was right behind her, smiling broadly, her expression ordering him to *lighten up*.

Not a chance. Josh had never felt more coiled and aroused in all of his days. Every part of him was stirred by this young woman.

Pushing back his chair, Josh stood, ready for her, ready for anything as Peg said, "Whatever you two guys have been talking about, it can wait."

Tess Franklin couldn't have agreed more, though she hardly got the chance to express it as that pale, overdressed man frowned at Peg.

"No, it can't," he said.

"Sure it can," Peg countered, "just chill for a little bit. That's all I'm asking, Alan."

Alan wasn't convinced. As he whined and Peg refused to be impressed or intimidated, Tess continued to regard Josh Wyatt.

He was taller than she had expected, over six-two, with strong, masculine features and thick, dark blond hair that was long enough and tousled enough to give him a boyish look.

This was no boy. His creamy brown eyes, his gaze, spoke of a man's experience and need. His lean, muscular frame betrayed those years he had toiled in construction before hitting it big in real estate development.

Despite that wealth, Tess could see that he wasn't at all corporate uptight, not like still-yakking Alan. Josh's choice in clothing was confident and casual—dark beige chinos and a white shirt worn open at the collar with the sleeves folded back to mid-forearm.

That skin was bronzed by the sun, that flesh sculpted by labor.

His gaze was still on her, watching, waiting, while his dark brows were lifting in approval, or was it surprise?

Tess wondered if his surprise was as pleasant as her own. Although she had seen photographs of him in Internet business articles, she never would have believed that he could be even better-looking in person. Or that his male beauty in a business setting could so easily match those bad boy photos in *Keys Confidential,* which were strewn all over this office, even his desk.

Tess warned herself not to look at the tabloid, and certainly not to linger on it, but couldn't resist.

Wow. That cover may have been unauthorized, but it was still amazing—nearly artistic as it showed three large photos of Josh with each building on the last, telling a sensual tale.

In the first, he was emerging naked from his pool. Light danced over the water streaming down his broad, muscular back and that luscious tattoo that ran the length of his shoulders.

Tess suspected he had gotten tattooed during his construction days. It was a geometric pattern, possibly Celtic—tribal, bold, virile. It made her skin tingle.

In the second photo, his ass was finally bared with that flesh as hard and well-toned as the rest of him.

In the third, he was fully out of the pool, his strong legs exposed, his hands lifted to his head as he smoothed back his damp hair, his torso turned to the side as if he finally sensed someone behind him. The muscles in his thighs were powerful and taut, the right side of his chest was exposed, showing those hard pecs and that dark, silky underarm hair.

He looked like a modern-day *David*. Even the artist Michelangelo would have been impressed.

No wonder he needed protection.